Thrill of the Chase

Thrill of the Chase

Thrill of the Chase

ELLE KEATING

New York   Boston

Forever Yours
Hachette Book Group
1290 Avenue of the Americas
New York, NY 10104
hachettebookgroup.com
twitter.com/foreverromance

First published as an ebook and as a print on demand: December 2015

Forever Yours is an imprint of Grand Central Publishing.
The Forever Yours name and logo are trademarks of Hachette Book Group, Inc.

The Hachette Speakers Bureau provides a wide range of authors for speaking events. To find out more, go to www.hachettespeakersbureau.com or call (866) 376-6591.

The publisher is not responsible for websites (or their content) that are not owned by the publisher.

ISBN 978-1-4555-3500-2

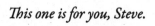

This one is for you, Steve.

Acknowledgments

I want to thank the incredible team at Forever Yours, in particular my editor, Lauren Plude, for taking a chance on me. I will be forever grateful.

To my family, this story would never have landed in my editor's hands if it wasn't for you. I want to thank my patient husband for allowing me to disappear for hours on end to write, to pursue a dream that I never thought was possible. You know you have it good when your guy has a glass of wine ready for you when you walk through the front door after tackling all those edits. And to Molly, Emily, and Jack, your support and love is what keeps me going. I love you!

Thrill of the Chase

Thrill of the Chase

Chapter One

The city was changing, the rigidity of the work day slowly unraveling and melting into night. Chase Montclair powered on the wall of screens and sat back in his leather swivel chair. He'd loosened his tie and started to roll up his sleeves when he saw her.

He reached for the intercom. "Lydia, please come here."

His secretary was at the doorway of his office within seconds. "Mr. Montclair, what do you need?" Lydia was old enough to be his mother. Her maturity and refined beauty were exactly what he wanted in a personal secretary. But her most coveted quality, the trait that Chase needed above everything else, was her loyalty. Her dedication to him was unwavering. And he couldn't...*wouldn't* have it any other way.

"Who is she?" Chase pointed to the screens on the far wall. Each monitor played the same image. Lydia stared at the large center screen. It took only moments for her to identify the mystery woman. Lydia made it a priority to know everyone on staff at Montclair Pharmaceuticals because Chase didn't have the time or desire to acquaint himself with the company's peons, though he did check on them every so often via monitor to ensure that they were doing their jobs and living up to his standards.

"She works in research and development. Her name is Erin Whitley."

He liked the sound of her name. It was both feminine and strong. Chase watched the woman tap the tip of her pen against the desk and then bring it to her lips. Her eyes remained fixed on her computer screen. There was a quiet confidence in her gaze, but there was also something lonesome about her.

"Bring her to me tomorrow…after my five o'clock," he said, rolling up his other sleeve. "And ask her to supply me with her latest report." Lydia bowed her head and left without uttering a word.

Chase had never sought out an employee to satisfy him sexually. An office relationship would be an unnecessary distraction. Instead, he chose to fulfill his needs with women he didn't need to see on a regular basis, women who didn't get attached or require him to give more than he was capable of providing. After what had happened last year, it was best he check his feelings at the door and enter each sexual relationship emotionally barren.

Chase stood up and walked over to the monitors. He watched the woman closely, his intrigue growing. Only a small strip of fabric fell below her lab coat, followed by long, athletic legs and black high heels. Her blond hair was pulled into a smart ponytail, though he could imagine what it looked like unbound, when she threw her head back at the moment of climax. The thought of her beneath him, in nothing but those high heels, aroused him. He felt his trousers grow tight around his mounting erection. And it only got worse when Erin Whitley rose from her chair and started to walk toward the other side of the lab. The swing of her hips and the sight of that tight little ass made his cock beyond stiff, and he determined that he would need to remain seated when she arrived tomorrow.

Chapter Two

It's not you, it's me?' Is that what I'm going to hear next?" Paul asked, half-sarcastic, half-hurt.

"I think it's time."

Erin had told her brother that the arrangement wouldn't be permanent when she moved in, but she was aware that Paul would try with everything he had to convince her not to move out. He had always been overprotective, even when they were kids. But things were different now and he often took his overprotective nature to an unhealthy level. She remembered how he'd grilled her after her first day on the job. Paul wanted to know who was in her department, if they were male, if anyone gave her the creeps. Erin wouldn't have been at all surprised if he hadn't believed her when she told him that her colleagues appeared normal and had gone ahead and conducted a background check on every individual in research and development. Erin wondered what Paul's reaction would be if she actually made plans to meet up with a friend and behave like a typical twenty-five-year-old single woman. Would he be tempted to pat down the poor unsuspecting friend who dared to have a drink with her or encourage her to have a social life? He *had* dropped Josh's name a few times over the past several weeks.

Erin's life was painfully simple. She woke up, went to work, worked out, picked up dinner from Whole Foods and came home to an empty apartment. Her brother often worked late due to his first-year status at the law firm. He was putting in all kinds of crazy hours, hoping it would pay off in the end. And it would. He always landed on both feet.

"Erin, the plan was for you to live with me while you went to med school."

Erin had put med school on hold, maybe indefinitely. Her desire to be a doctor had been extinguished months ago, and she wasn't going to enter med school now and attempt it half-assed. But her decision to suspend her dream plagued her, so much so that it had become a recurring theme in therapy in recent months. Dr. Cahil had to be sick of hearing her bitch about how it enraged her to think of her former classmates attending medical school one minute, and the next do a one-eighty and adamantly defend her choice to work at Montclair Pharmaceuticals.

Her heart pounded as she tried to retrieve the words she had practiced in therapy, but they weren't coming. The panic started to percolate, but she fought through it and said, "Sometimes, plans…change." She forced a smile, which seemed to prompt him to stand down. His skeptical expression softened and she knew she had him.

"I need this, Paul."

Paul got up from his chair and grabbed a beer and a bottle of Chardonnay from the fridge. He poured her a heaping glass of the chilled wine and then opened the Heineken for himself. They stood at the island in their modern kitchen and stared at each other, wondering who would break the silence. As always, Erin gave in first. She didn't want tension between them. But more importantly, she needed him on her side, she needed him to support this.

"I just need to start my life. That's all. I already found an apartment and I want you to come see it, make sure it lives up to your standards."

He took a hearty swig and set his beer on the counter. "Right now?" he asked with a raised brow.

Stay strong. You can do this. Pull up your big-girl panties, strap on a set, whatever you need to do, but don't back down.

"Yes, as a matter of fact. Right now." Erin grabbed her wine glass and Paul's hand.

He was just about to reach for his coat when she stopped him. "No need. But bring your beer."

His brow relaxed but his eyes had grown squinty and suspicious...and very lawyer-like. They reached the elevator and Erin pressed the circle for the seventh floor. Paul was leaning against the elevator wall with his arms crossed and staring at her. His penetrating gaze was relentless and she quickly looked away. She reached inside her hoodie pocket and withdrew the silver key. She held on to it, squeezing it into her palm until the metal was warm and saturated with her sweat. They descended three floors and when the doors opened, Erin led him down the hallway to apartment 715. She took a deep breath and attempted to unlock the door, but the key slipped through her trembling fingers. Although she couldn't see his face, she could feel Paul behind her, analyzing her. She shook her head in self-disgust and bent down to retrieve the key. She jammed the key in the lock and threw open the door.

Erin already had it painted with soothing earth tones and even had the living room and bedroom fully furnished. Not that it was a tremendous feat. Ethan Allen deserved most of the credit. With a few clicks of the mouse and a confirmation number, an espresso queen-sized bed frame and quilted mattress and matching bureau and nightstand had been delivered and assembled. A visit to Target.com resulting in artwork, two lamps and bedding completed the clean, earthy look. Erin shut the door behind them and Paul instantly went to the windows and checked the locks, analyzed the front door for any potential problems and surveyed the rest of the apartment without a word. Finally, he put his beer on the granite countertop in the kitchen and sat on one of the bar stools.

"So, I have no say in the matter? You've made your decision?"

"You do have some say." Erin smiled, although she knew how hard this was for him. He would always feel responsible for her, always have that need to protect her. She knew that it killed him that he hadn't made it in time. The image of her lying on the ground in that cemetery haunted him. Erin often heard him from her bedroom in the dead of night screaming her name and cursing. Erin had asked him if he would like to accompany her to one of her counseling sessions, to dispel those demons he wrestled with, but he flat-out refused. Erin didn't want to push him, so she backed off after that. "You get to choose the security system."

He raised his eyebrow and downed the last swig of his beer. "Well, prepare to live in nothing less than Fort Knox."

Erin walked over and gave him a hug. She felt Paul sigh and return the gesture. He rested his chin on top of her head. For the first time in her life, her rock, the impenetrable force she called her brother, was standing down and willing to concede. Because he trusted her. Because she was ready to turn the page and leave that dark chapter of her life behind. "I was counting on it," she said.

Chapter Three

The morning flew by, not because her work was so engaging, but because she was determined to meet a deadline that many people in the department deemed impossible. The report was almost complete and Erin was very satisfied with the results so far. Was it pathetic that completing a report could do it for her these days? That pressing SAVE and watching tiny dots circulate signifying a successful save could bring about an adrenaline rush?

She would have kept going, but she had promised to take Paul out for an "I'm sorry I'm moving out but I'm trying to be a big girl" lunch. She slid her white lab coat off and hung it on the hook behind the door. Erin adjusted her black pencil skirt and confirmed that her blue oxford blouse was securely tucked in. She didn't bother changing out of her black heels into more comfy foot attire; their lunch destination was only a stone's throw away from the Montclair Building.

Monty's Dips was definitely a guilty pleasure. It was home

to the best sandwiches in the city, as the crowd waiting to be seated confirmed. Paul must have arrived early or called ahead, because there he sat in the booth housing a bucket of salt-and-vinegar fries and sipping on a bottle of root beer. He had ordered her a vanilla soda.

"I assume you ordered already?"

He swallowed a mouthful of fries and raised his eyebrow. "Were you planning to deviate from your old standby?"

Erin scooted into the booth. "Not a chance in hell."

"Thought so."

She greedily gulped her soda and munched on some fries. Erin wanted to make this outing casual, no big deal. But Paul quickly identified the elephant in the room and just put it out there.

"You think feeding me delicious food is going to make me forget that you're moving out this weekend?"

His tone was serious, but Erin saw the acceptance of the situation in his intense blue eyes. "Is it working?" she asked, her voice steady, and with just a touch of playful sarcasm.

"It will take more than just one lunch date, I'm afraid. I see many of these outings in your future." He smiled, which he seldom did around others.

"Well, I guess I can make room in my hectic schedule." Erin grabbed her cell phone and pretended to plug him into her calendar.

"That reminds me," Paul said as he grabbed the phone from her hand, "we need to do something about that."

"About what?" Erin eyed her phone and then watched as he sifted through her contacts. Sadly, it didn't take very long.

"About the fact that you have no friends, that you spend every waking moment either working, sleeping, eating or exercising." Erin didn't like where he was going. Yes, she wanted to reclaim her freedom. But at her pace. "Ah, there he is."

No, she didn't like it at all, and before Erin could even stop him, Paul had already pushed his number. It wasn't difficult to deduce who the "he" was. The only other male in her contacts was sitting across from her, looking smug as hell. She reached for the phone, but it was too late.

"Hey Josh. It's Paul." Her eyes shot daggers, which only made Paul's smile widen. "I have to be quick. Erin and I are out to lunch. She just left for the bathroom and I was finally able to get my hands on her phone." Erin could hear Josh talking through the phone, though she couldn't make out any words. But just the thought of Josh on the other end made her heart ache a little. She had been a terrible friend to him over the past year.

"Look, I want to surprise Erin. She's been working like a dog at her new job and she needs to get out, have fun, see an old face, even if it is your ugly mug." Erin could hear Josh laugh on the other end. His carefree nature always brought a smile to her face. "Sounds great. Meet us at that that new club on Fifty-Second, Charo's. Say tomorrow, around eight o'clock?"

This was not part of the plan, at least not yet. Calling Josh, bringing someone back into her life who had the potential to remind her of her past, was at least number five on her mental checklist. Participating in therapy had claimed the top spot, finding a job had come in second and declaring that she was moving out of Paul's apartment had been number three on that list. She had achieved all three and was proud of herself. She wanted to bask a little more in that accomplishment and not prepare to take on another demon so soon. She also despised being told what to do.

Paul smiled, again a rare occurrence. The sight quelled her rage, but only temporarily. "Excellent…and Josh, be easy on her. She's a raging workaholic, getting out of the office and out of her apartment will be a culture shock for her."

They exchanged a few more pleasantries before they ended the call. Erin glared at her brother, though she was no match for his own icy stare. She hated lawyers.

"And what exactly am I going to tell him? Have you thought about that?" Erin paused when their waitress came into view. She set the two plates of heaping goodness in front of them and left. The waitress must have been swamped; she didn't utter a word nor did she check to see if they needed a refill on drinks before she rushed off. "'Oh, hi, Josh. So sorry I dropped off the face of the earth. So sorry that I have only returned a few texts and emails over the course of this year. So sorry that I have avoided you and any other person that could remind me of that night.'" Luckily, Paul couldn't see that her heart was racing, but he would see her trembling fingers. She quickly thrust her hands beneath the table and let them shake freely, undetected.

Paul sighed. "Look, you said you wanted to start your life. You have a good job and as much as it will keep me up at night worrying about you, you are moving into your own apartment. That's a step in the right direction. Now, let's include a friend or two in the mix, shall we?" He scooped up the first half of his sandwich and devoured a quarter of the massive concoction in one bite.

Erin sat in silence, knowing her brother was right. She just didn't know if she was ready for item number five on her checklist, a checklist Paul knew nothing about. It was better that way. Paul didn't need to know how difficult it was for her to even consider leaving his apartment. He would blame himself. He always did. It was best to let him interfere and allow him some semblance of control. Because that was what *he* needed right now.

Erin recalled a night when Paul wasn't in control, but numb and utterly distraught. Erin hadn't been prepared to lose both her parents in an accident that was so ridiculous, an accident that spawned more anger than grief. Erin was supposed to have been with them that night. Her parents had been celebrating their twenty-eighth wedding anniversary and had wanted her to join them for dinner at Rocco's, an upscale Italian restaurant located on a pier overlooking the Delaware River. Erin made up an excuse not to go because she thought they hadwanted to be alone on their special night.

Erin had just drifted off to sleep when she heard the knock at the door. She had opened the door to her dorm room to find herself face-to-face with a man resembling her brother. His eyes were red and vacant. To his left was a policewoman. Her brother had opened his mouth to speak, but no words would come to him. It was the policewoman who had come to his rescue and explained to Erin that her parents were dead; the pier on which they had dined had collapsed into the rough waters of the Delaware River. Their bodies had been recovered a half mile downstream. Fifteen people had still been unaccounted for.

"Josh is a nice guy. One of the few guys I would even put in that category. You'll just have to suck it up, sweetheart, and suffer through an evening in the company of two of the best-looking guys in New York City." Paul took another bite of his sandwich and winked at her. Erin sat back in the booth and breathed a long, dramatic sigh. Yes, it was going to be a long night.

Erin made it back from her lunch break with six minutes to spare. Determined to finish the report, she retrieved her lab coat and hunkered down in front of her computer for the next several hours. It was pushing five thirty when Erin had the strangest feeling that someone was watching her. An unnatural chill slithered up her spine, triggering the tiny hairs on the back of her neck to stand upright. She looked up from her computer screen and surveyed the lab. Everyone was gone for the day, which only contributed to her uneasiness. Erin massaged the base of her skull with her fingers, in an attempt to knead away the tension and to put those tiny hairs back where they belonged.

Erin's eyes gravitated to the corner of the room and the globe-shaped security camera. She worked for a pharmaceutical company, where drugs were there for the taking; security cameras were standard operating procedure. Without Big Brother watching, it would be very easy for employees to pocket the experimental drugs for personal use or to make a profit by selling the unmarked pills to countless addicts on the streets.

You're safe. This room is being watched by a security guard, maybe multiple guards. No one is going to hurt you.

Erin looked down at her trembling hands and swore out loud. Her hands never shook before the attack, but now when she felt threatened or found a situation to be particularly uncomfortable, Erin had noticed that her hands would begin to shake. The therapist she was seeing said it would subside and disappear over time. But until then, she would just have to deal with the annoyance.

Pissed off that she was letting her paranoia get to her, Erin finished the last two pages of the report, saved it to her flash drive and then pushed PRINT. She got up from her chair and started down the aisle. Erin was halfway to the printer when she heard the door to the lab close.

Chapter Four

Erin had never been summoned before, not by a boss nor by a professor. With report in hand, Erin walked behind Lydia, Chase Montclair's personal secretary. Erin kept her head down, taking note of the rich mahogany hardwood floors. They rounded a corner and Erin found herself in what appeared to be a lobby. A set of simple, but what she suspected to be very expensive, chairs atop an Oriental rug served as a centerpiece for the space. She was worlds away from her research lab, a space that gave off a hospital-like feel that was cold and devoid of character. Erin looked to her right and saw a large desk. A wall fountain with recessed lighting illuminated what Erin assumed was Lydia's work space.

What was she doing here? Did she screw up somehow? Erin's head was going a mile a minute as she tried to figure out what she possibly could have done wrong to earn a trip to the boss's office. All her reports had been completed on time. She had never been late to work or even called out sick. What the hell was happening? She had worked so goddamned hard to fly under the radar. But here she was, being escorted to the office of the CEO, a man she had never met before.

A large conference room was positioned to Erin's left, though the lights were out within the room, its occupants long gone. Lydia guided Erin to the only lit office on the floor and as they reached the doorway, she announced Erin's arrival to the man behind the desk and promptly left Erin alone with Chase Montclair. He didn't stand in her presence, but simply gestured Erin to a brown leather chair situated directly across from him with a wave of his hand. The plush leather enticed her to sit back and relax, but she rebelled and sat on the edge, positioning herself to hightail it out of there the first chance she got. He was on his cell phone and apparently confirming dinner reservations for two. A moment later, he ended the call and set the phone on his desk. His attention shifted completely to her and it was then Erin got a good look at one of the most beautiful men she had ever seen. It wasn't his perfectly tailored suit or the subtle scent of his cologne that she tried desperately not to detect, but his piercing blue eyes that caused her to suddenly lose the ability to breathe. Although it was the end of a long work day, every brown hair on his head was magically in place. She tried to picture what he would look like with his hair mussed, or better yet, what activity could cause his hair to become disheveled. The naughty thoughts this man seemed to evoke were coming rapidly, and it took everything she had to appear composed. Erin took a deep breath, convinced herself that this man was just that—a man—and sat up in her chair, her chin held high.

He leaned back in his chair, appearing to make himself comfortable. Despite his broad shoulders and frame there was still room for one more on his swivel chair—on his lap to be precise. A slight smile appeared on his face and Erin cringed. Was he reading her mind? Getting a bird's-eye view of her scandalous thoughts? His smirk morphed into an all-business expression and Erin relaxed somewhat. "Ms. Whitley, thank you for coming. Were you on your way home when Lydia came for you this evening?"

His voice was smooth and steady, which only made the situation more frustrating. He was calm and poised. Inside, she was anything but.

"I wasn't leaving until I finished my report on Cabraxol." Her stomach was churning and she was unraveling swiftly. Erin tightened her grasp on the report on her lap. She was clawing for solid ground and the one thing that she was certain of: her report.

"May I see?"

"Of course." She handed the packet to him, but as he reached for it his fingers brushed hers and she felt what could only be described as a charge pass between them. She felt hot and on the verge of breaking into a sweat. In her mind, she was not just sitting on his lap now, but straddling him and taking the first steps to muss up those chocolate-brown locks. That damn smirk had returned to his face. Erin sat back in her seat, her face hot and, she suspected, the color of crimson.

He leafed through the first few pages and then found her conclusions at the back of the report. "Will you be presenting the drug to the board?"

"No, Mr. Montclair, someone else will be presenting the findings." A year ago, Erin would have been up for any challenge, but not now. She was comfortable remaining in the lab with two research assistants who usually minded their own business, researching new medicines and compiling reports. Erin enjoyed flying below the radar. But she couldn't dismiss a nagging, unrelenting feeling that her solitary life in the lab was about to change.

"This research must have taken you months. The presentation should only be given by someone with such intimate knowledge of the drug."

Intimate.

As he uttered that word, Erin saw the last thread that was holding her dignity intact unravel, leaving her dangerously exposed. Erin hadn't desired a man for some time. Not once in the past eleven months had she yearned for the company of another, nor the easy release her own hand could provide. Erin crossed her legs, trying to thwart her body's pitiful response. But she was already wet with need and she again blushed. His eyes grew dark as they drifted to her legs and then to her eyes. Fortunately, Sex God's secretary buzzed in through the intercom.

"Mr. Montclair, I'm leaving for the evening. Will you be needing anything else?"

His eyes never left Erin's. His stare was intense, and Erin almost got up and walked out. "No, thank you, Lydia. That will be all."

And with Lydia's dismissal, Erin's body switched gears. A moment ago, she was a horny mess, imagining him screwing

her any way he wanted in his swivel chair and on top of his
very expensive desk. Now they were alone, his secretary gone,
the entire floor devoid of life, and even though she hated it,
Erin felt her fight-or-flight response come to life.

Erin stared down at her hands and noticed the hint of a
tremble. She grabbed the hem of her skirt with both hands, in
hopes of steadying them, or at least keeping them occupied.

"Have dinner with me tomorrow night."

Were these the dinner reservations he was making when she
first walked into his office? What a presumptuous ass!

It wasn't a question, but a command. She could give Paul
some latitude regarding his domineering nature, but
Chase…she didn't owe him anything. Erin fisted her hands in
an attempt to calm them. "I appreciate the invitation, but I
don't date. I mean I don't date people I work with, or for." She
bit her lip and shook her head.

He eyed her closely. He wasn't looking at her legs or allowing his eyes to peruse other parts of her body. No, he was
looking directly in her eyes as if he was searching for something. The needy feeling had been replaced with fear, and all
she wanted to do was run.

Get out of my head. You won't like what you'll find.

"No, I think you were telling the truth the first time when
you said you don't date, period," he said, folding his hands in
his lap.

Now she was pissed off. Her therapist was the only person
she had given full access to her unfiltered thoughts. For Paul's
sake and sanity, she had given him the PG version. Chase
Montclair had no jurisdiction here. Boss or no boss, she wasn't

backing down. "I don't see how my social life, or the lack of one, is any of your business." His smirk grew, along with the heat in his eyes. He seemed to be enjoying himself and the challenge she was presenting. But this was not a game. She had worked too hard. She had come too far. Erin stood from her chair, her legs almost buckling beneath her.

"Erin, everything is my business, including my employees and the people they may or may not be fucking."

Erin felt her jaw drop and her breathing hitch. She knew she was staring at him, but who the hell did he think he was? And even more disturbing, why was she so turned on at this very moment? Her emotions were in disarray. Erin wanted to smack him across the face. But she also had the insatiable craving to allow him to take her right there, in any position of his choosing. She wasn't thinking straight, which meant she had to get out of there, and quickly.

There was no response to one of the most inappropriate things Erin could imagine a boss saying to his employee. There were laws prohibiting such behavior in the workplace, weren't there? But as their stare-down continued, Erin realized that the law probably didn't apply to him. He was too confident, too relaxed.

She couldn't work for a man like that, so demanding…so arrogant…so incredibly sexy. It was a deadly cocktail, one of which she couldn't risk even a sip. "With all due respect—not that you deserve any—I quit!" Erin stormed out of his office and though she didn't turn around, she could feel his eyes boring into her.

How was it possible that a man could simultaneously trigger her defense mechanisms and send her into a sexual frenzy? With every step, she put more and more distance between her and Chase Montclair. It wasn't until she was alone in the elevator that she exhaled and realized what the hell had just happened. She was proud that she had stood up for herself and shut that cocky son-of-a-bitch down. But as the elevator descended, so did her mood, and she realized that she was suddenly very unemployed.

* * *

Eleven Months Ago

"Pencils down, everyone."

Erin could hear a handful of groans a few rows back, and she silently shared the sentiment. Normally, she was confident with her test-taking abilities, as her 4.0 grade point average showed. But this was no ordinary final exam. It was the last test Erin would take as an undergrad.

A long line had already formed down the aisle. The professor insisted that his students hand deliver their tests. She had heard a few classmates say the old man was paranoid and purposefully looked for cheaters. But Erin found him to be meticulous and, as she discovered during her freshman year, a man of compassion unrivaled by all others. Dr. Farrell wasn't just her professor; he doubled as her advisor. He had been there for her from the very beginning, seeing Erin through the toughest moment of her life only four months into her freshman year.

Erin noticed that the tightly woven knot in her stomach had finally started to unravel. Her nerves were shot from the hours of studying and pulling all-nighters. Erin was slowly shuffling along when she felt a hand tap her on the shoulder. "Coming with us, Erin?"

"What watering hole are you frequenting tonight?" She smiled at Josh, and though he flashed a huge grin encouraging her to come out with their study group to celebrate the end of finals, he already knew her answer.

"You need to ask?"

"You should buy stock in that place. They shout your name every time you walk through the Irish Pub's doors."

Josh put his arm around Erin's shoulders and sighed. "Yes, I'm like Norm from Cheers. *I've spent a lot of money and time to obtain such notoriety. I'll miss that place when we graduate."*

Erin sighed, knowing she should spend one of her last nights in Philadelphia as an unruly and carefree college student. But she just didn't have it in her tonight. All she wanted to do was go home to her one-bedroom apartment, open a bottle of cheap wine and eat leftover Chinese food. "Will you guys be going out tomorrow night?" she asked.

"Well, for you, I guess I'll have to commit to two consecutive nights of being a drunken mess."

Erin gave him a quick jab to the gut. "You spoil me, you know. How chivalrous of you to take one for the team."

"Like I said, anything for you, Erin."

Josh never took her rejections personally. He had been a good sport and an even better friend over the past few years. He was the first guy Erin had met at the University of Pennsylvania. From the moment he sat next to her in Dr. Mazano's Chemistry class, the phrase "Misery loves company" had definitely pertained to them.

Josh gave her a little nudge, and she found herself next in line.

"Ms. Whitley, you did well, I take it?" Dr. Farrell asked. The professor reminded her of an older Morgan Freeman, not in looks, as he was Caucasian, but in demeanor. Dr. Farrell had a way of calming her nerves with just the sound of his voice. And although he wasn't a large man, there was a quiet confidence about him that demanded respect.

"I think I did okay." Deep down, Erin knew she had aced the exam. But it wasn't like good grades came easy to her. She always had to work for them, which, she admitted begrudgingly, only made them sweeter.

He chuckled as he shook his head. "Would you mind staying a moment after class?" he asked as he collected Josh's test booklet.

"Sure, no problem."

Josh and Erin walked over to an empty row of chairs. She plopped her book bag on one of the desks, but before she could say anything, Josh gave her a quick hug. He suddenly appeared a little melancholy, as if the end of final exams and college graduation signified the dissolution of their friendship. She gave him a hug and a peck on the cheek. "Have fun tonight. If you pace yourself and you're not too hungover, we can do it all again tomorrow. Promise."

"Promise?" He was persistent, she had to give him that.

"Yes, now go toss a few back for me. And do me a favor?"

"And what would that be, beautiful?"

"Although you will be three sheets to the wind at some point this evening, try to keep an eye out for my brother tonight. He found

out he passed the bar exam this afternoon and is planning to hit the bars with some of his buddies. Paul's not a big drinker, but when he does go out, the Irish Pub is usually where he ends up."

"Babysitting duty...wouldn't be the first time I had to monitor the alcohol intake of a Whitley."

Erin pushed him playfully with both hands to the chest. "Must you remind me of that night every chance you get?"

"Oh, what night might that be? Hmm...the one I had to hold your hair back as you puked behind a tree in Rittenhouse Square?" He tapped his finger to his chin. "Or maybe it was the night I found you doing a keg stand in that frat house. You were so proud that you accomplished such a feat—that was, until you ran out onto the porch afterwards and I witnessed you heaving over the balcony. That was not a fun walk home for either of us, I recall."

"Pot calling the kettle black, my friend. You can count on one hand the number of times I have been black-out drunk. Don't even get me started on your own track record."

"Yes, there aren't enough minutes in the day..." Josh looked away, smiling to himself. His cell phone chirped in his pocket. Josh retrieved his phone and read the incoming message.

"Another one of your 'friends' in need of your attention tonight?" Erin asked. Though Josh was a perfect gentleman, he had more women and more opportunities than anyone she knew.

"She'll never hold a candle to you, sweetheart," he said, flashing her a smile that could truly melt a woman.

Erin rolled her eyes. "Just text me when you get in tonight." Erin gave him a squeeze and he reciprocated with a kiss to the forehead.

Josh looked at her. "Hey, I don't mind waiting around. Let me walk you home."

"And leave your 'friend' waiting? Absolutely not," she said. She was tired of the escorts, the universal belief that Erin Whitley was incapable of making it from point A to point B all by herself.

"My 'friend' can wait," Josh said. His tone had changed from playful to serious. Erin knew the reason for the sudden shift, and she softened instantly. She wasn't the only one that was haunted by the past.

"I have no doubt, but I'll be fine," she said. Erin kissed him on the cheek and gave him a gentle push toward the door. "I'll see you tomorrow night." He turned around and gave her a disbelieving glance. Erin folded her arms across her chest and gave him a look that told him not to doubt her. Josh sighed but complied.

Erin watched Josh leave the auditorium and then turned to see Dr. Farrell collect the last of the exams. He shuffled them into a neat pile and placed them in his leather briefcase. Only when the room was completely clear of students did he speak.

"So are you ready to close this chapter of your life and start a new one in New York?"

"Are you trying to tell me that Penn hasn't prepared me for med school?" she teased, trying to keep the conversation light.

"Quite the contrary, young lady," he answered in an equally sarcastic tone. He cleared his throat and diverted his eyes from hers. He mumbled, "You're the most prepared premed I've ever met. I just wish Penn's medical program had been able to woo you into staying here." They must have had this conversation over a hundred times.

Erin couldn't help but laugh at her professor. She knew the

program at Penn would give her as good an education as NYU School of Medicine but if she was determined to start her future she needed to do it in a place that wasn't haunted by memories of her past. Her smile faded. "You know why I'm going."

Dr. Farrell looked her in the eyes and sighed. "I'm just being selfish; I'm going to miss you, you know?"

Erin was going to miss him too. She wrapped her arms around his neck and gave him a hug that said it all. Thank you, I'll miss you, I love you. She sighed. "Paul is going to be there so we will have each other and take on that big, bad city together, just like we promised each other after our parents died. I'm going to be fine. You know how protective Paul is."

"Yes, and rightfully so."

Which reminded her that she had forgotten to text her brother when the exam ended.

Erin took one final look around the classroom. She could feel the tears begin to form, signaling that it was time for her to leave. She reached for her book bag and slung it over her shoulder. She turned to say one last goodbye to Dr. Farrell, expecting to see melancholy and, she hoped, pride, but instead his eyes wandered past her, staring suspiciously out the door.

"Everything okay?" she asked. Erin instantly followed his gaze, but there was no one there.

Dr. Farrell shook his head and replaced his glasses in the proper position on his nose. "It's nothing, Erin. An old man's tired eyes playing tricks on him."

"Okay, old man. I'm heading home, but only if you promise that I can stop over this weekend, maybe have some tea before I leave?"

"Promise, but only if you bring those cookies I like." Dr. Farrell was a sophisticated and well-bred gentleman with more letters after his name than anyone Erin knew, yet he was highly addicted to Thin Mints.

"You got it."

"Very well." He snapped the gold-plated buckles on his briefcase shut and started for the back door. "Erin, would you like a lift home tonight? It's dark and I'm not comfortable with you walking home alone."

She turned and gave him a stern look, though he knew it was all a farce. "You sound like Paul." His expression was of fatherly concern, and Erin was touched that he cared about her. "No thank you, professor. I'm a big girl and I'll be careful."

Dr. Farrell waited a moment and again said, "Very well." His favorite saying, she had concluded over the years. He smiled once more and then left the auditorium.

Erin shot her brother a quick text, assuring him that she was on her way home. Paul responded immediately in caps that she was to stay where she was and that he would come and walk her home from class. Frustrated by his hovering, the years of not believing she could take care of herself, Erin texted back: "I THINK THIS POOR, HELPLESS LITTLE GIRL CAN WALK HOME ALL BY HERSELF!"

He didn't respond. Erin instantly felt badly. Paul was just being himself, his overbearing but big-hearted self.

The building was quiet, lifeless in the barely lit hallway. Erin found herself oddly relieved as she exited the building and felt a warm May breeze wash over her face. It was a beautiful night. She smiled as she thought about the next chapter of her life. Her dream of becoming a doctor was that much closer. She crossed the cobblestone street and stepped onto the sidewalk.

* * *

The first thing Erin felt was his hand covering her mouth from behind. He pulled her into his body and it was then she felt a cold steel blade pierce her flesh. He muffled her screams and twisted his knife further into her side. She gasped for air, but nothing except his scent, a mixture of soap and mint, entered her nostrils. She kicked and thrashed her arms, but that knife turned once more and she suddenly felt warm liquid trickle down past her hip. She froze.

He hustled her into what appeared to be one of the oldest cemeteries in the nation and lifted her onto a three-foot stone wall encircling the eighteenth-century tombstones. She looked up and stared at her living nightmare.

He wore a black ski mask, though his mouth remained completely uncovered. He loomed over her and she estimated him to be close to a buck eighty and over six feet. His hand still covered her mouth, the knife still warning Erin not to scream. She felt his muscular legs spread her dangling ones apart and instantly found his mouth on her neck. She jerked away, but that fucking blade paralyzed her and she winced in pain. She whimpered into his laundry-fresh gloved hand. Though her body seemed to be frozen in time, her mind was racing. Please, please don't do this. Please! He didn't kiss her, but caressed the space below her right earlobe to the spaghetti strap of her sundress with his warm lips. His breath felt hot against her skin, and as he nav-

igated upward, Erin knew that she was not dealing with just a horny asshole who enjoyed taking advantage of women. He was controlled. And he didn't seem to worry that he could be caught at any moment.

"I'm going to take my hand away, but do not scream, Angel. Though I cherish your body, I will not hesitate to silence it if the need arises," he whispered. He removed his hand from her mouth and she sat there on that wall, her lips quivering, the tears already falling. "Shh, don't cry, Erin."

Erin's eyes widened at the sound of her name. The bastard knew her. This wasn't a random attack. She stared back into brown, feverous eyes. The control she saw there only moments ago was starting to wane. She felt the cool blade slide out of her. But this movement did not quell her fear. He was morphing into the animal that she knew he was. With his hands at his sides, he watched her, as if waiting for her to make the next move. She leapt off the wall and started running. With tears streaming down her face, she screamed for help, for anyone to save her from this living hell. Disoriented and clutching her side, she ran deeper into the cemetery and tripped over a partially submerged tombstone. He was upon her in moments. He grabbed her by the ankle and dragged her across the grass. He flipped her to her back and pinned both her hands over her head.

"I love that spirit, that strength. You're perfect, Erin. But I will kill you if you leave me again." He secured both her hands with one of his and again the knife found its resting place at her side. He didn't pierce her skin this time, but he didn't have to. Begrudgingly, she heeded his warning. He had the eyes of a killer, a doll's eyes, lifeless and cold. He reached under Erin's dress and

tore her panties down, ripping them in the process. Erin wanted to escape her body, just jump out of it for a few minutes. Her begging only aroused him more, making his erection through his black jeans even more pronounced.

"I've waited for you, Angel. I had to make sure you were pure, that you waited for me as well." He unzipped his pants and exposed his pulsating cock. "You are such a good girl." He reached into his back pocket and withdrew a condom. "Put it on me, Angel." His voice was gentle and almost loving. She wanted to be sick. Erin tore open the foil packet and slid the slimy ring around the wide girth of his penis. He closed his eyes as she sheathed him. This was it. She wasn't going to get another chance. She felt it in her soul. With one hand still on his cock, she squeezed and yanked at his balls, hopefully hard enough to rip them from his sack.

"Fuck!" he screamed. The knife dug into her, much deeper than before, and she released him. The pain radiated through her and she screamed. His hand swallowed her cries as he attempted to catch his breath. She knew she'd hurt him, but was it enough to make him incapable of finishing this?

"I know you are clean, my love, as am I, but I suspect you are not on birth control." His breathing steadied, and she felt her fight leave her, like the blood that was seeping from her side. "I need to get inside you."

Erin felt the bile rise in her throat.

He wasted no time and plunged into her. His hand at her hip tightened, but the knife-toting hand slacked somewhat. That fire, that fight she believed had been extinguished, awakened, and she took that opportunity and screamed bloody fucking murder. He either didn't realize that he had dropped the knife or didn't care because he was having too much fun violating her in every way possible. Erin thought it was the latter.

Two hands grabbed her attacker from behind and threw him to the ground. Erin heard punches thrown and the unmistakable thud of rock hitting bone. It was all a blur and she took those few seconds to cover up what would be forever tainted. It was at that moment that Erin saw blood flowing down her leg and staining her yellow sundress. Erin hugged her legs to her chest, laid her forehead on her knees and sat there in silence. She felt numb and more than willing to escape from reality.

"Miss, are you okay? Are you hurt?"

His voice was gentle and way too familiar.

Erin looked up feeling several emotions at once. Pain bled into anger…but it was the embarrassment that overtook her. Paul rushed to her side, his voice cracking as he said her name. His eyes found the blood and she cried into his embrace. "I'll be okay, Paul."

Paul stood and moved with purpose. He stood over her attacker, who was now quivering and moaning in pain, and smiled with a hatred that would bring anyone to his knees. Paul kicked the bastard in the stomach to rouse him. It was as if he wanted the asshole to be aware, cognizant of his surroundings and the beat down that would ensue. Erin watched her brother smash the man's head repeatedly against the same tombstone she had tripped over and then follow it up with blows to every inch of his now bloodied body. Paul was screaming and cursing, and Erin just looked on, wishing that she had the strength to join him in the massacre.

Paul threw her attacker to the ground. "Who are you? Show your fucking face!" Paul screamed.

"No!" Erin yelled. The sound of her voice, her raspy and tired plea, seemed foreign to her. "I want to be the one to remove his mask." Clenching her side, she stood up and instantly regretted her decision. The cemetery and all those goddamn stones started to spin, and she fought for balance. Paul ran over and caught her. His eyes grew wide as he found the wound. Despite the beautiful spring temperature, she felt cold and clammy...and eager to close her eyes.

"Stay with me, honey," Paul begged as he gathered her into his arms. "There's a hospital right around the corner."

Her eyes grew heavy and she disobeyed her brother. And as she let herself slip away, she heard Paul's footsteps quicken, carrying her farther and farther away from what could have been her final resting place.

Chapter Five

Erin's usual Saturday morning routine consisted of a seven o'clock start, a workout at the gym and a skinny Frappuccino at Starbucks as her reward. Today, she decided to bypass it all and sleep in. She also felt the need to stew over what had transpired last night in her former boss's office. The full implications of her actions hadn't hit her until now. Erin closed her eyes, rolled onto her side and played the scene over and over in her mind.

Although her encounter with Chase had been brief, she had experienced more human emotion in those five minutes than in the past eleven months combined. Yes, she unloaded frequently on her therapist, but that was a controlled setting and therefore didn't count. Last night, she had not had a safety net. And she had survived. Maybe her fingers had shaken a bit, and she'd panicked when she realized that Lydia had left and she was completely alone with Chase, out of earshot for even the most piercing of screams, but she had stood her ground. And it wasn't just fear that she was presented with in Chase's office, but also good, old-fashioned desire. The lust in his eyes, the way he had looked at her as a woman, not a victim, not damaged goods, made her feel alive and wanted. It didn't take long for Erin to notice the first effects of her thoughts. Her hand wandered to her thighs. She hadn't even touched herself yet and she was already wet with need, her panties soaked through due to her thoughts of *him*.

Erin imagined his full lips on hers, his hands cupping her breasts and plumping them until they formed easy-to-suck-on points. Her fingers found her clit, and it took only a moment to establish a rhythm that had her gasping and moaning his name. With her other hand, she inserted two fingers. She knew that it wouldn't take much to get there. It had been close to a year since she had taken the time to enjoy herself. God, she'd missed this! Just letting go and feeling her blood pumping through her veins. She felt every stroke, the palm of her hand delivering that perfect amount of friction to a part of her body that had been numb for too long. In her mind's eye, she could see Chase Montclair raise the skirt she wore last night and prepare her with his tongue. Her body shuddered and arched as her orgasm took hold, subsiding only after the third wave released her from its grip. Fully satisfied, Erin pulled the covers to her chin and fell back asleep.

She awoke an hour later to knocking on her bedroom door. "Er, you up?" Paul asked from the hall.

Erin looked over and checked the clock. Knowing Paul, he had probably been up for hours and had already been to the gym. Erin instantly felt like a slug for staying in bed and pleasuring herself. But then she remembered just how good it was and who the inspiration to send her way over the edge had been, and her guilt faded completely.

"Yeah, come in," she said. With water bottle in hand and dressed in full workout getup, he entered her room and sat on her bed.

"You feeling okay?" He put his hand to her forehead. Satisfied that she didn't have a fever, he continued, "Don't even try to get out of tonight."

Erin groaned and buried her head under her pillow. She had no desire to go clubbing with Josh and her brother. But before she could bask in further self-loathing, Paul grabbed her by the arm, ripped her out of bed and pushed her toward the bathroom. "Get showered, Sleeping Beauty, and make it fast. You're booked solid for the rest of the day."

"What?" She rubbed her eyes, shedding the remaining effects of sleep.

"You'll see."

Erin gave her brother the evil eye and disappeared into the bathroom. Wincing at her reflection in the mirror, Erin decided that she would be in need of more than a simple shower to look at all presentable tonight—she needed full pregame prep. After showering and shaving every part of her body, she returned to her room where she changed into black yoga pants and a fitted gray t-shirt. Paul called for her from the kitchen and when she finally emerged, a plate of eggs, bacon and home fries was laid before her.

"What's the occasion? Why are you making me breakfast?"

Skeptical of his motives but ravenous nonetheless, Erin dug into her home fries.

"Why must I have a motive to make my sister breakfast?" His brows were raised and his eyes were wide, feigning innocence. She glared at him, but all that did was make him chuckle. He turned toward the stove and flipped his own over-easy egg from the pan to the plate in his hand.

"Oh please. You're just guilting me into not cancelling our plans tonight with Josh. Bailing out on you after you've made me breakfast would make me look like a real ass."

"Correct. And not just breakfast, my dear. A day of pampering and shopping awaits you. Cancelling on me after all that would indeed make you look and feel like a real asshole. Mission accomplished."

Paul poured her a cup of coffee and slid it across the counter in her direction. She shook her head at him and his smile grew. He could be arrogant, demanding and straight-up obnoxious at times. But she loved him dearly. And she had no desire to disappoint him and ruin all the plans he had made for her today. He was being incredibly sweet. But he was also putting himself out there, leaving himself vulnerable and attempting to let her go, even if it was just for one night. She didn't need Dr. Cahil to tell her that tonight was not just a big night for her, but for Paul as well. Erin sighed and sipped her coffee. Did he have any idea how much he meant to her? She had told him many times that she loved him, but did he have the slightest clue how much she cherished their relationship? Erin took another sip, set her mug on the counter and smiled. "You look quite pleased with yourself."

Paul sat down on a bar stool and pulled his plate of steaming eggs and potatoes closer to him. He was beaming and looking proud and content. She hadn't seen him like that in ages. He didn't respond. Instead he took a bite of his eggs and smiled, all the while chewing. She had missed this, how relaxed they could be together, when he wasn't checking locks and sweeping each room. She would agree to pampering and shopping every weekend if it brought him the peace he truly deserved. Tonight, they would have fun and laugh and attempt to resurrect two people that needed to start living.

Chapter Six

Our limo awaits!" Paul shouted from the living room.

Limo. This was way over the top.

Erin had already agreed to a manicure, pedicure, facial and haircut earlier that day. Not to mention her shopping trip to Roberto's. Erin settled on a short black dress that hugged her curves and strappy heels that made her legs look like they went on for miles. She wore her hair loose and, thanks to the makeup artist at the salon, her smoky eyes definitely had that come-hither look. The whole ensemble gave off a sexy, but not slutty, vibe.

They arrived at the club around seven thirty and due to the early hour, they didn't have too much difficulty finding a table. Erin looked around and took in the swanky atmosphere. She was thankful that she had gone with the dress she had chosen. The other one, the dress that was definitely more comfortable and didn't show as much boob, would have looked frumpy here. Reminded of her cleavage, she looked down to make sure that her girls were still in place and not misbehaving.

Paul ordered her a glass of wine and a beer for himself. He knew her too well. She wasn't a big drinker. If she started her night with wine and then switched to beer with the occasional shot thrown in the mix, she would last longer and not get too drunk or sick.

The first glass of wine went down quickly, and Erin soon found herself getting reacquainted with the hum and buzz that only a club can bring. People were filtering in now. A line had formed outside, and she was thankful that they had arrived before the crowds had set their sights on the place.

She had just checked her phone for the time when a waitress came to the table with a lemon drop shot and a bottle of Heineken. Paul raised his beer and Erin lifted her shot in return. "To new beginnings, a new life."

Erin smiled, knowing how much was behind his words: a combination of pain and hope that they could both move on from the past. She picked up the shot and threw it back. The sweet liquid scurried its way down her throat. The warm sensation that followed transported Erin back to happier, more carefree days.

And as Erin slammed the shot glass back down on the table, she heard a familiar voice from behind. "That's my girl."

It may have been almost a year, but Erin would have known it anywhere. She turned and found her best friend smiling at her.

Erin tore across the aisle and ran straight into his arms. She was laughing and crying all at once. Erin didn't know how much she had missed him, missed that put-life-on-hold atti-tude until now. Josh hugged her tight, appearing equally happy to see her. After a minute of "I can't believe you're heres" and "I missed yous," she grabbed his hand and pulled him over to the table. Paul was already standing, his hand extended to Josh.

Looking at Josh, Erin was shocked. She'd known he'd be here, but she was shocked at how good it felt to see her old friend, to be okay with coming face-to-face with a part of her life that she had tried desperately to forget, to check off item number five on her list. Josh symbolized her life at college and the moment when her innocence had been taken from her. And until now, Erin had thought that allowing Josh back into her life would somehow awaken the memories of the rapist that had lain dormant for the past several months, since she had started therapy. Though occasional nightmares and trem-bling hands still plagued her at times.

Josh ordered a round for their intimate little gathering and they instantly started reminiscing about their college days. Erin forgot how great a storyteller Josh was, and before she knew it, he was sharing the keg stand story with her brother. Paul smiled and interjected at appropriate times during the retelling, but she couldn't fight the feeling that her brother was studying her. When Josh excused himself to the bathroom, Paul seemed to seize the opportunity and reached for her hand. "Time for me to head out."

"What…where are you going?" she asked, clearly missing something.

"I have no intention of being the third wheel. My plan was to hang out here until I felt you were comfortable enough to be with Josh and just have fun." Paul stood up, not allowing her to disagree or try to convince him to stay. "The limo will take you wherever you need to go. I'll have my phone on me at all times. Call me if you need me." Erin knew how hard it was for him to let her go. He wanted to stay, to never let her out of his sight if he could help it. And again, she loved him for it.

Paul kissed her on the forehead and walked to meet Josh, who was just returning from the restroom. Erin watched from the table and though she couldn't hear the conversation between her brother and Josh, she gathered that the conspirators deemed Operation Get Erin Back to the Land of the Living a success. Erin smiled at her brother as he left, thanking him and giving him the confirmation he needed that she would be alright.

Josh came over to the table with two beers in hand and Erin happily accepted. "If my calculations are correct, you are just one beer away from agreeing to dance with me. So drink up, sweetheart."

Josh's estimate was dead-on. Erin was working on a great buzz, feeling the wine and shots, which were giving her that lightheaded, carefree feeling that all was right in the world. The beers were going down like water and the next thing she knew, Josh was pulling her out onto the dance floor. It didn't take long for them to find their rhythm.

They would grab a beer during the songs they both despised and then immediately return to the dance floor. Erin was loving every minute of it. People were bumping and grinding on all sides of her, leaving no space for worries or memories to crowd in and haunt her.

One song bled into another, and suddenly Erin felt two hands grab her waist from behind. Her body grew rigid and she repelled the stranger's touch. With her fists clenched, she swung around, fully prepared to wallop the guy who thought it was okay to be the other half of an Erin sandwich. Erin felt her breath leave her as she stared into piercing, deep blue eyes. Lust and desire resonated there, and they pleased her. She liked how he looked at her. But she was also aware that this was a man who probably always got what or whom he wanted. She had denied him—and rightfully so—and turned down his invitation to dinner. She'd then followed it up with her resignation. No, this was a man who didn't get rejected often, and he was most likely viewing her as a challenge, his next conquest in a long line of adoring women.

"Dance with me?"

Chase's voice was husky and so goddamned sexy. He wore dark jeans and a black button-down shirt with the sleeves rolled up, exposing muscular forearms. His thick brown hair had that I-just-woke-up look, but on him it absolutely worked. And the subtle smell of his cologne all but made her weep, for good reasons.

Josh reached for her hand. He wasn't one for confrontation, but would happily lay a guy out if Erin asked him to. Erin looked at Chase and then at Josh. She didn't want to cause a scene. It would get back to her brother and he would kick himself for leaving her at the club, for organizing the entire evening, a night that had been awesome up until this point.

"Do you know this guy, Erin?" Josh asked. Josh could be

protective, but he was also respectful of her choices and knew when to back down.

Erin nodded. And then with a little more confidence, she looked at Josh and said, "Josh, it's okay."

Josh let go of Erin's hand and told her that he was going to grab a drink at the bar. He smiled, indicating that there were no hard feelings. She wasn't too worried about him. He would be snatched up immediately by some chick, or three. Josh was incredibly hot. Seldom was his bed empty during their college years.

Chase's one hand was still on her waist; the other had navigated down to her wrist. He pulled her close and they started to dance. Erin discovered quickly that the man knew how to move. Not surprising.

That painful fact would make it all the more difficult to tell him off. But she had to try.

"I don't like confrontation. That's the only reason why I'm giving you this one dance." She was such a piss-poor liar. She wanted this dance. She had wanted to feel him…*taste* him ever since she had entered his office. Erin's voice was shaky as he grinded against her. She could feel every ripple of his washboard abs. It took everything Erin had not to continue her quest southward and learn if he was just as firm elsewhere.

He leaned in closer. "Are you with him?" Even amongst the noise of the club, his whisper was crystal clear and so very tempting. His breath against her neck caused her to shiver and she whimpered. She prayed he had not heard her.

Erin swallowed, hard. For some reason, she had a very

strong feeling that he already knew the answer. "No, he's a friend from college. Why?"

And just when Erin thought he couldn't get any closer, he did just that. His grip tightened around her waist, confirming that he was just as hard below the waist as he was above. He found her neck and for a second, Erin thought he was going to kiss her. His lips traveled upward, with a teasing motion that left her skin hot and wanting. When he reached her ear, she felt his own breathing shudder.

"Because I don't share...ever."

Demanding, arrogant, full-of-himself asshole.

Sexy asshole.

Her body halted, though the music continued to pound. "I would have to be yours, first off. And that is never going to happen," she said.

"Are you absolutely certain about that, Erin?" Erin tried to step back, but he was too quick. His hands encircled her waist and she was flush against his chest. "Kiss me. If you feel nothing, I'll walk away."

The desire, the heat between them, was too intense. And it wasn't like Erin was going to see him on Monday; she had quit her job at his company. There really wasn't anything to lose. One kiss and she would walk away. One kiss to help inspire her when she was alone and pleasuring herself.

"No." Erin shook her head. "You kiss me," she said.

He didn't hesitate. She felt his lips on hers. His breath was a heady mixture of mint and Scotch, and she welcomed his tongue as it eagerly explored her mouth. His hands had taken the liberty of cupping her ass. It felt like he didn't just want her, but needed her. It intrigued her that she didn't tremble in fear at the thought. Erin heard him groan and it only fueled her desire to go even further, right there on the dance floor. Erin tried to care about how many people had to be watching them but could think of nothing beyond Chase. Erin heard herself whimper as his kiss drew deeper. She reached down and felt his cock through his pants.

He grabbed her hand and groaned. "You will make me come if you continue to touch me." Erin loved how powerful she felt. It wasn't the alcohol that was giving her the courage. It was the sudden realization that she hadn't died that night in the cemetery, though her current day-to-day routine ever since suggested otherwise, that prompted her to seize this moment and take control of it. It was an aphrodisiac just watching him come dangerously close to losing control as she cupped his balls. "Erin, we can't do this here." His voice was firm and dark.

Erin wanted him more than she wanted anything. "Yes," she whispered. He took her hand and led her through the club and out the front door, where a limo was idling. The driver opened the door and they both got in. For Chase, it was probably a daily occurrence to be driven around in a stretch limo, but Erin she could count on two fingers how many times she had found herself seated in such luxurious surroundings: once on the way to the club just this very night, and back when she was eighteen and going to her senior prom with a guy Paul had threatened to castrate if he didn't behave himself. But she didn't feel intimidated now; rather, her confidence soared and she was determined to live out the fantasy she had started on the dance floor.

Chase pushed the button for the intercom and told the driver to take them to the penthouse. Chase blacked out the glass with the push of another button. They picked up right from where they left off, but this time Erin kissed him. He laid her on her back and within seconds, Chase undid the two snaps that were holding her bodice intact and exposed her bare breasts. Her nipples were already hard and needy. He caressed one while he took the other in his mouth, sucking on it ravenously. Erin groaned, as the pain was intoxicating.

"I need to taste you…and I will not wait." His voice was gruff and wanting.

Chase pulled up her dress, her black silk thong in full view. He looped his fingers under the smooth fabric of the waistband and shuffled the undergarment down her legs. The action was gentle but determined. He started to kiss her thighs and as he reached her entrance, she felt her juices flow shamelessly down her legs. Each heated kiss left her begging for another. He wasn't just kissing her thighs, but tasting her with his lips and tongue.

"Oh my God, you're so wet for me, Erin. I need to make you come. It's all I've thought about."

Erin saw what looked like desperation—that need for her—in his eyes, which only made her own desire to be claimed by him mount with each passing second. She was panting for him. "Please Chase…touch me." Her legs fell apart, giving him the personal invite to satisfy her feverish need.

He slid his tongue into her tight slit and she instantly jolted and cried out. Chase parted her folds to gain greater access, which almost did her in. He ate her greedily, and she let him know how good it was. Erin moaned, begging for more, pleading for him to stop because she didn't think she could possibly stand it any longer. Erin was on the verge of the most powerful orgasm of her life when she felt him slide a finger into her, and she immediately clamped down around his finger. "Erin, you're so fucking tight. So snug. I need to get inside you."

Erin froze. It was as if someone had transported her back to that cemetery, her body exposed and being penetrated. "No…stop!"

He ceased immediately and she sat up in her seat. Her heart was pounding and her fingers trembled as she pulled her dress down and attempted to snap her bodice shut. Due to her shaking hands, she couldn't grasp the final snap between her fumbling fingers and out of frustration, she yanked at the material and ripped the snap clear away from the fabric. Without that final snap tucking the girls in for the night, she would definitely be giving off that slutty vibe now. Erin was so mortified that she couldn't even look at him. But it had nothing to do with her boobs. She was angry at herself. That one fucking phrase could put her back in that dark place she'd foolishly thought she was crawling out of.

"Erin, I'm sorry, I thought you…"

Erin stopped him from finishing his thought. "You didn't do anything wrong, Chase. It's me, fucked-up little me." She stared out the window, avoiding his gaze at all costs. Erin didn't want him to see her cry. She pressed the intercom button. "Please take me back to the club. I'll go home from there."

Erin released the button, and then with a barely together voice, she simply whispered, "I'm sorry."

He reached over, taking her trembling hands into his. "Please don't apologize. If I pushed you in any way, I…"

Erin pulled her hands away and he stopped talking. The limo came to a standstill, and she was happy to see that they were back at the club. The driver opened the door, and though it would have probably been in her best interest to leave without another word, Erin turned only enough for him to see her profile.

"Trust me when I tell you this, Chase. You did nothing wrong." She stepped out of the car and entered the club in search of Josh and an ending to a horrific night.

Chapter Seven

Erin awoke to the smell of coffee brewing and the sound of someone making way too much noise in the kitchen. She swung her legs around, feeling the cold hardwood floor beneath her bare feet, and stood up. She could barely detect a hangover, thanks to the two Advil she had taken before bed and the late-night munching at some grease truck. Erin still couldn't believe she let Josh talk her into eating a gyro, which was prepared by a man named Rudolph Monk, at two o'clock in the morning.

Erin stepped out of her room to see Josh and her brother having coffee and watching SportsCenter. Erin looked over at the couch she had converted into a bed after they had stumbled in late last night. The sheets and comforter she had given him were neatly folded and lying on the arm of the couch. What time did Josh get up this morning? More importantly, what did he tell Paul about last night? Hopefully, they had been discussing sports and not the fact that she had gotten down and dirty with Chase Montclair on the dance floor and then disappeared for a half hour in the back of a limo. Josh didn't ask for the details when she had reemerged and entered the bar looking disheveled, but he didn't attempt to conceal his shit-eating grin.

The exact grin he was sporting right now. He looked smug and pleased with himself. But Paul was acting normal. Sipping his coffee and watching the highlights from last night's Phillies game, Paul was behaving like his typical self and not a man who had learned his sister had gotten it on with someone in the middle of a club. Josh must have omitted her little tryst on the dance floor and the lost thirty minutes. Erin mouthed the words "Thank you," and he winked at her. Yep, he was too good to her.

"Nice of you to join us, sunshine. We have a big day ahead of us."

Erin groaned. Moving day. She was going to need a bagel and a lot of coffee. Immediately.

"It won't take too long. Two hours…tops," Josh said as he sipped his coffee. He appeared to savor the taste, and she grew envious. She needed her daily jolt of liquid bliss desperately, and she retreated to the kitchen.

"Oh no, you are not helping me move." Erin poured herself a cup of coffee, grabbed an Asiago bagel and slapped on the cream cheese. "I'm not putting you to work," she said.

"Too bad," Josh said. She childishly stuck her tongue out at him.

"Kids, kids. Enough," Paul playfully scolded them both as he set his coffee down on the counter.

They devoured their coffee and bagels and got to work. Erin was completely moved in within an hour and a half. Not that it was a huge feat; they only had to travel three floors down and she didn't own a whole lot of stuff. But nevertheless, her new apartment was ready to be lived in, and Erin smiled at this first taste of true independence, postcollege.

She was sitting cross-legged on the floor of her bedroom and folding clothes to put into her empty chest of drawers when her thoughts were hijacked by Chase. With Paul and Josh long gone, she was alone and free to envision herself with Chase on the dance floor, her body melting into his, his hands fondling her ass as they kissed. Erin let her mind relive the scene in the limo, and she dropped the shirt she had attempted to fold for the third time. He had been gentle but clear about what he wanted. She could still feel his breath against her thighs, how his tongue slipped past his teeth and tasted her while she moaned for him. She threw the godforsaken shirt into the drawer and stood. She contemplated getting a shower for the sole purpose of releasing her pent-up frustration. But that would only be a temporary fix. She needed to stop thinking about him. She wasn't ready to throw herself into a relationship, as she'd proved last night. She had been whisked back in time, to that hellish place, with six simple words.

She chose plan B, stress-induced eating. The safer choice. Her refrigerator bare; Erin grabbed her purse and decided to head to the market. But when she opened the front door, a delivery man stood there, his hand fisted and ready to knock. "Oh, sorry," Erin said.

"No problem, miss. I have a package for you." Erin looked

down at the large paper bag in his hand and recognized the Whole Foods ogo. It had to be from Paul. He knew about her healthy obsession with their salad bar and, more recently, the new Mexican bar with the help-yourself pan of guac.

"Who is this from?" she asked, taking the bag from the man.

"I'm not privy to that information, but he or she did leave this card." Erin thanked him and took the card. When she tried to tip him, he adamantly refused and left. Erin removed the card from the envelope and read the message…and almost dropped the bag on the floor.

Erin,

Thought you might be hungry after your move. I'm sorry about last night but I do not accept your resignation. See you on Monday.

—Chase

Arrogant asshole. Why would he assume that she would just renege on her decision to quit and show up to work tomorrow morning, as if nothing had happened? And how the hell did he know she had moved into her new apartment today?

The smells coming from the bag temporarily distracted her, and she contemplated whether she should just throw its contents in the garbage. But her stomach won out, and unless he had someone spying on her from the balcony, he would never know that she had gorged herself with the food he'd had delivered.

Erin had just ingested her second enchilada when she heard her phone vibrate. She looked down at the text and winced. *So proud of you. You were right. Time for us to look to the future. Enjoy your new digs!*

Staring down at her brother's message, Erin decided then and there that there was no way she was going to mooch off her brother or tap into her parents' wrongful-death-settlement money to pay for the apartment. She would have to continue working at Montclair Pharmaceuticals, but that didn't mean she wouldn't be job hunting in the meantime. She had survived things much worse than Chase Montclair.

She was a survivor and though it might cost her her sanity, she could do this. She could work with Chase Montclair. Or at least she'd find out in less than twelve hours.

Chapter Eight

It took a level of restraint he didn't know existed to stay away from her. Chase looked across his desk and stared at the empty leather seat that Erin Whitley had vacated in a huff that had left him both intrigued and aroused. She was still here, in this office, in his head. He could still taste her, and his thoughts immediately went back to what had happened in the limo. The whole situation was unnerving. One moment, Erin Whitley appeared to be a confident woman who enjoyed a challenge and took risks. The next, she seemed fragile and ashamed. Of what, though? What had caused her sudden shift? What haunted her?

Chase stood, walked around his desk and sat in Erin's chair. He looked across the desk and tried to picture what she had seen the night he had Lydia retrieve her. What was going through her mind as she sat there? He knew he had made her nervous. Her pink cheeks and jittery hands were normal signs of distress, common reactions he invoked in many people he summoned to his office. But there had been other emotions at play. There had been fear and anger, and they'd flip-flopped back and forth with what he'd hopefully detected correctly...desire and want.

Why the hell did it matter who Erin was and what was in her past? It just wasn't possible to feel a connection with someone that quickly. And he couldn't, wouldn't, put himself in a situation that made him vulnerable and susceptible to inconvenient emotions. It had been a little over a year since Gabrielle had betrayed him in every conceivable way, which also marked the moment he decided never to trust another woman or his heart again.

Chase ran his hand through his hair, turned on the monitors in his office and waited. Would the confident, headstrong woman come in to work this morning or was she buried under the covers in her newly acquired apartment? Chase was leafing through her skinny personnel file when he spotted her on the screen. Erin had entered the main lobby and was heading for the elevator. She wore a black pinstripe knee-length skirt that highlighted her curvy figure and a gray button-down shirt with cropped sleeves. Black high heels and an upswept hairdo completed the ensemble. She climbed into the elevator along with a sea of other employees. He watched her until the doors closed and he lost sight of her. He quickly adjusted every monitor to show the lab. In less than a minute she hustled into the research department and went straight to her desk. Erin put her purse in the bottom drawer of the desk and retrieved her lab coat from its hook. She looked stunning and he couldn't help but stare in awe.

And he was almost convinced that she was all business today, until she glanced at the camera for an extended moment and then went back to her desk. Her hands were trembling slightly as she turned on her computer. She appeared nervous...maybe even frightened. Did the camera spook her? Did the knowledge of being watched make her slender fingers shake, like they had when she'd tried desperately to snap her bodice closed in the back of the limo? Or was it him? The thought that he could be the one to cause her distress bothered him. Chase could have watched her all morning if he wasn't booked solid until at least five o'clock. He switched off the monitors and reluctantly went to his first meeting of the day.

* * *

The first text came around midmorning. Erin didn't know why she was surprised that he knew her personal cell phone number. Chase Montclair owned the building and had access to every employee file. But it still frustrated her, and it needed to end. It read: *"Nice to see you at work. Have dinner with me tonight?"*

Erin wanted no part of this. At least that was what her brain was telling her. Erin's body, however, defied her once more, and she felt that familiar warmth radiate through her as she looked down at her phone. Even after a minute or so, Erin still couldn't come up with a witty response: *"You were right before. I don't date, period."*

But the moment she pushed the SEND button, Erin knew

she had unintentionally opened Pandora's Box. He simply asked: *"Why?"*

Erin had been wading in dangerous waters for the past several days and it appeared that she'd just dived in headfirst. She kept her response generic: *"Not worth sharing. Need to get back to work."*

Erin wanted to heave when she saw the next text: *"I don't think that is the case. I will find out, Erin."*

Erin's energy drained from her body and the only thing she could type in response was: *"Please don't."* The texts stopped after that, and though she was grateful for the reprieve, Erin knew that it was only a matter of time until Chase, a man with unlimited resources and power, would start digging and possibly unearth her heinous past.

Chapter Nine

Erin breathed a sigh of relief. She had made it through the next day without incident. It had to be this way. She couldn't risk Chase nosing around in her past, discovering her secret.

The phone at her desk startled her and she grabbed it immediately. "Ms. Whitley speaking."

"Yes, Ms. Whitley, this is Lydia, Mr. Montclair's personal secretary. Mr. Montclair is requesting your presence in his office."

Erin gulped and started to sweat. "Um, sure. I am on my way." Erin returned the phone to its receiver, sat back in her chair and glared into the camera mounted on the wall. She knew he was watching her right now. She could feel it. Exhilaration mixed with anger at being beckoned. Erin broke contact, reached for her notepad and pen and begrudgingly reported to the Master's chambers.

Cocky, arrogant ass.

Lydia didn't announce Erin this time, which she preferred.

Announcing someone's arrival seemed so pretentious. Lydia silently shut the door behind her when she left. Chase was sitting at his desk, looking regal but relaxed. Again, images of Chase between her thighs flooded her thoughts, and she felt her face grow hot.

"You must be hungry." Chase's grin was irresistible, and Erin fought like hell to not get lost in it. He stood up and walked over to a large conference table and gestured for her to join him. Two place settings were arranged at the far end of the table. Containers of Chinese food were stacked between them.

"No, I already had lunch. But thank you." Erin looked down at the floor and adjusted her skirt.

"Don't lie to me, Erin. I know you've barely stopped to breathe today."

Erin glanced at his wall of monitors and raised her eyebrow. "Oh, because you've been spying on me."

"Please sit. You refuse to go to dinner with me. The least you can do is agree to a working lunch here in my office. I promise to keep this meeting…professional."

Erin felt a little more at ease, though the sexual tension buzzing in the air was suffocating her. She took a seat, trying to avoid his probing gaze. She detected his cologne, the same scent that, among other things, had driven her crazy on the dance floor. It was having the same effect on her now and she summoned all her strength to be professional.

"I wanted you to know that I have assigned you the Cabraxol presentation." He reached for one of the large white containers and began to scoop out steaming brown rice onto a plate. Chase offered her the container, but she just sat there, staring at him.

"Why are you doing this?"

"Why did I give you the assignment or why am I pursuing you?" He had no difficulty just putting his intentions out there and abandoning his promise to keep things professional. His confidence was disturbing and extremely sexy. Erin hated herself in that moment, as she sat there desiring him, craving his touch and wanting a repeat of that kiss from the dance floor. She wasn't ready. His words alone had triggered her, as if they had been spoken by the rapist himself. How would Chase react if he ever learned of her secret? Would he be disgusted? Pity her? Either response would devastate her.

"Nothing is going to happen between us again. I wasn't myself the other night and I apologize if I gave you the wrong impression," Erin said. She swallowed. Flustered and needing to do something, anything but be the recipient of his gaze, she grabbed a random container from the table and shoveled its contents onto her plate. His eyes were boring a hole into her forehead as she stared at Mongolian beef and broccoli.

"Why didn't you go on to med school like you planned?" he asked.

"You found that in my personnel file?"

"No." He speared a piece of beef with his fork and continued, "I learned that from your college professor, Dr. Farrell."

She looked at him, not even trying to disguise the rage this pompous, obnoxious man evoked. Chase sat back in his chair, his expression calm, his body poised. In what universe did

Chase Montclair think he had the right to track down her former professors?

"You what?" she seethed.

"I paid Dr. Farrell a visit last evening, introduced myself as your boss, and we got to talking." He folded his hands across his lap, appearing relaxed, as if preparing for her impending wrath.

"Who the hell do you think you are? You think because you have more money than God, that because I work for you, you have every right to invade my privacy…my life!" This was an outrage she refused to take sitting down. Erin stood up, sending the chair clattering to the floor behind her. But she couldn't be bothered with that now. His gaze did not waver, nor did his breathing. He sat there calmly, taking her and her tantrum in. She bit her lip and his eyes narrowed.

"Why does it upset you so, that I know that prior to coming to work here, you had every intention, every ability to be a great doctor?" His brow was raised and he truly appeared interested in solving this mystery.

"You just don't get it, do you?" she asked. Erin shook her head and started for the door. She may not have heard him get up from his chair, but she definitely felt his hand on her elbow and his arousal as he pinned her against the wall. Her breath staggered with both shock and anticipation. Fear overtook her, but she wasn't scared of him. She was afraid of being exposed, and of the revulsion he would surely feel when he learned of the secret she was keeping.

"I want to know who you are," he whispered. His lips hovered over hers. She bit her lower lip, but found the courage to at least return his heavy gaze.

"It's safer…easier…if you don't."

"What do you mean by 'safer,' Erin?" He drew even closer, his eyes never leaving hers. Many expletives came to mind as soon as he uttered the word "safer." Of course he would focus on that. Her slip would only fuel his intrigue.

"Please let it go," she whispered against his cheek.

"I can't." Although his voice was steady, his tone was dark and tempting. "I want to know the woman who can let go and take control, and the woman who hides away from the world."

Erin couldn't think straight. She had been watching his lips formulate the words, and she ached to feel his mouth, his tongue, explore hers. His hands were at her waist, his erection evident even through his trousers. She should break free of him, walk right out his door, and make her way to the unemployment line. But her desire to taste him one last time dominated her common sense and she foolishly leaned in. He met her halfway and Erin instantly went wet as their lips touched with an intensity that had them both groaning with need. His hands moved to frame her face as he made love to her mouth. He pressed his cock against her core and she knew she could come, just like this, standing and with no skin-to-skin contact. Erin whimpered as his thrusts came in strategic waves and she threw her head back, giving him the opportunity to explore her neck with his hot kiss. He obliged her immediately, and she felt quick and demanding little nips at her ear and then lower on her neck.

It felt incredible and every nerve in her body tingled. If

she didn't stop this now, Erin knew they would be screwing against the wall in a matter of seconds. Her arms felt like lead as she pressed her hands gently to his chest. His body grew taut and he stepped back. His ability to turn his desire down to a simmer made her feel safe. Chase would never push her further than she wanted to go. He gave Erin a glimmer of hope that not all men were animals.

But even that hope wasn't enough to make her stay. There was too much at stake; she had to find the strength to walk away. Erin stepped away from him and whispered, "Good-bye, Chase." Then she gathered all her willpower and left his office.

He didn't stop her and she was thankful that he allowed her to leave gracefully. Erin didn't know how truly grateful she was until she reached the elevator and felt her eyes begin to well. She felt ridiculous for crying. Crying over what, really? Being smart enough not to make out with her boss? Or was she crying because she had finally accepted the cold hard fact that she would never be able to let someone in?

Chapter Ten

Erin didn't need to mark her calendar or program her computer to remind her, she just instinctively knew that the anniversary of her rape had arrived. She and Dr. Cahil had talked about the upcoming anniversary at last week's session. Erin leaned against the elevator wall and thought about its significance.

It's just another day. No big deal.

Erin hadn't heard the term Thirsty Thursday since college and was disappointed that people were still using it, especially grown-up people with grown-up jobs. But apparently the saying was alive and well, as Tori, her coworker, asked Erin to celebrate Thirsty Thursday with her and another employee from the research department.

"We plan on hitting Fire tonight. Come with?"

The elevator was packed, and it seemed to taunt her as it stopped at each floor, giving her ample time to give Tori an answer. Erin was pretty sure things couldn't get any worse until the elevator doors opened, putting her face-to-face with Chase. As usual, he looked incredible in his suit and tie, and again his scent wafted over to her, always tempting her, making her needy and unable to think clearly. Erin's cheeks were on fire with a blush that he surely noticed. But his smile disappeared as their eyes locked and was replaced with desire. His heated blue eyes appeared to darken until they matched his navy tie perfectly. Clueless Tori continued her conversation as if Erin wasn't in the middle of a paralyzing state of arousal and longing for her boss, a man whom she needed to stay away from for both their sakes.

"Pick you up around eight? Tori asked.

Pick…up…what? Erin hadn't been paying attention to anything Tori was saying, not since Chase had walked into the elevator and disabled the part of her brain that allowed her to deliver coherent responses.

So Erin did something completely asinine, something that she knew she would regret, and nodded, her eyes still locked on Chase.

"Great!" Tori squealed like a little girl.

What the hell did she just agree to? Shit. Erin shifted her gaze to Tori, completely prepared to clarify that she would not be joining her at club Fire tonight or any night, but the elevator doors opened and Tori escaped before she got the chance.

Fuck.

Chase had also stepped out of the elevator, but not before flashing Erin one of those grins that left her both frustrated and hungry for what she knew would shatter her completely.

Erin had no right to be frustrated. Chase had adhered to

their agreement. It had been two days since she had said good-bye to him, two days since they had almost lost it in his office and given her two nights' worth of vivid and mind-blowing dreams. She had awoken both nights and again this morning wet and aching with need.

He had kept his distance and made no attempt to contact her. So, when she saw the lust in his eyes when he looked at her in the elevator—when she saw that the desire, the heat, had not dissipated, she was intrigued and undeniably pleased that she had caused it.

And she could only imagine what he saw in her own gaze. But she didn't know how to look at him any differently, or if it was even worth trying to suppress her longing. The smile he had given her as he left told Erin that he was more than satisfied, if not completely aroused.

Chapter Eleven

He had stayed away, though it almost killed him to do so. Chase could tell that Erin wanted him as much as he wanted her. He could feel it whenever she looked at him with those haunting blue eyes. But for some reason, she kept him at arm's length and it was beyond frustrating.

What the fuck was he doing? Why wasn't he listening to that voice in his head that had steered him correctly for the past year? The one that told him it was safer to date multiple women, screw them and move on. The one that told him not to get attached to another woman because she would surely hurt him, maybe not right away, but down the road, when he least expected it.

Chase knew he shouldn't go, that if Erin spotted him it was likely he would come across as some sick stalker. But something told him to go to Fire. Something wasn't sitting right and he couldn't put his finger on it. He arrived at the club around nine o'clock and found a dark nook off the main bar.

From that vantage point, he could see her at one of the table-tops on the far side of the club. The woman named Tori was trying to convince Erin by pulling gently on her arm to join her and two guys on the dance floor. He couldn't read her lips from that distance, but it was obvious Erin was letting Tori down easy and that she didn't want to dance. Tori gave Erin a pouty face, turned on her heel, and took the dance floor by storm.

The waiter had just cleared their table of two empty glasses and two beer bottles when Chase noticed Erin resting her head against her hand. Her eyes were droopy, as if she was tired or on her way to being wasted. Chase intercepted the waiter and threw a fifty on the tray he was carrying. "How many drinks has that girl had tonight?" Chase asked, pointing to Erin.

"This was her first drink of the night and she's been here for at least forty-five minutes."

It didn't make sense. Chase watched her stumble off her stool and shuffle to the back of the club, toward the restrooms. All apprehension about her seeing him vanished and he pummeled through the crowd to reach her. Erin was walking down a narrow hallway when she tripped over what appeared to be nothing. Chase caught her right before she took a header onto the tiled floor. He gathered her in his arms without a word and continued out the back door to where his Bentley was parked.

His driver opened the car door and Chase gently placed her in the backseat. He sat down next to her and directed his driver to take off. Without warning, Erin straddled him and snuggled into his chest. Her fingertips brushed over the ridges of his abdomen, making his cock stiffen instantly. At any other time, he would have been more than willing to let her ride him, allowing him to sink deep into her tight heat.

She started to kiss his neck and when she nibbled close to his ear, she whispered, "I want you inside me."

He almost came on the spot, though he knew he wouldn't take her, not here, not now. "Not like this, Erin."

She whimpered as if she was disappointed and nestled into him once more. "Don't you want to touch me? I need this. And I want you to give it to me."

She was making it extremely difficult. He disregarded her question with one of his own. "Did you have any drinks before you came to the club…or take anything?"

Erin's eyes began to close. "No, just the one." Her voice trailed off and her breathing had changed. At first he thought she was falling asleep, but when he listened to her shallow breaths he knew something was terribly wrong.

"Erin, wake up. Erin!" He jostled her, but she was in some sort of dreamlike state, mumbling and saying things that didn't make sense.

So when he told his driver to turn the car around and go to the hospital, he was shocked to hear her whimper, "No hospitals!" Though her eyes were closed, Chase could see the tears flowing down her cheeks.

Chase was torn. He knew she needed medical assistance, but as he watched her cry, begging him not to take her to the hospital, Chase withdrew his cell phone and dialed one of the few people he could trust.

"Robert. Yes, I need your assistance. Twenty-five-year-old

female, no known health concerns. I believe her drink was drugged." Chase looked at Erin and was immediately filled with fear. The crying had ceased and she had slipped into a deep sleep, one from which he could only pray she would awaken.

Chapter Twelve

How much was in her system?"

Erin recognized the voice but her surroundings were foreign. The enormous king-sized bed that she must have slept in appeared miniscule in the massive bedroom. She looked in the direction of the voice and saw Chase standing next to a window that overlooked a beautiful skyline and talking on a cell phone. "Chase?" Her voice sounded froggy and weak, even to her, and he turned when she called for him.

"She's awake," he told the person on the other end of the call. "See you in a few minutes."

Chase placed his cell phone on the nightstand beside the bed and sat down next to her. Erin rose to a sitting position, but immediately knew that it was a mistake. Her head pounded and her vision was a little blurry. This was without a doubt the worst hangover Erin had ever experienced.

How much did she have to drink? How much alcohol had been in her system?

And for the first time, Erin couldn't remember. Couldn't remember anything about last night. Erin's eyes gravitated to her attire and she flinched, knowing that she definitely didn't go to the club in a man's t-shirt and black lounge pants. "How did I get here? Did we…" Erin couldn't finish her thought. She was too embarrassed.

"I found you at the club and brought you home. And no, we didn't do anything. You slept here. I slept over there on the couch." A pillow and blanket were strewn about on the oversized loveseat, and she sighed with relief.

"But I don't remember you being at the club." Erin pulled her knees to her chest and laid her head in her hands. Why couldn't she remember?

"What's the last thing you *do* remember?" he asked, his voice steady, yet gentle.

Erin shook her head, hoping to dust the cobwebs off her brain. "I remember sitting at the table with Tori, Jonah and his boyfriend Greg. We ordered a round of drinks. I think I had a cosmopolitan. I always order that when I plan on having a one-drink night and have no intention of extending my stay."

"Can you remember anything else?"

Erin sat in silence for a moment, trying to think of what came next, but nothing surfaced. Absolutely nothing. She just shook her head and closed her eyes. After a moment of self-pity, Erin stood up, in search of a bathroom. But the moment she became vertical, Erin instantly felt like she was going to vomit. Erin ran for what she hoped was the master bath. Luckily, she had made it in time and was hugging porcelain within seconds.

Chase was crouching behind her and holding back her hair as she emptied the contents of her stomach into his toilet. This wasn't happening. Her boss wasn't fisting her hair as she squatted on her hands and knees in his oversized t-shirt and lounge pants! A knock at the door interrupted her humiliation for a split second. But Chase ignored the person at the door, giving Erin his full attention. Three heaving episodes later, Erin finally felt like she had nothing left and it was safe to ask for a toothbrush and a glass of water. Chase disappeared and returned a minute later with the items she had requested. "Erin, I'll be just outside the door. Dr. Marshall is here and he wants to talk to you, make sure you're alright."

"What? Doctor? I don't need a doctor for a hangover, Chase."

His eyes were like steel, serious and unwavering. A chill slithered down her spine as he uttered his next words. "You don't have a hangover, Erin. You were drugged last night."

Chapter Thirteen

Erin liked Dr. Marshall immediately. He reminded her of Professor Farrell and she couldn't dismiss a twinge of regret—or was it guilt?—that she had not been in touch with the man who had counseled her through some dark days.

"You gave us both a scare, young lady," the doctor said as he returned the stethoscope to his leather bag.

"How do you know I was drugged?" It sounded like a ridiculous question, considering she couldn't remember anything and had just spent the morning throwing up, but Erin had a feeling Dr. Marshall could provide her with a concrete answer to her question and hopefully some insight into her missing hours from last night.

"Although you were in and out of consciousness last night, you were able to provide me with a urine sample."

Oh God. Erin felt her stomach churn once more. He must have sensed her mortification, because he did not elaborate on how he obtained her urine, and simply patted her hand like last night was no big deal.

"I tested it for several things, in fact, but it came up positive for GHB."

Erin's embarrassment morphed into anger as she came to the realization that someone at that club had slipped her one of the most powerful date rape drugs on the market. But she felt more than pissed off, she felt violated…again.

The doctor sat down on the bed, held her wrist, and took her pulse. Satisfied, he laid Erin's arm back down, but not before giving it another pat with his hand. "It was fortunate that you ran into Chase last night. That drug can leave one completely incapacitated and vulnerable to…well, to men that do not respect women."

It was difficult to dismiss the warmth in the doctor's voice as he spoke of Chase. Erin looked at the bedroom door. Though he was nearby, it would be next to impossible for Chase to hear her if she kept her voice low. Erin didn't know if she would have another opportunity to learn more about the mysterious and godlike CEO. "How long have you known Chase?"

"All his life." The doctor smiled and reached for his bag on the floor.

"Are you family?" Erin knew the question was personal, but she really didn't care at this point.

"Practically." With a sly smirk, he continued, "Now it's your turn. How long have you known Chase?"

"Almost a week." Erin's face flushed with embarrassment. She knew what he probably thought. Didn't take long for you to hop into Chase's bed and become just another notch on his expensive bedpost, huh?

"Interesting."

That wasn't the response she had expected.

"I beg your pardon?" Erin didn't say it with sass, but with curiosity, hoping he would clarify.

"I was here last night, checking your vitals, ensuring that you remained stable. But Chase, well...he never left your side." He stood up and walked to the door. But before he left, the good doctor said, "What I find intriguing is that I have never in thirty years seen him so shaken." Dr. Marshall winked at her and left before she could respond. Erin could hear the two men exchanging words in the hallway and then the opening and closing of an elevator.

Chase walked into the bedroom a few moments later with a tray in his hand. "Hungry?"

Erin didn't think it was possible to consume food after her productive date with the toilet this morning, but her stomach had a mind of its own. It rumbled on cue, and Chase smiled. "We'll start you off with something safe: dry toast and tea," he said.

He laid the tray over her lap like she was some hospital patient. Erin reached for a piece of toast and took a bite. She could feel him staring at her, as if she were going to combust at any moment. And as much as Erin wanted to tell him to stop treating her like an invalid, she was grateful that he had gotten her out of that club and sought medical attention. Erin kept her smart-ass comments to herself and simply said, "Thank you."

She scarfed down the toast in record time and took a sip of tea. Erin figured that she might as well get it over with and ask Chase how she ended up at his penthouse. "I don't remember seeing you at the club last night. When did you get there?"

Erin's mind must have been compromised all morning, because only then did she notice how incredibly sexy Chase looked. Barefoot, he sported dark jeans with a simple white t-shirt. The subtle scent of his cologne mixed with pure, virile male made Erin all too aware of her own sad and disgusting appearance. Erin pulled the covers closer to her body. "I arrived around nine, minutes before I found you in the hallway at the back of the club. You could barely stand at that point, so I carried you out of that place and brought you here, though I had every intention of taking you to the hospital."

The mention of a hospital made Erin grow pale. The last time she had been to a hospital was the night of the rape, when she had agreed to a rape kit and answered the police's embarrassing questions. "What made you bring me here instead?"

Chase ran his fingers through his hair, and even in the state she was in, Erin could imagine those fingers running their way over her body. Suddenly, a vision of her straddling Chase in the backseat of a car flashed in her mind, and she wondered if that actually had happened or if it was just a replay of one of many fantasies she had about Chase. "You were adamant about not going to the hospital." He paused for a moment and then asked the question she had hoped he wouldn't. "Why?"

Tread lightly. Make it believable.

"Hospitals just creep me out. Always have." Keep it simple. A lot of people hate the sights and smells of a hospital.

Chase stared at her, as if analyzing Erin's every move, dissecting the tone and possible double meaning of her words. "You begged me not to take you to the hospital."

Nope, he didn't buy it. Shit.

"And when you began to cry, I just couldn't get you home fast enough." Erin wanted to melt right there. He was being so sweet, so attentive.

"I find it hard to believe your excuse that hospitals repel you. You were going to be a doctor, remember?"

Sweetness gone.

Erin shook her head, but kept her eyes down. She was a shitty liar. So it was best that she keep her mouth shut. Erin pushed the covers back and got out of bed. Again, the room started to spin. "Can I use your shower?"

Erin could see his jaw clench. Obviously the conversation was not over in his mind, but he remained a gentleman and helped her to the bathroom. "Are you steady enough to stand in the shower, or will you need my assistance?"

His question forced her to look him in the eye. There was a hint of a smile, but she knew that he wasn't taking advantage of the situation. He could have had her every way possible last night and no one would have been the wiser. "I think I got this. Thank you, though."

Famous last words.

Erin was in his shower for only a few seconds when she thought she saw the multiple shower heads rotating, proving that her equilibrium was off. Erin reached for the railing, but missed and went down, hard. Chase threw open the glass door, his face panic-stricken.

"Christ! Did you hit your head?" He stepped into the shower, clothes and all, and picked her up.

Mortified, Erin just shook her head. She couldn't be more exposed. Naked and recovering from a drug-induced state. "That's it," Chase said. "You will let me shower you. And then you will go right back to bed."

"Chase, this is, this is…"

"What? Embarrassing? I have seen or touched most of your body already, Erin. I can handle it if you can."

Erin could smell a challenge when she heard one. She reached for the railing, successfully this time, to steady herself and then she looked at him. The water was pouring over her body and soaking him through as well. He wore that smirk that got her heated and thinking very naughty things. "I can handle it." Surprisingly, she sounded confident, in complete contradiction to the throbbing between her thighs.

He started with her hair. His fingers gently massaged her scalp as he worked in the shampoo and then the conditioner. Erin kept her eyes closed most of the time, but when she did have those momentary lapses of judgment and looked at him, Erin was amazed that his gaze did not wander to other areas of her body. He seemed to be in complete control, his attention focused on the task at hand. He rinsed her hair and then began lathering her body with soap, which Erin determined complimented his cologne in an extraordinary way.

The shower sponge moved in hypnotic circles on her back, and she felt him draw closer. Chase moved her hair to one side as he washed the back of her neck. His touch was tender and soothing. His touch made her feel…safe. It was this realization that allowed other emotions in, and she let her desire for him take hold. He was just inches away…and she was losing it. He turned her around and it was then Erin noticed that he too was struggling with the challenge he had proposed. His erection was even more prominent through drenched jeans, and she felt her breath catch. Erin's gaze lingered there, but it was disrupted by the first touch of suds and steady hands on her breasts. She looked at him and noticed that the playful smirk had been replaced with intense desire. His fingers were meticulous as he soaped up her full globes and brushed over very firm nipples. Erin allowed a soft moan to escape, which prompted his own breathing to stagger.

With sponge in hand, he navigated south. This time her body didn't stiffen as it had in the limo that first night. She wanted his hands to touch her there. But it had to be on her terms. Without a word, Erin took the sponge from him and soaped it up thoroughly. He watched her move the sponge in slow, circular motions over her well-trimmed mound, and into each fold. She swept the sponge across her clit and she nearly came from the sensation. Her body was so wound and ready, and she groaned with satisfaction and want.

"Erin, you're not playing fair." His voice was gruff, as if in pain. He kept his hands to his sides, though his fists were clenched.

Erin slipped one finger into her tight entrance and massaged her clit with another, and immediately felt the climax building. Breathless, she answered, "No more games."

That was all the invitation he needed. His hands found her waist and he kissed her against the shower wall. With her help, he tore his shirt right off his body. She unbuttoned his jeans and inched them down, exposing his throbbing length. Erin licked her lips, wanting his cock in her mouth, wanting him as needy as she was. She just hoped she could please him. She had never done this before. Reading erotic romances had given her an idea what to do, where to touch and lick, but nothing could have truly prepared her for Chase Montclair. But it was worth the risk. *He* was worth it.

Erin sank to her knees, cupped his balls in one hand and wrapped the other firmly around his shaft. His entire body undulated and he groaned. "Erin, oh God!" Not that she needed it, but the sound of his anticipation gave her the encouragement to take him deep. She stroked the underside of his cock with her tongue, sucking and licking the salty liquid that seeped from the head. "Ah, suck it hard. Oh, you feel so good!"

Erin couldn't get enough. The sounds he was making were an aphrodisiac for her. She could feel her cunt grow wet with need, but all she wanted was to please him. His cock swelled, growing thicker between her lips as it hit the back of her throat with each forceful thrust. The thought of them in the shower, the image of her on her knees taking him deep while he rammed into her mouth, taking what he wanted, only made her more crazed.

"You take it so good...your mouth. Ah, *Erin*!" His voice was a guttural growl. Semen exploded into her mouth, which at first was overwhelming, but she quickly adjusted to the onslaught and swallowed each and every drop. Erin licked him clean and stared up at him. At first, she thought he was going to lift her to her feet. Instead, he placed her on the shower bench, parted her legs with a sense of urgency, and began to lick her clit with such precision that she knew she would come very soon. Erin screamed his name as his tongue speared her, and she heard him groan in satisfaction. Erin grabbed his hair and rocked into him. "Chase, harder, more, more!"

Erin felt his fingers on her cunt, but this time she didn't freeze. She still needed some control, though, and she laid her hands over his, guiding them inside her. "You are so tight and wet for me." The combination of his two fingers inside her and his tongue lapping against her sensitive flesh in that deadly rhythm drove her straight to the edge.

"Come for me, Erin. Now." Erin never thought she would be able to come on command, or that it was even humanly possible, but then the warm rush of pleasure poured over her, and her orgasm took hold in unremitting waves.

Chapter Fourteen

Erin didn't know if it was the incredible orgasm, the insurmountable spread of food Chase's housekeeper had prepared or a combination of both that had her feeling almost human again. They sat in his king-sized bed, legs crossed and eating burgers and cheese fries, and sipping on root beers. Barefoot and wearing lounge pants and t-shirts, Erin thought that they probably looked like a couple of teenagers gorging themselves after a night out.

"Think we'll get in trouble for playing hooky from work today?" Erin asked. She had already polished off her burger and was now working on the fries.

"Not if the boss doesn't find out," Chase said. Smiling, he dipped a fry in some heavy-duty melted cheese and fed her. A bit of cheese had spilled onto his finger and she licked it off. Even after the orgasm he had given her, Erin could feel her body respond as her tongue slid over his fingertip.

"Continue and I will have you flat on your back." Though

his tone was playful, he was dead serious, and Erin gave him a quick kiss on the lips.

Round two would have to wait. Erin knew there were a few things that had to be discussed. "I want to thank you for last night and for bringing me here, instead of to the hospital. I can be stubborn at times and probably thought that a hospital visit wasn't necessary." Wait for it. Maybe that excuse was more believable. He seemed to study her for what felt like an eternity. Erin imagined he was looking for some flaw in her guise. "It was fortunate that Dr. Marshall was able to come over on such short notice."

The mention of the doctor's name seemed to relax Chase, and he reached for a second burger. "He's like an uncle to me. Robert was my father's best friend. He helped raise me after my mother died."

"Oh, I'm sorry. I didn't know." Erin wondered if he knew about her parents. It wouldn't take much to find out. An internet search would unearth their names, classifying them as victims of a horrible pier accident. She might not be able to share everything with him, but Erin figured the subject of her parents was safe.

"Do you know about my parents?" He didn't flinch at the question, but nodded. And then before she could ask how he knew, he told her about his one-on-one visit with Dr. Farrell at the coffee shop in Philadelphia.

Erin didn't know whether to be angry, concerned or flattered that he had traveled to Philly to track down her former professor. "Why go to Philly? What were you looking for?" she asked.

He laughed, which was a sound that Erin was not used to from him. "It's not like you're an open book. Sometimes one must resort to unconventional methods to gain the information needed."

"Do you always get what you want?" she asked.

He sipped his root beer and placed the glass bottle on the nightstand. His gaze grew dark and haunted. Red flags went up and waved…violently.

"Not always." His answer was abrupt, telling Erin that it was probably wise to switch conversation topics.

Erin resorted to one that she knew had put him at ease before. "Dr. Marshall reminds me of Professor Farrell. Genuine and loyal to a fault."

"Loyalty is everything to me, Erin. Without trust, you have nothing."

That haunted look had not dissipated; in fact it seemed to intensify. She could only assume that he had been burned in the past, maybe by a business partner, or a woman, perhaps. But before Erin could ask why he appeared agitated, a knock sounded at the door. Chase answered the door and was greeted by his housekeeper, Charlotte.

"Mr. Montclair, these came for Ms. Whitley. Where would you like them?" Charlotte looked around the room for the proper place to secure an enormous bouquet of exotic flowers.

The flowers were beautiful and Erin was taken aback by how sweet he was. She had never been sent flowers before, at least not by a man. Parents and brothers didn't count. "Chase, they are gor…"

"I didn't send them, Erin. Though I wish I had, considering

the smile on your face." Chase took the flowers from Charlotte and politely dismissed her. She bowed in compliance and left them alone.

Confused, Erin walked over to him and searched the bouquet for a card. Tucked neatly into the green foliage, she found a yellow envelope with her name written simply on the front. Erin withdrew a matching yellow card. Her hands trembled as she read the two sentences:

Hope you are feeling better. See you soon, Angel.

Chapter Fifteen

Erin's first instinct was to take the bouquet and throw it against the wall. But she couldn't, and she knew that she had to be very careful. Chase would be scrutinizing every move she made. Erin's stomach began to roil and she fought desperately to keep down the contents within. She had to get to Paul. Erin folded the card in half and tucked it into her pants.

"Who are they from?" Chase asked, his tone laced with jealousy.

She couldn't tell him the truth. So what *would* he believe? Stalling, Erin walked over to the small bedside table where Chase had placed her belongings. Erin retrieved her purse and slipped on a sweatshirt and a pair of flip-flops that Charlotte had purchased for her earlier that morning at a boutique just around the corner from Chase's building.

"Erin?" He was growing impatient and, in all honesty, she couldn't blame him.

"Apparently, my ex thought it would be amusing to send

flowers to me here. Cocky son-of-a-bitch." There was so much disdain in Erin's voice that it would be difficult not to believe her. And truth be told, she wasn't really lying. The son-of-a-bitch that sent the flowers was an ex, just not an ex-boyfriend.

"So he's stalking you? He must be if he knows you're here." He slammed the flowers down on the nightstand. Water seeped from the spider cracks. "May I see the card?" he asked, through gritted teeth.

Shaking her head, "Trust me, it's not worth it, he's not worth it." There was no way he was going to see that card.

Erin slung her purse over her shoulder, prompting an already-agitated Chase to take his frustration to the next level. "Where are you going?"

"To put an end to my ex's antics."

"You're not leaving, and you are certainly not leaving me to go speak with your ex."

Erin didn't take kindly to demands, and out of sheer defiance, she glared at him and walked toward the door. Chase blocked her exit and she went into a panic. Erin didn't like feeling trapped, and when his hands found her wrists, she instantly was back there. Held against her will in that cemetery. Erin began to cry and she screamed for him to let her go. Stunned and possibly fearful of what he'd evoked, he instantly let her go. Erin pushed him away and ran out the door and onto the elevator before he could stop her.

Erin yanked open her purse and withdrew her phone. She had four missed calls and three texts, all from Paul. She read through the last text. Apparently someone—or maybe it was her and she didn't remember—had answered him. It was obvious that he was worried about her. Luckily, someone responded to his, *"WHERE THE HELL ARE YOU!"* with *"Out with friends, having fun, talk to you soon."* His calls and texts ceased after that, suggesting that he was satisfied with her response.

Erin decided to nail down who had actually sent the texts to Paul at a later date. Right now, she needed to get to Paul. He answered on the first ring. She didn't even say hello. Erin took a deep breath and said the words that she had hoped she would never have to utter.

"He's alive, Paul. And he has found me."

Chapter Sixteen

Scott Morris was a man of means. He never wanted for anything, including women, yet he enjoyed the deprivation, the withholding of sexual intimacy. However, it wasn't like he was holding out for "the one." Rather, he indulged only when a current fixation aroused him enough to succumb to his dark and demented desires for control and the complete domination of innocence.

Looking back into his childhood, there wasn't an event that had set him on his path. He didn't mutilate animals or imagine himself kicking puppies and kittens. He had never been witness to domestic violence, as his mother and father always spoke lovingly to one another.

No red flags would have clued anyone in that he would become who he was. Well, maybe there was one person who had an idea, a feeling, possibly, that he engaged in such a pastime. But that person had remained silent, which was wise on his part.

Scott did not like to lose. Though when it came to Erin Whitley, it was all he seemed to do. She brought out the worst in him and, because of his fascination with her, he had been brought to within an inch of his life.

Scott watched Erin from the tinted windows of his Audi as she left the Manhattan high-rise building. For the first time in his life he was willing to forget his own rule. There was a very real possibility that his Angel was no longer pure and that she had fucked Chase Montclair last night. But he could forgive her transgressions and chalk it up to the fact that she was out of her mind, due to the drug he himself had slipped into her drink.

She was talking on her cell phone and appeared anxious as she walked to the curb and waved for a cab. Even in her laid-back attire she still looked beautiful, though the dress she had worn last night had left him breathless. And he had almost succeeded. If it wasn't for her new boyfriend, Erin would have been his last night and willing to do anything in her drug-induced state.

Erin's cab pulled away from the curb and headed in the direction of her apartment building. Scott put the car in drive and followed her. But it appeared that her apartment was not the destination, and the cab continued down Fifth Street and eventually turned onto Worthington Place. The cab came to a halt in front of the Pierce and Stone Law Firm. He watched her hand the driver a few bills, glance around as if to ensure that she hadn't been followed, and ascend the few steps to the law office. But before she could enter the building, the door swung open, revealing Paul Whitley.

The sight of Erin's brother threw him into a silent rage. And as he watched that arrogant prick embrace his Angel, it took everything Scott had not to exit his vehicle and inflict the same pain on her brother that he had experienced in that cemetery.

Be patient, be patient, he willed himself. His time will come.

Paul Whitley looked around, as if he too was surveying his surroundings, and escorted her into the law firm. But she turned around once more, and Scott noticed that his Angel had begun to cry.

Chapter Seventeen

Stop her!"

"I'm sorry, sir. But the woman you described just stepped into a cab and is heading east on Fifth Street."

Chase released the button on the intercom and paced his grand foyer. What the fuck just happened? One minute they were eating burgers in bed and the next she was screaming for him to let her go. And to top it off, her ex-boyfriend sent her flowers to his penthouse. That arrogant fuck!

Chase retrieved his cell phone from the nightstand and dialed an old friend. "Sam, yeah, I need your help. I need you to run a background check on someone."

"Time frame?" Sam asked. "When do you need it by?"

"Yesterday." Chase answered.

"Not a problem, Chase. You know that."

Chase raked his fingers through his hair and sat on his bed. He was lucky to have someone like Sam in his life. They had been friends since the first grade. And though work and life in general prevented them from meeting up often, Chase knew that he could count on Sam for anything, especially with matters that required the utmost discretion. If anybody could provide him with a thorough background on Erin Whitley, it was Sam, the son of a former high-ranking CIA agent. Sam was not CIA, but he had definitely learned a few tricks of the trade from his old man before he had passed. Getting the dirt on someone while remaining invisible was now a hobby of his, which seemed to contradict his rather predictable day job as an accountant.

"Her name is Erin Whitley."

Chase felt like he was betraying her somehow. He wasn't comfortable asking Sam to look into Erin's past, but something wasn't right. Erin had screamed and started to cry when he tried to prevent her from leaving his apartment. He had let go of her immediately, but he couldn't get the image out of his mind. It was as if she was frightened that he might hurt her. And it was definitely not the first time her reaction had sent up red flags. Chase thought about their encounter in the back of his limo, how she put on the brakes as soon as he mentioned that he wanted to be inside her. She proceeded to apologize and said that he had done nothing wrong. That it was her—"fucked-up little her." Her choice of words was disturbing.

Chase shook his head, remembering more of her cryptic responses. She had basically told him not to dig, to leave whatever was in her past alone. And he would have honored her wishes, but some innate response coaxed him on. She had been drugged last night to the point where she couldn't remember a goddamned thing. And then this morning, an enormous bouquet of flowers from her ex arrived for her at his apartment. It could be a coincidence and the two events could be unrelated, but Chase was willing to bet his entire fortune that they were without a doubt linked somehow.

He didn't like the look on her face when she had received the flowers from her ex. She had appeared more than annoyed. She looked frightened.

Chase told Sam about Erin's parents' death, informed him of her sudden career change upon graduating from college, and identified the handful of people that were in her life, including Dr. Farrell, Josh and her brother Paul. Again, Chase felt guilt wash over him. He was disclosing personal information about Erin without her knowledge. But it had to be done; it felt as if her safety depended on it.

"Got it. I'll see what I can find," Sam said.

Chase sighed. "Thanks for doing this."

After a brief silence, Sam said, "She must be important to you."

"Why do you say that?" Chase asked, clearly agitated.

"Because you haven't been this rattled over a woman since Gabrielle." Another moment of silence passed and then he said, "I'll give you a call soon."

"Thanks." Chase hung up the phone and cursed. He was frustrated for a multitude of reasons, the most recent being Sam's spot-on observation.

With the investigation underway, Chase felt he could put all his attention into finding Erin. He quickly changed into jeans, sneakers and a t-shirt. Chase decided her apartment was a good place to start. Chase approached the doorman at her building and asked him if he had seen Ms. Whitley that morning. The older gentleman smiled and told Chase that he hadn't seen the lovely Ms. Whitley since last evening.

Chase looked across the street and was relieved to see a coffee shop with outdoor seating. Chase purchased a mug of half-decent coffee and planted himself at one of the small tables, giving him an unobstructed view of the entrance to her building.

Chase decided that the only thing he could do at that point was wait, which he knew was not going to be an easy task for him. He could be patient, especially in matters of business. He was known in the business world as a man who always got what he wanted. And at first, what he had thought he wanted was Erin. But he had been wrong. He *needed* her. Although Gabrielle had been skilled in bed and could at times hold his attention, he had never needed anyone to make him happy, to complete him or other bullshit like that.

But as he envisioned Erin taking him deep in the shower, with her mesmerizing blue eyes searching his as she pleased him, he couldn't help but feel like a man possessed. In just one week's time, he went from swearing off relationships, which gave him the freedom to fuck whomever and whenever he pleased, to needing to claim and be claimed by Erin Whitley. How the hell did that happen? If he was feeling that territorial about a woman he hadn't even slept with yet, it scared him to think how he would feel after he had actually been inside her.

But even Chase, a man who'd had more women over the last

several months than he cared to admit, knew that sex wasn't what was solely driving him this time around. Yes, he wanted to experience what it was like to claim her body, feel her heat as she surrounded him, hear her scream his name and beg for pleasure that only he could give her. But there was something else that landed him at the coffee shop, waiting for a woman who was at the moment meeting with her ex-boyfriend. The sudden surge of jealousy prompted him to slam his coffee mug on the grated tabletop, causing it to shatter to pieces. A couple at the table to his right looked over at him for a moment, but immediately went back to their conversation. Chase was just about to get up to retrieve some napkins and clean up his mess when a waitress came over with a bin that busboys tend to carry.

"I'll get that, sir," she said, her fake eyelashes batting at him. She appeared to be around Erin's age, maybe a little older, and as she bent over to gather the ceramic shards with a dustpan and brush, the girl smiled at him while giving him a private showing of her breasts.

He sat back in his chair, not even giving the waitress a second glance. Chase had thought that she would have taken the hint, but his standoffish demeanor only seemed to coax her on. "You didn't hurt yourself, did you?" she asked.

Ignoring her hadn't worked. Maybe quick, clipped conversation would get his message across. "No, but thank you."

Before he could stop her, she reached over and grabbed his hand. "Are you sure you don't need me to look you over?" she asked, turning his hand in hers, looking for an abrasion that she knew didn't exist.

Chase withdrew his hand from hers and somehow forced a smile. "Just a little clumsy is all," he said.

"Clumsy...and very cute," she said, emptying the ceramic pieces into the busboy bin.

"Clumsy...and very taken," he said. Short of telling her to get the hell away from him, he couldn't have been more transparent. He wasn't interested...not anymore, not since Erin. Yes, the waitress would have most likely pleased him physically, allowing him to fuck her in multiple ways, but that would be it. He wanted...no, needed more, now. What he needed was Erin and what only she could give him.

"Such a pity," she said, pouting.

"Can I have another cup of coffee?" he asked, ignoring her last comment.

"Of course. And if you need anything else, you only have to ask," she said.

Chase didn't bother to force a smile this time. No matter what he did, it only seemed to encourage her. He sat back in his chair and stared at Erin's apartment building, thinking about just how natural it was to tell the waitress, a virtual stranger, that he was, without question, taken.

Chapter Eighteen

What are we going to do?"

Paul scratched his head and looked at his sister, his inspiration in what could be a very cruel and dark world. He had hoped that the rapist would have either succumbed to his injuries or slithered back into the hole from which he had come, leaving Paul free to avoid the consequences of his own involvement. But apparently he had survived and was making himself known.

"You are moving back in with me, for starters," Paul said.

Erin shook her head. "No. If I do that, he wins…again."

Paul didn't want to scare her, but the sick bastard had proved that he could get to her. He had drugged her and then had the balls to send her get-well flowers the morning after. "Where did you say you spent the night?"

"My friend Tori's house…a girl from work." Paul noticed that she didn't look at him and immediately gathered that she was lying about something. He would explore that later.

"What is important is that you're protected. We need to go back to the police. I know they came up empty-handed last time, but…"

"No. We're not involving them again. You heard them, just as I did, that this…shit is a ghost. No physical evidence was found during the rape kit. And the blood they discovered in the cemetery didn't belong to any perp in the system."

Paul sighed. He had hoped the piece of shit had suffered and experienced a slow and agonizing death. They had left him in excruciating pain and bleeding out amongst the tombstones. When the police had come back and told him that the man he admitted to beating was not in the cemetery he himself had identified, Paul panicked. Erin had been in no condition to travel that night, but her safety trumped caution, and upon her discharge from the hospital, he packed their things and fled to New York. But he knew even then that he would always be looking over his shoulder, that he had failed to give Erin the peace she deserved. The fact that he hadn't removed the mask and identified the bastard would always haunt him.

"Okay. You can stay in your apartment. But you leave me no choice but to assign a bodyguard to you," Paul said.

"You're not serious?" she asked.

"Very." Paul crossed his arms and stared down at her.

"I will not be followed around all day. How will I explain that when I go to work?"

As much as he adored his sister, she could also frustrate him like no one else. Erin had a stubborn streak a mile long, and it seemed that he had the unfortunate ability to bring it out.

"You could work from home. Your qualifications are unique and in demand. It wouldn't be too difficult to find a job that would enable you to…"

"Be a prisoner in my own home?" Erin interjected.

His heart ached for her.

"This is all my fault. I should have finished him off when I had the chance." Paul's nightmares were still consumed with that missed opportunity. He had dreamt of killing the shit in multiple ways, some slow and agonizing. Other times he envisioned himself killing the rapist swiftly.

"Just stop. Don't go down that road again. We can't change what did or didn't happen." Erin stood from her chair, and he noticed how tired she looked. Coupled with her casual attire and messy bun, it appeared she'd had a long night.

"Alright. No bodyguards. But there is no harm in reporting this to the police, Erin. At least agree to that?"

She sighed, but nodded.

Although he was the lawyer, he rarely felt like the victor when they argued. She had a way of getting what she wanted. He looked at Erin and said firmly, "Good. I will escort you to and from work every day. You will also promise me that you will never go anywhere alone. And I mean anywhere…lunch, bathroom, to the gym. Understood?"

Erin smiled. "Yes." She walked over and hugged him. Erin reached for her purse and then started for the door.

"And it starts right now," Paul said.

She raised an eyebrow.

Paul phoned his secretary and told her that he was taking an early lunch. "Shall we?"

"Where are we going?" she asked.

"We are going to the police station to make a report and then I'm taking you to Monty's for lunch. After that, I'm escorting you home. Trust me when I tell you that you could use a greasy sandwich and some rest."

Erin playfully elbowed him in the gut and then latched on to his arm. Smiling she said, "You are such a pain in my ass."

"Right back at ya, love."

* * *

He had waited for nearly two hours, but there was still no sign of her. Thankfully, the brazen and very eager waitress who had practically thrown herself at his feet must have gone on break or something, because he hadn't seen her for some time.

Chase had called his housekeeper and asked her if she remembered who had delivered the flowers that morning. According to Charlotte, a young boy, no more than seventeen, had hand-delivered the flowers. When she tried to tip the boy, he refused and said that it was not necessary. Charlotte said he left on a bike, never asking her to sign for the flowers.

Chase had just finished his call to Charlotte, which turned out to be a dead end, when he saw Erin pull up in a cab with her brother. Chase had never seen Paul Whitley in person. However, a quick internet search had provided Chase with a photo of the young attorney. He watched the pair enter the apartment building and then gestured to a young man, who may or may not be serving as his waiter, for the check.

Chapter Nineteen

Watching Paul search each nook and cranny of her apartment for an intruder or anything suspicious made everything seem frighteningly real. He secured the locks and checked the windows, a common practice of his when they had lived together, but now that the threat was upon them, Erin thanked God for Paul's inclination to smother her. He gave her a quick kiss good-bye and told her that he would be coming by later with her favorite takeout.

Paul wasn't gone for more than five minutes before Erin's phone started to ring. She looked down at the display and saw that it was Chase. She dismissed the call. Erin instantly felt guilty about her childish act of avoidance. But she needed time to gather her thoughts...and to get her story straight. Right now, Chase was under the impression that she had an ex-boyfriend who apparently wanted back in her life. Erin would have to hone her skills in deception, providing Chase with just enough detail to convince him that her fictitious ex, though persistent and obnoxious, was completely out of her life.

And if hiding her past weren't challenging enough, Erin had other things on her mind that were also weighing in. Her thoughts instantly went to the encounter in Chase's shower. She had never been more exposed or bared to anyone, at least not willingly, than she was with Chase that morning. She remembered his hands running along the curves of her body and how all she wanted to do was please him. She stepped into the bathroom and was horrified at the reflection in the mirror. Paul was right, she was a hot mess.

As the bathroom gathered steam, she was again reminded of the most erotic morning of her life. Erin needed to clear her head. She took a quick shower, knowing it was best for her body and mind not to linger and think of him while she was covered in suds.

Safely out of the shower, Erin threw on some yoga pants and a tank, and decided to veg in front of the TV, to allow some mind-numbing movie to lull her to sleep. But before she could drift off, her cell phone chimed, signaling that she had received a text: *"Can I see you?"*

It was a simple text, one that Erin shouldn't read into, but Chase seemed concerned, and again she felt bad for how she had left things. He had taken care of her last night, asking his own personal doctor to make a house call. But equally important, he never once took advantage of her or the situation. And she had returned the favor by leaving abruptly, but not before screaming for him to take his hands off of her. Erin wouldn't be surprised if he was wondering if she suffered from a mental illness, a split personality perhaps.

Erin had a feeling that Chase's texts would just continue if she refused to answer. She sat back on the couch and decided to keep her side of the conversation short and simple: *"I'm home and very tired. Sorry about this morning."*

His response came within seconds: *"Can I come up? We don't have to talk about this morning, at least not right now."*

He was being incredibly sweet, which made Erin want to cry. The truth was that she wanted him with her, here in her apartment, here in her bed. This realization gave her hope. Despite her freak-out prior to leaving Chase's apartment, she still wanted him and longed to be in the safety of his arms. But she needed to get her head on straight and there were too many emotions in play. Reluctantly, Erin responded: *"Not right now, okay? I just need the weekend to recoup."*

This time he took over a minute to answer: *"Do you still want him?"*

Erin cringed at the five little words. The thought of wanting the man who had sent her those flowers, the piece of filth that had stolen everything from her, made Erin want to throw up. She didn't know if it was out of anger, impulse, or just plain honesty, that she texted back: *"No. What I want is to finish what we started in the shower. I'll see you at work on Monday."*

Erin pushed the SEND button and laid the phone back on the coffee table. After several minutes, she received one last text for the night: *"Forgiven."*

Chapter Twenty

Erin spent the weekend wondering what Monday would bring. The last time she had seen Chase, they had been rudely interrupted by a bouquet of flowers while enjoying breakfast/lunch in his bed after the most incredible orgasm of her life. She didn't know what to expect when they saw each other. As Erin stepped onto the elevator at work, she felt that same heat, that dark gaze fixed on her, undressing her in front of the five other people who occupied the space. Erin felt her face grow hot, and she looked down to keep anyone from noticing that she had turned ten shades of red.

The elevator stopped at three more floors, causing the elevator's occupants to get very cozy. That was when Erin felt something very hard, something very determined, nudge her from behind. Erin's breath hitched and she felt that familiar throbbing between her legs intensify. Erin felt his hands on her waist and she silently begged him to press into her. The elevator stopped at the next floor, allowing one more person to enter and giving Erin the excuse to back into him even more. She felt his hand travel from her waist and beneath her black, flowing skirt. A small cough escaped him as his hand reached her garter. Erin looked at the dozen or so people around them, but nobody seemed to notice that the CEO's hand was up her skirt and now making its way between her legs.

Her heart was beating so quickly Erin was certain that the woman in front of her could hear it. And then she felt him slip one steady finger inside her. She embraced the intrusion, but she wanted more. She didn't want him to stop, nor did she feel the need to control his fingers with her own. She wanted him to touch her. And that thought made her feel strong and empowered. Erin bit her lip so hard that she thought she drew blood. She let out an audible whimper, though it was muffled by the ding of the elevator door opening to the next floor. He gently removed his hand and smoothed her skirt to its original position as if nothing had happened, as if she hadn't nearly come just a moment ago.

The withdrawal of his hand made her suddenly feel empty, craving his greedy touch. She looked at the floor number and was thankful that they had reached her destination. Even if they hadn't, she had already decided that she would get off and hit the stairs. She could use a moment to cool down. But before Erin could hustle out of the elevator, he leaned in, his lips dangerously close to the back of her neck, and whispered, "A word, Ms. Whitley?"

Erin knew she was flushed and was very grateful that he was behind her, unable to see the expression on her face, what he was capable of doing to her. Her voice low, but clear enough for him to hear her, Erin said, "Um…of course." She felt his hand on her elbow as he escorted her out of the elevator and led her in the opposite direction from her lab.

He didn't speak while they walked down the hallway. Erin was just about to ask him if everything was alright when he pulled her into the stairwell. He pushed her up against the wall, the cool concrete a direct contrast to the warmth emanating from between her legs, and covered her mouth with his. She felt his tongue enter, and Erin instinctively began to suck and nip at that very talented part of his body. She heard him groan, which encouraged her even more. He took her hand and pressed it against his hard cock. Chase bit her lip gently and then whispered, "This is what you do to me, Erin."

And before she realized it, Erin heard herself not asking, but *telling* him to touch her. Complying immediately, Chase lifted her leg, exposing the strap to her garter belt. She felt his fingers fondle the material. "This is dangerous," he said, tugging at the strap, "and very naughty."

His hand released the strap and Erin felt two fingers caress her clit through the thin silk cloth of her panties. Her back arched and she knew it wouldn't take long to find her climax. Erin moaned shamelessly, which made one of those smug smiles take form on that perfect face of his.

"God, you're so wet for me, so ready." His words only heightened her need and within seconds, she felt the pad of his thumb stroke her clit in a motion that could only be achieved through ample experience. Erin pushed that troublesome thought aside, along with those pangs of jealousy she had no right to harbor.

His finger lingered at her entrance and she felt herself leaning into him, wanting him to come inside. Erin heard him chuckle, and if she wasn't so turned on, she probably would have been embarrassed by her obvious lack of self-control. Only one word escaped her, but it was enough to make that smile on his face disappear. It was replaced with something much more delicious.

"More," she demanded. Erin felt the heat of his gaze. A finger slipped inside her silky warmth and she moaned his name.

"So snug, so..." He groaned, unable to finish his thought.

Erin was wet, her slick heat ready and wanting so much more. Her hand was on his belt when Erin heard the distinct sound of the stairway door open just a few flights below. She inhaled abruptly, but he didn't release her right away. With his hand still in between her thighs, he whispered in her ear, "Dinner. Tonight." She didn't respond; the fear of getting caught in such a compromising position with the boss left her in a state of frozen panic.

He pushed a second finger into her, stretching tender but wanting flesh. Erin bit down on her lip, muffling her obvious pleasure. She nodded, accepting what she knew wasn't an invitation; it was clearly a command. Only then did she feel him release her leg from the propped and ready position it was in. Erin quickly adjusted her skirt and retreated to the stairwell door. She looked back to see him walk down the steps, toward the voices below. But just before he was out of sight, he returned the glance with a grin that suggested that although he had just enjoyed himself, it was only a precursor to the evening ahead.

* * *

Her desk was a welcome sight; the mound of paperwork was a healthy distraction from Chase and everything else in her life. Erin logged into her email and found that as of seven o'clock that morning, she had been officially assigned to the Cabraxol account. Erin would be presenting the drug to the board this coming Friday. She swallowed and felt a twinge of nervousness grab hold of her stomach. The anxiety wasn't due to incompetence or a lack of knowledge about the drug she would be presenting; its source was much simpler. Chase would be sitting among the board, watching her with that heated stare, with the look that always left her wanting. She sighed, knowing that Friday would be a challenge.

Erin answered a few emails and then clicked on her calendar. She blocked out the next few nights, needing the time to prepare for the presentation. It had been over a year since she'd had to get up in front of a room full of people and present, which was kind of unfortunate since she had always been comfortable speaking to a crowd about a subject that she knew like the back of her hand. But it didn't take a rocket scientist or a visit to her therapist to gather why she had gravitated away from more public forums. Erin knew the effects of the rape would linger. But for how long? That was the million-dollar question she would love to have answered.

Erin worked straight through lunch and would have probably continued if it wasn't for the phone call. She picked it up on the second ring and melted at the sound of his voice.

"Erin, you skipped lunch again."

Erin looked up at the camera and scowled. She spoke into the camera, though all he would be able to do was read her lips. "You're stalking."

"I'm watching out for your well-being…quite a difference."

"Hmm. Not so sure about that," she said, smiling.

"Let me take you to lunch."

Erin shook her head, still looking at the camera. "I have a lot of work to do, preparing for Friday's presentation, remember?"

"I can order in then, a quick lunch in my office and you'll be back to work," he said.

"We tried that before. I ended up pinned against the wall."

He sighed, which only made him more sexy, if that was even possible.

Erin didn't want to spoil the playful mood, but she had to ask him if he knew why the other research assistants in the lab had not shown up to work today. "Chase, you wouldn't know where Tori and Jonah are? I haven't seen them all day."

"As a matter of fact, I do know. They have been transferred to another site."

"And why is that?" Erin asked, though she had an idea why her two carefree colleagues had been shipped away to another lab, probably another state.

"I can't be too careful when it comes to you. And according to your texts, your brother feels the same way. That's why I answered his multiple texts when you were asleep the other night. I can imagine how concerned he was. As for Tori and Jonah, they were with you at the club. Though I doubt they were responsible for drugging you, well…I'm not taking any chances."

Erin didn't know if she should be appalled or completely turned on. He was demanding and possessive, two qualities she should steer clear of. But he could also be gentle, showing her concern and patience. Erin didn't know what to say. On one hand she was angry over how controlling he could be, and on the other…well, her heart skipped when she thought about how he made her feel. Wanted…claimed.

"I'll see you tonight," she said. Erin hung up the phone, instantly regretting losing the opportunity for a midafternoon replay of their stairwell encounter.

Chapter Twenty-One

Nothing?"

"Believe me when I tell you this. I couldn't find anything in her history," Sam said with obvious confidence.

Chase scratched his head and turned off his computer. He didn't know whether to be relieved or concerned that Sam's search had not unearthed a single red flag. Because that uneasy feeling at the pit of his stomach still lingered.

Sam continued with the debriefing. "She graduated within the top five percent of her class, which gained her acceptance at numerous med schools across the country. She volunteered in the pediatric cancer unit at a hospital in Philly during her junior and senior years. And in her spare time, though I have no idea how it was even possible, she held a part-time job at a mom-and-pop-type bookstore in the city."

"And the boyfriend?" Chase asked.

Sam sighed. "I found nothing that would indicate she was

in a relationship. But her bank statements are quite interesting."

"How so?" Chase asked.

"Let's just say, I don't think you have to worry about her pursuing you for your money."

"You mean, she's…"

"Extremely comfortable," Sam interjected. "Her parents' accident left her with a little over a mil in the bank, though she spends like someone on a tight budget:; a few shopping sprees, totaling a few hundred dollars here and there; weekly food orders from Whole Foods the occasional bottle of wine; a membership to a gym on Manker Avenue. Nothing suggests that she travels or even goes on vacation."

"I can't believe you didn't find anyth…"

Again, Sam cut him off. "There were a few things I noted, though. Her bank statements indicate biweekly debits of two hundred twenty-five dollars each to a Dr. Susan Cahil."

Chase pushed the SPEAKER button on the phone and placed the receiver back into a resting position. He stood up from his desk and walked over to his office window, wondering why Erin consulted a doctor every other week. "What kind of doctor is this Susan Cahil?"

"She's a psychiatrist, Chase."

That was indeed noteworthy. Chase decided that he would explore the purpose of those visits in the very near future. "You said a few things. What else?"

"Well, this is more subjective than my other findings…but…"

Chase could tell that speculating was not Sam's forte. His

friend liked concrete evidence, drawing conclusions from black-and-white sources, such as bank statements. "Sam, just say it," Chase said, trying to disguise his frustration.

"The thing is, Erin finished her finals on a Wednesday with graduation scheduled for the following Saturday. She completed her final but never attended the graduation ceremony."

"So? A lot of people choose not to walk," Chase answered.

"Maybe, but she was scheduled to speak. She was second in her class and was selected to deliver a speech as the salutatorian." Sam was silent for a moment and then continued, "But what is really interesting is that not only did she ditch her own graduation, she up and left her apartment sometime between that Wednesday night and early Thursday afternoon."

"What do you mean 'left'?" Chase asked, turning toward the speakerphone.

"I mean she packed up all her belongings and vacated her apartment. I checked with her landlord at the time. He didn't mind that she went AWOL. Her rent was paid in full and she left the place in perfect condition."

"What about her brother, Paul?"

"Same thing. He up and left his apartment as well. His bank statement indicated a hotel charge for a three-week stay, starting the night after Erin's last final exam, here in New York."

Chase paced around his office, trying to wrap his head around what Sam had just divulged. He must have been trapped in his own thoughts for some time, because he suddenly heard Sam ask, "Hey, are you okay man?"

"Yeah, I'm fine. Just thinking things through."

After a short silence, Sam said, "You know, the last time you asked me to do a background check, it didn't turn out so well."

"Erin is not Gabrielle," Chase answered, his voice clipped.

"I didn't mean to insinuate that she was. You know, it could mean absolutely nothing that Erin decided to forego her graduation. Maybe she gets skittish at the thought of public speaking, maybe she wanted to get a jump on the next chapter in her life. Who knows? All I'm saying is that from outside looking in, it seems strange that her plan to attend med school was on the straight and narrow, and then for some reason things changed, which led her to the research lab of your company as opposed to NYU Medical School, where she accepted entrance months before graduation."

Chase didn't mean to sound so harsh. Sam was just the messenger. The messenger who he himself had asked to dig and find anything that could shed some light on the woman he couldn't stop thinking about. She was a mystery to him, though she let him in on occasion, which only fueled his addiction. She was like a drug to him. Each glimpse, each unfiltered moment when she would just let go and allow him access to more than what was on the surface, was stronger than the previous one. "I'm sorry. I didn't mean to jump down your throat. I just need some time to process all of this."

"I hear you. But due to your hissy fit, I think a beer and a sandwich from Monty's are in order."

Chase smiled. "Meet you there in thirty?"

"Sounds good. And Chase, in case you didn't read between the lines, you, my friend, are buying."

Chapter Twenty-Two

Erin followed Paul through each room of her apartment as he made his nightly inspection.

"All clear," Paul declared after checking the last room. Erin felt terrible that he felt the need to babysit her. Maybe she should have agreed to the bodyguard. At least then Paul could have a life.

"Have a date tonight?" Erin asked. He was already walking toward the door, and it wasn't like him to not stay and chat for at least a few minutes.

He hesitated for a moment and then said, "I wish that was the reason why I need to cut out early." Paul gave her a quick kiss on the cheek. "Heading back to work for a bit...need to tie up some loose ends on a case. Will you be alright?"

Erin's thoughts went to Chase and the preview he had given her of what could happen on their date tonight. She felt a blush coming on and immediately was grateful that her brother was making himself scarce. She had no idea how to describe her relationship with Chase to her brother. What could she say? *Paul, I technically haven't slept with my boss yet, but the foreplay has been outstanding. I'm hoping my skittish tendencies can be kept at bay while I attempt to fuck Chase's brains out tonight. Fingers crossed.* Yeah, best Paul didn't know that she was dating.

So she lied. "I'm fine. I have a presentation to prepare for anyway."

"Okay." He gave her hand a squeeze and left her apartment.

Erin sighed, feeling guilty for keeping something from Paul. They were always honest with each other, and Erin wondered what else might lie around the bend for which she would feel the need to skirt the truth. Erin looked at the clock and gulped. Chase would be picking her up within the hour.

* * *

"I am sorry that I can't let you up to her apartment but I have my orders." The gentleman behind the desk appeared embarrassed. He eyed Chase up and down and then telephoned Erin's apartment. "Good evening, Ms. Whitley." Chase could hear a female voice through the receiver, but was unable to make out any words. "Yes, I am sorry to disturb you. But I have a Chase Montclair here to see you."

The gentleman smiled and then blushed. "Very well." He returned the phone to its cradle and looked at Chase. "Ms. Whitley will be only a moment."

The receptionist looked to be in his midsixties. He seemed to be a seasoned staff member, as he carried himself around his station with confidence and pride. Chase watched the man greet everyone who walked through the glass doors by name. They reciprocated with their own warm smiles.

"Security here is tight, yes?" Chase asked, watching the man closely.

"Yes, our tenants' safety is our utmost concern."

The receptionist nodded toward the open elevator and whispered, "Especially Ms. Whitley's." Chase detected a touch of admiration and what sounded like concern in the man's voice, which didn't sit well with Chase. Was her safety in jeopardy?

Chase put the unnerving thought aside the moment Erin came into view. She was stunning. She wore a black strapless gown that hugged every sweet curve. Her blond hair hung in waves down her back, and he instantly envisioned how she would look splayed across the backseat of his waiting limo.

No, not yet, he chastised himself. Be patient.

His earlier conversation with Sam gave him pause. Erin's past was a mystery, to say the least. For the first time in his life, he was going to try to slow things down, refrain from acting on every sexual impulse that was now screaming. But as she walked over to him, close enough that he could smell her alluring perfume, he had tremendous doubts that he would be able to adhere to his plan.

Chase reached for her hand and she smiled, taking his breath away. He leaned in, her neck mere centimeters from his lips, and whispered, "You are beautiful." Erin blushed and simply thanked him for the compliment.

Chase held out his arm, which she latched on to immediately, and the two made their way to the limo. His driver opened the door and they slid into the backseat. Chase pulled her close to him, inhaling the heady scent of her hair. He was losing it.

"I like this," she said, twirling his tie between her fingers. His breath caught and he wondered if she took notice. She threw one leg over his and straddled him.

Yeah, she noticed.

Her breathing escalated and she laid her hands on his chest. Her heaving breasts practically spilled over the flattering bodice of her dress. Chase couldn't hold back any longer and took her deep, his tongue stroking hers with a sense of urgency. She moaned and he felt her hips churn in a rhythmic motion against his hardening cock. He released her mouth and navigated to her neck, kissing smooth, heated skin. His hands were cupping her rear and pulling her into him, increasing the incredible sensation against his mounting erection.

"I want you, Chase," she said, her voice breathless. She grabbed his palms and urged them toward her breasts.

He found her nipples and began to knead and tug at them, the stimulation making her groan against his mouth. But what he wanted was to take each breast in his mouth, where he could suck and bite at each hardened point.

He looked out the tinted windows and then back at her wanting stare. "I will take you, but not here. I want you in my bed." Chase pushed the intercom button. "Marcus, to my penthouse, please."

"Yes, sir."

Without warning, Chase flipped her onto her back. A small

and playful whimper escaped her lips. His hand glided along her leg until he reached the lacy end of her thigh-high stocking. Further exploration led him to a garter belt and strap. "Did you wear these for me?" he asked, pulling at the black strap.

"Do you like them?" she asked, her glance dark and needy.

He released the strap. "Yes." Her eyes grew wide as the pad of his thumb swiped her clit through her soaked panties and she quivered beneath him.

She grabbed him around the neck, bringing his lips to hers, and whispered, "More…please." She rolled her hips, stroking her cleft against the rigid length of his cock.

"My God…"

Somehow Chase had enough wherewithal to gather that the car had stopped and they were now in front of his building. Marcus's voice came through the intercom confirming that they had reached their destination.

Erin sat up and pulled her dress down. Chase didn't say a word. He grabbed her hand, helped her out of the limo, and briskly walked to the elevator. The seconds it took for the elevator door to close were agonizing. The last sliver of the outside world disappeared, and he pushed her up against the wall, his lips grinding into hers.

"What are you doing to me, Erin?" he asked, his voice shaky. He felt her hands grab his hair as she pulled him closer. "Christ, you feel so good, so…"

The elevator came to a gentle halt and the doors opened into his foyer. He picked her up in his arms, not wanting to waste another moment, and took her to his bed.

Chapter Twenty-Three

Erin was in his grasp, kissing him as if she needed him as much as her next breath. Once in his bedroom, he placed her on her feet and turned her around so her back was to him. He unzipped her dress and with just a soft tug, the dress slid to the floor. Erin stepped out of the dress entirely and when she turned around, she heard a slight gasp.

Erin had never felt absolutely certain about anything, the unconditional love from her family excluded, until those elevator doors in her apartment building had opened. Chase had been standing in the lobby looking at her with such intensity that she almost kicked off her three-inch stilettos so she could run into his arms. Instead, Erin had looked down, smoothed her dress with steady fingers and exhaled. Her hands hadn't trembled, from fear or even just normal jitters. She had felt in control and confident.

"Christ, Erin." He stared at her, his eyes moving from her head to her black stiletto heels and then working their way back up, hovering for an extended period of time at her breasts. "You are so fucking beautiful," he said.

Erin knew how she probably should have felt right then, standing in front of him with just her black lace bra and panties while he remained fully clothed in a suit and tie that screamed sex. She should have felt intimidated, but just like before, in the lobby of her apartment building, she was empowered, and she felt the need to embrace that newfound freedom.

Erin put her palms upon his chest, letting her fingers caress his muscular torso. She needed more; she needed to feel him. As if he'd read her mind, he slipped off his suit jacket and began to unbutton his white oxford shirt. The anticipation was too much. Erin helped him with the task and finished with the buttons in record time. She pulled his shirt off and then dug her fingers into his trousers, grabbing his white undershirt and lifting it up over his head. She stared at his body, naked from the waist up, and licked her lips. "Touch me, Chase."

He grabbed her by the waist and held her to him, her breasts pressing against his chest. His hands found the clasp to her bra and unhooked it. He tore the fabric away from her body and she instantly felt his lips around a taut and needy nipple. Chase sucked and nipped on the hard peak while he tugged gently on the other with his fingers. Erin moaned, feeling the incredible sensation travel to her sex. She quickly undid his belt, and as he shuffled out of his pants and socks, Erin knew that she couldn't wait another moment.

"I want to feel you inside me," she said, slightly above a whisper.

Groaning, he took off his boxer briefs, exposing his impressive cock. Erin swallowed, not knowing how she was going to physically accommodate not only its length, but also its width. He kissed her again, but this time the urgency had been brought down to a simmer. He laid her on the bed and she felt his pelvis grind against the thin and soaked cloth of her panties. "I need you," she begged.

He removed her heels, thigh highs and panties in what seemed to be one motion. Erin felt the pad of his thumb stroke her clit. Her back bowed as she screamed his name. He slipped a finger inside her and then a second.

"My God, you're so fucking tight." And before she could answer him, if his comment even warranted an answer, he asked, "How long has it been, Erin?"

Erin knew what he was asking and she certainly didn't want to get into her sex life, or the lack of one, at that moment. So she gave him a generic, but very true, answer. "A while."

His fingers moved in and out, stretching tender, sensitive flesh. It took Erin a moment to realize that he wasn't just engaging in foreplay anymore. "I don't want to hurt you, Erin. So we'll need to take this slow, okay?"

She melted. The sweetness in his tone, the way he was able to put on the brakes so she wouldn't experience any pain, made her want him even more. Though he exhibited admirable restraint as she lay there moaning with pleasure, her sex wet and ready, his breathing became staggered, his eyes lit with an emotion that she could not identify. Chase brushed the hair from her face and said, "I want to feel all of you, Erin."

Erin bit her lower lip. "I'm on birth control," she said

through small, breathless pants. Erin looked in his eyes, knowing that the next admission would be a little more difficult. "And I…I've been tested. I'm fine." After the rape, Erin decided to go on birth control. Not that she was predicting a repeat occurrence of such a heinous event, but if she ever found herself in a similar situation, Erin wanted to be protected, at least in that regard. As for being tested, Erin voluntarily subjected herself to testing every month, even though she was told by multiple doctors that she was healthy and hadn't contracted anything from that asshole. Dr. Cahil told her that it was a coping mechanism that she would eventually let go of. And maybe it was, since she felt relieved and not as dirty each time the doctor told her that her blood results were normal.

He lowered his head, his lips brushing over hers. A shadow swept across his face and then he whispered in a tone that was serious, but gentle. "I've been tested too, Erin. I'm okay."

Erin nodded, looking into beautiful blue eyes that seemed to be hiding something. She would have to remember to ask what could cause, though temporarily, the haunted expression on his face.

"I need you, he whispered, his voice raspy. "Open for me, love."

Erin spread her legs wider, inviting him in. With his hand, he guided his cock to her entrance, and she drew in a breath. "Breathe, Erin," said Chase. Erin smiled sheepishly. "I'll be gentle."

And she believed him. Erin was beneath him, his weight pressed against her, his cock straining to gain access, yet his voice was soft, his caress patient. She exhaled.

"I know you won't hurt me," she said. The words echoed in her mind and she smiled. Erin felt safe, a feeling she would never take for granted again.

His mouth sealed over hers and she licked at his tongue in leisurely strokes. His hips swayed forward and she felt his cock first slide across slick folds and then enter, one glorious inch at a time. The look on his face told her that he was restraining himself, taking it slow so he didn't cause her pain. A few inches in, he stopped and looked at her. "Are you alright, love?"

Erin didn't know if it was the term of endearment or the delicious burn between her legs that caused her to spread her legs even more and raise her hips to meet his. The result of that sudden move made her whimper as she felt his cock slide all the way in, deep against her core. "Don't…" he moaned. She felt his testicles pressed against her entrance. "Oh Erin, I'm so deep!" he yelled. The twinge of pain that she'd induced quickly dissipated and was replaced with unrelenting pleasure.

"You feel so good…so good," she said, between pants. Her blood was on fire for him.

His elbows fell to either side of her head as his thrusts came in slow, strategic strokes. She arched her back and screamed, wanting all of him. "More…I need…."

"Tell me what you need, Erin, and I'll give it to you." It was like he needed the green light, the undisputed signal from her, to tell him that he had the go-ahead to take her…hard.

"I need more…I want…harder, Chase, harder!"

His breathing intensified and she felt him drive into her, each plunge bringing her closer to climax. "Oh God…yes…fuck yes!" she screamed. His finger circled her clit and the additional sensation almost sent her over the edge.

He grabbed her ass and thrust even deeper. "Mine, mine," he grunted. "You're mine, Erin." Her heart skipped. He was unraveling her, breaking down every wall she had built to protect herself...and she didn't care.

"Tell me you're mine, Erin," he said, his breathing mimicking her own.

Erin didn't even hesitate. "I'm yours, Chase...yours."

He groaned and then said, "Come for me. Now!" Her orgasm came almost instantaneously, happily submitting to his demand.

"Ah Christ...Erin!" His own climax rippled through him and she felt his heat overtake her. Erin wrapped her legs around him, holding him close to her, taking all of him. His head dipped to the side, nestled in her neck. They held each other for a while, in silence, as their bodies remained intimately connected.

Chapter Twenty-Four

Erin would never have guessed that Chase Montclair would be one to spoon. And if she was being truly honest with herself, based on their first interaction in his office, she would have pegged him as being one of those fuck-'em-and-leave-'em types. But there he was, his arms holding her tight against him, one leg weaved between hers, his breathing slow and mesmerizing as he slept. She hated to disturb him, as he looked so peaceful, but nature called. Erin slowly squirmed out of his embrace and when she stood from his bed, she looked down to see if she had been successful. He rustled a bit, but then rolled to his other side, still asleep, still painfully beautiful.

Erin smiled and as she crept to the bathroom, she felt a slight ache between her legs, a reminder that Chase was still with her. She was actually a little surprised that she wasn't really sore, considering his size and the fact that after she had given Chase the green light, he'd rammed into her with determination and such lovely force.

Out of habit, Erin looked at the toilet paper holder before taking a seat. Finding it empty, she peered into the cabinet below the sink, but there was no TP to be found. Across the room stood a full-sized door, which seemed odd, since linen closet doors were usually not as wide. She hadn't taken notice of the door the last time she was in Chase's master bathroom. The fact that her mind had been a pile of mush due to her drug-induced state could explain the oversight. She shrugged, walked over to the door and twisted the knob.

Locked.

Before Erin could theorize as to why Chase would lock a door in his bathroom, she was interrupted by a voice that was laced with a definite edge. "Erin, what do you need?" Chase was standing in the doorway, his eyes dark, his hands clenched at his sides.

"Um…toilet paper…was just looking for a refill," she said, nodding to the empty roll.

His eyes softened and that dark, penetrating glare dissolved. Chase walked over to another cabinet in the expansive bathroom and retrieved a new roll of toilet paper from inside. "Here you go," he said, handing her the roll.

"Thanks," Erin said, still unnerved by the darkness she had witnessed. "Sorry I woke you."

He caressed her cheek with three fingers. "You can wake me up anytime you like." He smiled and then grew serious. "But I learned that there is nothing I hate more than waking up without you next to me."

Erin felt her face grow warm in response to his intense statement. They had moved this relationship, or whatever was happening between them, to the next level. It was scary, exhilarating and what Erin could only describe as highly addictive. She liked how he made her feel. She loved the person she was when she was with him. Someone who took risks and wasn't so goddamn afraid all the time. Someone fearless and growing stronger with each heated gaze he gave her. The soreness between her legs was replaced with need, and she was wet with desire. Erin stood on her toes and planted a kiss on him that could only lead to naughty things. His body responded, his rock-hard cock pressed against her and he groaned. Erin found the strength to break free and said, "I'll be right out." Smiling, she backed away from him. "And Mr. Montclair, be ready for me." She reached down and touched herself, then revealed two glistening fingertips. "Because, as you can see, I am very ready for you."

He swallowed, his gorgeous face revealing what appeared to be ravenous want. "You will be the end of me, Erin," he said, his tone serious and incredibly sexy. He left the bathroom, shutting the door behind him.

At least they were on the same page.

Chapter Twenty-Five

Erin moved little throughout the night, with the exception of the four times Chase was deep inside and completely enveloped by her. Chase's need to have her was insatiable, as his growing erection now indicated. She was lying on her side, her smooth ass peeking its way out of one of his t-shirts. With her hair mussed and her lips swollen, she was beyond sexy. He had to have her again.

Chase kissed the back of her neck and she began to stir. He cupped her rear, kneading the soft flesh. She moaned softly and reached behind her, finding his hand. Erin brought his hand to her breasts, which made him even more aroused. He stroked her taut nipples, pinching them, inducing that perfect amount of pain, the kind that morphs into pleasure.

Chase rolled her to her knees and bent her over so her face rested on the pillow. "I want you like this, Erin, with your sweet ass exposed to me." He reached around, sliding a finger into her cunt. He was met with incredible heat, signaling that she was, like every time before, ready for him.

"Oh yes, please, take it," she whimpered. He grabbed her waist and with one smooth motion, he plunged into her from behind. She gasped and then cried out. "Chase!" she screamed through rapid pants.

"Your body was made for me, Erin." He could have come at that moment, but fought to hold out. It was a monumental task not to submit as she clamped down on him. Chase watched his slick cock slide in and out of her, each thrust producing a jolting sensation that seemed to travel to every part of his body. "You're mine…mine," he grunted, his orgasm mounting.

The lips of her sex clenched and her entire body shook beneath him as she climaxed. "Just yours," she screamed. Chase came at once, spilling his seed deep inside her, and then collapsed at her side.

He was falling quickly…and breaking every promise he had made to himself.

Fuck.

* * *

The morning sunshine was not a welcome sight. Panicked, Erin sat up in Chase's bed and looked at the alarm clock on his nightstand. "Shit," she said, a little above a whisper. Erin looked over at Chase, who was sleeping peacefully, and stood up. The sudden movement seemed to emphasize the soreness between her legs. But it was pain brought on by incredible pleasure, and she sighed happily at the thought of their active evening.

Erin contemplated whether she should just let him be, his beautiful body enjoying much-needed sleep. But she remembered what he had said about waking up without her. Erin searched his chest of drawers and found a pair of sweatpants that would definitely be huge and make her look ridiculous, and crawled over to him. She stared at him, appreciating the view. A white sheet covered him from the waist down, but his ripped chest and tight abs were gloriously exposed. His brown hair flopped in every direction and as she bent down to kiss him, his scent—that fantastic mixture of soap, cologne and pure male essence—washed over her. Erin wanted to peel back the covers and jump back in bed with him.

But that was definitely not a possibility. She had less than an hour to get home, shower, dress, and be ready for Paul when he arrived to take her to work. Erin knew that she would have to have "the talk" with Paul; she was delaying the inevitable. She just needed more time to figure out how to explain to her brother where Chase fit into her life.

Erin felt his arms wrap around her, taking her by surprise. He returned her soft kiss and it was apparent that if she was to make it home on time, Erin had better put an end to it. She broke away and whispered, "I need to go and get ready for work."

His sigh was reminiscent of a pout, and he pulled her to him and kissed her. "Let's call out," he said.

Erin pressed her hands to his mouthwatering chest. "I have a presentation this Friday and I need to be prepared. My boss can be a real dick when his employees disappoint him."

He grabbed her ass and before she knew it, he was on top of her, his expression wild…hungry. "I'll let you leave, as long as you agree to have dinner with me tonight."

Erin tapped her finger to her chin. "So, we are going to try once more? Think we'll be successful this time?"

He smiled. "Maybe it's best we stay away from limos?"

Erin nodded. "Most definitely."

"That's a yes?"

Disheveled and worn from a night of unbelievable sex, he looked incredible at that moment, a far cry from his pristine businessman appearance. How the hell could she turn him down? And why would she want to?

She nodded.

He was closing in, disengaging every defense mechanism she had.

Shit.

Chapter Twenty-Six

Paul paced her small living room like some sort of caged animal. He was going out of his mind with worry. Where the hell was she?

He was just about to call her for the twentieth time that morning when he heard a key turn in the front-door lock. He held his breath, and when his sister came into view, a barrage of emotions flooded his mind and heart. Relief, anger, love, rage and grief swept over him, and he didn't know whether to run up and hug her or shake her senseless. But he found himself doing neither, and he just stood there.

"Christ, Paul...you scared me!" Erin gasped and put her hand over her heart.

"That makes two of us." He ran his hand through his dirty-blond hair. "Do you have any idea how worried I was...what conclusions I reached when I came here this morning to ask if you wanted to go to the gym and found you missing?" Paul sat down on the sofa and rubbed his eyes with his thumb and forefinger. It wasn't even eight o'clock and he was wiped out, drained from thinking the worst—that his sister had been abducted, raped…killed at the hands of that monster.

"I…I'm sorry," she stammered.

He looked up, the exhaustion he was experiencing temporarily put on hold, and stared at his sister. She was wearing sweatpants, flip-flops, and a t-shirt he had never seen before. Her face was clean and free of makeup. Her hair was pulled back into a haphazard ponytail, and he noticed that the more he studied her, the more uncomfortable she seemed to be.

And then it hit him. Like a ton of frickin' bricks. He knew that look.

"Who is he?"

Erin placed the plastic bag she was holding on one of the bar stools. Paul noticed the slender heel of a black shoe peeking out of the bag. "He who?" she asked, her eyes never once meeting his.

"Don't do this, Erin. We've always told each other the truth, even when it was painful to do so." He stood up and walked over to her. Paul lifted her chin with two fingers, forcing her to look him in the eye. "I think I can stomach the fact that you're seeing someone, but what I will not tolerate is you putting yourself in a dangerous situation."

"I can't stop living my life, Paul. I know that piece of shit is out there somewhere." Erin's eyes began to fill up. "I just want to feel normal. When I'm with…" She stopped and hung her head.

"Who is he, Erin?" he asked, gently this time around.

"Chase Montclair."

"Of Montclair Pharmaceuticals?" he asked with a raised eyebrow.

"Yes," she said, her voice sounding a bit more confident.

"How long has this been going on?"

"Not long…less than two weeks. Why?" she asked, backing away from him.

"I mean, he walks into your life right around the time that asshole reemerges. It could most certainly be a coincidence, but…"

"But what? What the hell are you saying, Paul? That Chase is the rapist? Are you out of your mind?"

Paul knew that deep-seated pain and frustration prompted her words. "What I'm saying is that we can't rule anyone out. Neither of us saw his face that night. The coward hid behind that fucking ski mask, his voice barely above a whisper." Paul went to the fridge and grabbed a bottle of OJ. "I should have torn off his mask and burned the image in my mind for future reference." He took a long sip of the juice. "No…all I could think of was getting you away from him and to the hospital."

"We've had this conversation before, and I know where this is going. We can kick ourselves hard and often if we like. But what we can never do is go back in time. I should have waited for you after the exam. Instead, I walked home alone, like some stupid teenager who thinks she is invincible…that nothing bad could ever happen to her."

He put his drink on the counter and hugged her. "We just can't be too careful. I mean…do you really know this guy, besides the fact that Chase Montclair is a millionaire and the CEO of a major company?"

"I know enough to rule him out as a suspect. Is that what you want to hear?"

He released her and leaned against the sink. "No. What I want to hear is how you know that. How can you be certain?"

Erin walked over to one of the bar stools and sat down. She sighed, as if she was choosing her words carefully. "Well, for one, Chase is a great deal taller than that asshole."

"And?" Paul pressed, and then sighed. "Look, I know this is awkward, especially coming from your brother."

"Understatement of the decade," she whispered, but then continued. "Asshole's flowers were sent to me at Chase's penthouse. And unless Chase is taking acting classes in his spare time, there is no way he could fake what I perceived as complete surprise and anger that somebody would send me flowers at his home."

"So, you didn't sleep at Tori's that night?" he asked.

"No." She blushed. "And I felt like I had no other choice but to tell Chase that the flowers had been sent from an ex-boyfriend who you and I both know doesn't exist."

Paul looked at her, fighting back the urge to scold her for lying to him. He took a deep breath and said calmly, "No more lies between us. Okay?"

She nodded. "Sorry."

He grabbed her hand. "Forgiven." Paul gave her a quick smile and then let the seriousness of the conversation sober him. "Is there anything else you can think of that would assure us both that Chase is not the asshole?"

She looked up at him and again blushed.

"Just tell me. Forget for once that I'm your brother."

Erin sighed and then shook her head. "Okay, you asked for it." She stood up and walked toward the French doors that led to her balcony. With her back to him, she said, "I would give anything to forget what that asshole smelled like, what he felt like, how he made me feel…what he took." She shook her head. "I've been with Chase. He is nothing like that monster."

Paul winced. She hadn't shared with him such intimate details about the rapist. He assumed that she saved those for her therapist, which was for the best. It infuriated him that her memories were so vivid and that she could be transported back to that night so easily. He wished he could rid her of her gruesome thoughts. He would gladly take on that burden alone.

"Okay. I believe you. But for my own piece of mind, I think I'll call in a favor."

"Ricky?"

"Yep. He owes me one."

Paul was tired of looking at Erin's back. He walked over to her and spun her around by the hand. "Don't worry. Ricky will be discreet. Chase will never know that I'm digging through his past, the night in question in particular."

She looked up at him. "Okay. But promise me this: The minute you find out that it was not him, you'll tell Ricky to stop. I want to learn about Chase on my own, not from one of your best friends."

He paused and then nodded. "Agreed."

Paul was pleasantly surprised that she was somewhat conceding. He knew he might be pressing his luck, but he had one last request. "Until I rule Chase out, I don't want you to be alone with him."

Erin stared at him and just when he thought that she was going to spit venom or rip him a new one, she smirked. "Well, you better get Ricky on the phone. Chase is picking me up at eight o'clock tonight, and I have no intention of canceling my date."

Chapter Twenty-Seven

Erin received a gift on the hour, every hour, throughout the day. The first one arrived at nine o'clock in the morning. She read the card and smiled:

To replace those I happily destroyed.
   Though I cannot promise that these too will not fall victim to the same fate.

—*Chase*

Erin lifted the lid to the blue-striped box and spread the tissue paper apart, exposing black lace panties. She hadn't noticed until this morning, when she was gathering her belongings from Chase's bedroom floor, that he had literally ripped her panties off her body the night before. She swallowed, feeling that familiar heat radiate throughout her body when she thought about Chase. It occurred to her that she was at work, and anyone could walk into the lab and witness her caressing her very naughty little present. Luckily, she was completely alone thanks to the sudden and most likely unwarranted dismissal of Tori and Jonah.

Erin looked at the camera and smiled. If he was watching her, then he would know from the expression on her face that she would be giving him more than just a smile tonight.

The next two gifts adhered to the same theme: black silk stockings and a beautiful corset. Each gift included a wicked little note from Chase, each one more tempting than the last. She had thanked him via text after she had received his first present. But as she stared at the third gift—a corset that promised a night of delectable things—she decided that a face-to-face thank-you was in order. Erin was walking toward the elevator when her phone made that annoying chime sound, signaling she had received a text. She looked down and saw that it was from Paul: *"Can you break away for lunch? Monty's? 1:00?"*

Erin's thoughts went to their early-morning conversation, the one in which Paul shared his concerns that Chase could be the rapist. There was no possible way. The man she was on her way to see, the man she'd had inside her multiple times throughout last evening, could and would never hurt her. Call it a gut feeling, but Erin knew that Chase was not capable of such a monstrous act.

Erin pushed the elevator button for the tenth floor and then leaned against the wall and responded to her brother's text. Paul didn't typically ask her to lunch. It was usually her asking him to stop and breathe and maybe ingest something healthy or at least not from a vending machine. Paul thought she was the raging workaholic. Pot, meet kettle.

So Erin couldn't help but conclude that he had heard back from Ricky. The thought of someone leafing through Chase's past did not sit well with her. Lord knew that she didn't want anyone nosing through hers. But if it was going to make Paul breathe easier, than it was worth it. Besides, Ricky was very adept at what he did for a living. Paul had nicknamed him "The Phantom." He said that he could come and go, physically or electronically, and no one was the wiser. Ricky had entered law school with Paul, but never completed his law degree. He had chosen a different route entirely for one reason or another, and had become a private investigator. Paul and Ricky had remained friends, despite Ricky's career change, and they would get together for a beer or a ballgame every so often.

But no matter how much Paul trusted Ricky and his ability to track down scum, Erin and Paul had decided that it was best not to involve anyone in their business, particularly the rape and the night in question. It was their secret, their burden to bear.

Investigating Chase, however, was much safer. Paul had probably told Ricky that he needed a background check on the CEO of Montclair Pharmaceuticals because of a pending lawsuit he was filing. It wouldn't be the first time Paul called on Ricky to look someone up or help him with a case.

Paul had told her once that he trusted few people in his life. Erin, of course, laughed and said sarcastically, "No, I had no idea you were so guarded."

He had smiled, but then said, "Ricky's someone you can count on too, Erin." She had given him a quick punch to the arm, relaying that she suffered from a similar affliction. In fact, Erin redefined the concept. Paul may have been guarded, cautious of others. But Erin went ten steps beyond that and just closed herself off from the world.

The elevator door opened and she made her way toward Chase's office. Lydia greeted her with what appeared to be genuine warmth. "Well, good afternoon, Ms. Whitley."

Erin smiled in return. "Please call me Erin."

"As you wish, dear."

"Would it be possible to speak with Mr. Montclair?" Erin asked.

"Of course. You have a standing invitation. You can head right in."

A standing invitation? Had he told his personal secretary about them? Just the thought that he had told another living soul that she was important enough to him to allow her entry at any time sent Erin into a mild delirium. She was falling...hard.

Erin felt the heat reach her cheeks and she blushed. There was no way Lydia didn't notice the blatant change in her complexion, but being the professional she was, she simply smiled and signaled her into Chase's office. Embarrassed, Erin thanked her and walked briskly to his office.

She stopped at the doorway and just watched him. He was standing at the window, his back to her, and talking to someone on his cell. He had removed his suit jacket and his sleeves had been rolled to his elbows. With his tie somewhat loosened, Chase Montclair was without a doubt the sexiest man she had ever seen.

Erin stepped into his office and closed the door behind her. The click of the door latch must have gotten his attention, because he turned from the window and looked right at her. His breathing hitched and his eyes grew dark. Erin licked her lips as she took him in. She wanted him again. Right here, right now. Erin felt her nipples harden against her silk blouse. There was no hiding her arousal, not that she really wanted to. Her eyes drifted across his body, but her focus remained on the growing bulge in his pants.

"I'll have to call you back, Sam."

His tone reflected the seriousness in his eyes. He ended the call, tossed the phone onto his desk and was on top of her within three strides. She needed him inside her. Erin released his belt and unzipped his fly. She reached inside his boxer briefs and stroked his cock from root to tip. Groaning, he picked her up, and as if on instinct, she wrapped her legs around his waist.

"I have to have you, Erin. I need to hear you come."

She moaned, wanting him to ride her deep and hard. "On your desk," she whispered. Erin had envisioned him there, pounding into her, doing whatever he wanted to her body, as she lay splayed out.

"Christ." He carried her to his desk and laid her down, her blond hair falling all around her. The coolness of the wood penetrated the thin material of her silk blouse, making her nipples taut, more willing. He had her blouse unbuttoned, her skirt hiked up to her waist and her panties on the hardwood floor within seconds.

"You're so beautiful, so fucking sexy," he said, looking down at her. Erin watched him yank his boxers down, revealing his throbbing cock. He spread her legs wide and rammed into her. She gasped, not at the sudden intrusion, but at the instant pleasure his thrusts evoked.

"Oh God, you're so wet…so tight around my cock."

Her climax was already so close, and if he kept talking like that she would come within seconds. The feeling was so intense that she could barely formulate words. Erin screamed his name, but thankfully he muffled her cry with a deep kiss. Still, she prayed Lydia had taken her lunch break.

Erin groaned into his mouth and he immediately grabbed her legs, scooted her down even farther on the desk and took her fiercely. "Mine…you're mine, Erin. You belong to me," he grunted, as he slammed into her over and over again.

Her fingers had been fisting the edge of the desk to maximize the friction between them. But as he uttered those words, she found the need to touch herself, to expose everything to him. She took her breasts in her hands and kneaded her nipples between two fingers. "Yes, Chase," she moaned.

"Never enough, it'll never be enough," he said, breathless, his pants becoming more erratic.

The impact of his words resulted in an orgasm so strong, so incredibly intense, her back arched with every sensitive ripple.

"Look at me, Erin. Tell me you're mine."

"I am…always yours!" she screamed.

And she was…completely.

* * *

Erin sat across from her brother in their usual booth at Monty's and wondered if he could tell that she had been ravished less than twenty minutes ago. If he had any inkling, he didn't let on. Thank God.

"His alibi for that night is tight."

Erin stared at Paul, trying hard not to give him a look that screamed, *I told you so.*

He leaned back in his seat and sipped his root beer. "I had to be sure." The waitress came with their order and Erin happily dove into the dripping roast-pork monstrosity. Paul took a bite of his own messy sandwich and then continued, "Chase Montclair was at a benefit that night. Witnesses, including multiple media sources, prove that he was in New York City supporting breast cancer research."

Again, she bit her tongue. But this time, Erin didn't suppress her smile.

Erin's smile faded quickly as she soaked in her brother's stern look. "Montclair may be ruled out as a suspect, but that only means that your rapist is still out there," he said.

"I know," she said, barely a whisper.

His eyes seemed to soften. "So, I guess I need to ask." Paul paused and then looked her in the eye. "How much did you tell Chase? I mean, what did you tell him?"

It was a fair question and one that she had expected him to ask that morning when he first discovered that she had been seeing Chase. "In a nutshell…he knows about Mom and Dad, that I switched career paths, and that I am not real…worldly when it comes to dating."

Paul cleared his throat. "Did you tell Chase that you were raped?"

"He knows jack about that night, and if I have to move heaven and earth to keep it that way, I will." Her tone took on an edge that she rarely used with anyone, especially her brother.

Paul's stare was unwavering, matching her fierce expression. "So you have no plans on telling him what happened to you?"

"No." Erin could feel the tears begin to form and anger taking hold because of her weakness. "And I can tell you this with confidence because I can't bear to see him look at me with pity in his eyes, or even worse, disgust, if he learns that I have been raped. He looks at me as if I'm beautiful...whole. Not broken or tainted. He treats me like...like..."

"How you should be treated?" Paul interjected.

Erin didn't know how to answer that. It was definitely a loaded question. "You sound like my therapist."

"And you are avoiding my question."

The conversation had grown increasingly uncomfortable. It was time to put an end to it. Erin looked down at her watch and grinned. "Guess we'll have to put this conversation on hold. I need to get back to work."

Paul sat back in the booth, appearing as if he had conceded. Erin one, Paul zero.

But she couldn't have been more wrong.

"Not a problem. I'll meet you at your apartment...say seven o'clock?" he asked, a mischievous twinkle in his eye.

"You know I have a date with Chase tonight," she said, her voice sounding a lot less confident.

"Yes, I'm aware. But since you cannot tell me that he is treating you like he should, then I guess I'll have to judge for myself. Cocktail hour at your place. If I deem Chase Montclair suitable for my baby sister, than you have my blessing to proceed to dinner without me tagging along." Paul stood up abruptly and threw a twenty on the table to cover their lunch.

Erin stood in silence, stunned that Paul had just invited himself over to her apartment that evening for drinks and a meet and greet with the guy she was sleeping with.

"Ready?" he asked, gesturing to the front door of the busy restaurant.

Erin somehow regained the ability to speak and answered, "Yes. But I'm telling you one thing: Behave tonight. Turn the overprotective brother act down a whole octave. It can be…intimidating, to say the least." Her comment was meant to lighten the mood, but he seemed to have his own agenda.

"I'll behave, Erin. But the one thing I will never agree to is being less than what you deserve. I will never let my guard down. And if Chase Montclair is intimidated in the process, then so be it."

Chapter Twenty-Eight

Chase was staring out his office window when he heard his cell phone chirp. He looked down and read the incoming text: *"Looking forward to dinner…and what comes afterward."*

He smiled at a sudden flashback of their midafternoon romp in his office. Chase had been in the middle of a phone call with Sam when Erin showed up at his door. He had taken her repeatedly the night before, but when he saw her in that fitted skirt, her nipples straining against her silk blouse, all he could think about was how much he needed to be inside her once again.

His cock grew hard at the thought of her. The image of Erin spread out on his desk, her wavy blond hair scattered haphazardly around her gorgeous body, made him wonder how he was going to make it through the rest of the day. He responded to her text: *"I will never look at my desk the same. Thank you."*

Another text came a few seconds later: *"You are most welcome. But I do have a request."*

His response was just as quick: *"Ask. It's yours."*

Her text didn't come through for at least a minute, suggesting that she was taking her time, choosing her words carefully perhaps: *"My brother wants to meet you. Call him old-fashioned."*

Chase stared at his cell, his curiosity mounting: *"I would require the same. Just tell me when and where."*

Again, a minute passed: *"Before dinner tonight…seven o'clock, my apartment?"*

Chase walked over to his wall of monitors and turned the channel to his favorite show. Erin had just walked into the lab. His erection pressed against his trousers. She was killing him. He texted: *"I'll be there. And Erin, wear my gifts tonight. I want to take my time peeling away each and every one of them from that tight little body of yours."*

Chase pushed SEND, but didn't wait to see her response to his text. He switched off the monitor in fear that if she looked back at him with one of those sexy smiles of hers, he would come right there. He was completely addicted to her, a habit that he had no intention of kicking anytime soon.

* * *

Erin stood in front of her bedroom mirror and sighed nervously. The butterflies in her stomach were fluttering every which way. No, she was more than nervous. She felt like she was going to be sick at any moment. Chase would likely be here within the next several minutes. He seemed to always be punctual, in and out of the office.

Paul had already arrived. He had helped himself to a beer, turned on the ballgame and taken a seat on her couch. Erin finally knew what it felt like to bring a guy home for fatherly approval. Paul might be her brother, but he looked after her, protected her like any father would. The transition from brother to father seemed seamless for Paul. She had wondered if the roles had been reversed, if she would have been able to take on such a responsibility. She had thought of it so often that she at times questioned whether she would be brave enough one day to have children of her own. Before the rape, she had envisioned having children with a husband she adored. Since, she worried over whether she was strong enough emotionally to take care of another human being when she was struggling to just take care of herself. But things were different now. She felt more like her old self, a woman who didn't dwell in the past, but who looked to the future.

Erin stared at the beautiful ensemble Chase had put together. The silver, beaded floor-length dress was breathtaking, hugging her body in all the right places. She didn't want to fathom a guess at how much it had cost. And that was just one of the gifts that had been delivered to her throughout the day. Erin was desperately trying to do the lingerie, shoes, and diamond earrings he had given her justice. She particularly cherished the earrings. They weren't gaudy, but classic and simple. He had great taste.

Erin heard the intercom next to her front door buzz. Again, her stomach churned. Chase was downstairs. Her legs felt like jelly as she left her bedroom and listened to the receptionist announce Chase's arrival. She pressed the button and told the sweet man that Chase was welcome to come up. Erin released the button and rushed back into her bedroom. The only thing left to tackle was her hair. She pinned up the sides, exposing the earrings, and left the rest wavy and flowing freely down her back. Erin did another makeup check, though it was not necessary, and walked out into the hallway only to hear a knock at the door. "I'll get it," she said, her voice shaky.

Erin took in a deep breath and opened the door...and nearly lost it at the sight of him. He was wearing black dress pants and jacket, and a white oxford shirt and silver tie that matched her dress exactly. She fought the urge not to leap into his arms and beg him to take her right there in the doorway. The mixture of his shower soap and cologne was deadly, and she forgot for a moment that they were not alone. He must have sensed where her mind had gone, because he smiled that devilish grin that made her cunt throb.

Not the time...most definitely not the time!

"You look...lovely." The sound of his voice momentarily brought her out of her stupor and she smiled, gesturing for him to enter her apartment.

Erin still hadn't gained the ability to speak. Luckily, Chase seemed poised and confident. He walked next to her as they made their way into the living room. Paul was already standing, beer in one hand and his other outstretched. Chase introduced himself and shook Paul's hand. It took Erin a second to realize that she hadn't said a word. She had practiced in front of the bathroom mirror how she would introduce the two most important men in her life, but when the moment came, she had failed miserably.

Though she sensed each man was sizing up the other, their conversation seemed to take on a life of its own. The ballgame in the background provided a relaxed ambiance, and Paul and Chase quickly worked through the pleasantries and shifted to sports. Erin asked Chase if she could get him a drink. Lord knew she could sure use one.

"Beer or wine?" she asked.

"I'll take a beer, thank you." Chase turned his attention back to her brother and continued talking about the Phillies, Paul's favorite sports team. And it wasn't like Chase was going through the motions or humoring her brother; he seemed to genuinely know about the game and the Phillies ball club in particular.

Erin didn't know what to make of the situation. It was surreal, and she found herself staring at the scene in front of her. Paul looked up at her and smiled. "Everything okay?" he asked. She must have looked like a complete idiot, gaping at the two men.

"Um…sure." Erin unglued her heels from the kitchen floor and walked out into the living room. She handed Chase his beer and took a much-needed gulp from her own bottle. Erin sat next to Chase, but was careful to keep her distance. She didn't trust herself, her body, to behave when she was close to Chase.

Paul shifted the conversation to work, though it remained lighthearted. Erin had the distinct impression that Paul cared little about what Chase had to say in regard to his company, and more about how Chase acted in his presence. Surely Chase knew he was under the microscope, auditioning for a role that

Erin wasn't completely sure he wanted so soon. They had just met. Regardless, Chase played the part perfectly, answering at the right times, interjecting and inquiring with his own questions about Paul's interests and career.

Erin's nerves eased somewhat.

Chase had started to tell Paul about her upcoming presentation when she heard her cell phone vibrate from the island in the kitchen. Erin excused herself to retrieve her phone. She looked down at the incoming text and instantly reached for the edge of the granite counter in an attempt to steady herself.

Erin looked up to see Paul staring at her, his eyes dark and foreboding. Erin quickly glanced at Chase. His eyes narrowed as he studied her. Paul stood up and walked over to her, but instead of asking her what was wrong, he smiled and said, "So, where are you two going for dinner?" Erin knew what Paul was doing. He was trying to draw attention away from the fact that all the color had drained from her face.

Smile…breathe…play this off…please…please!

Erin reached deep within and flashed Chase a broad grin. "Better ask the man you had set your sights on intimidating tonight."

Paul too could play the part. "And you wouldn't have me any other way." He smiled, though a shadow remained on his face.

Chase looked at her and then back at Paul. The crease between his eyes deepened and Erin got the feeling that Chase wasn't convinced that all was well. He had witnessed something, but just couldn't put his finger on it.

Chase smiled but it didn't reach his eyes. He took her hand

in his. "*Amore Bella*. But we could always cancel and look else-where if you're not in the mood for Italian."

"Sounds fantastic. I've never been there, but always wanted to go. I'll get my wrap." Erin walked to her bedroom and grabbed a black shawl from her closet. She felt someone be-hind her and turned around. Paul was standing there with her phone in his hand.

"This has to end. He's getting more brazen. Cocky son-of-a-bitch." He reread the text aloud: "*How cozy. Though I would tell Chase not to get too comfortable.*"

"Should I cancel my date?" she asked.

"My preference would be to lock you in a panic room." Paul walked to the balcony and checked the lock on the French doors. "No, go ahead. But be careful. Don't leave Chase's side."

"So, you approve?"

"Leave it to you to ask that at a time like this." He shook his head, though Erin could see the remnants of a subtle smirk. "Yes…for now."

Paul sighed and looked down at her phone. He started to tap on the screen.

"What are you doing?" she asked.

"I'm forwarding the text to my cell. I suspect that the num-ber that came up will probably be from a disposable cell, but it's worth investigating anyway."

Guilt and anger washed over her. "You should be preparing for your next case or getting ready for a date of your own. In-stead, your life is consumed by the fallout of my stupidity."

"When's the last time you went to your therapist?" he asked.

Embarrassed, Erin looked to the floor. "Just last week," she said. "Seems like the only time I feel the need to degrade my-self or dwell in self-pity is when the asshole rears his ugly head."

"Make an appointment with your therapist," Paul said. He walked over and handed her the phone.

"Should I make it for two?" It was a risk, but she had to ask. Paul was dealing with his own demons and she had no idea how he was coping.

Paul looked at her and though his face was hard, his eyes softened at her plea. "Okay, Erin. Make it a family session."

Erin was too surprised to respond verbally, so she hugged him. He held her tight before releasing her. "He seems like a good guy," Paul said. "But I still want you to call or text to let me know where you are…and if you're not coming home tonight."

"I will," she said, her face growing warm. They were both grown adults, but it was still difficult to talk to Paul about her new social life.

They walked out into the living room to find Chase with his suit jacket back on and watching the Phillies. He looked amazing. The contrast was mouthwatering: He was dressed to the nines in a suit worth more than her entire wardrobe and watching a ballgame on TV. "Utley just homered. We're up by one."

Paul leaned into Erin and whispered, "We'll keep him…for now."

Erin smiled, giving him a playful jab to the gut.

Chase adjusted his tie as if out of habit and walked over to Erin. "Ready?" he asked.

She nodded. Her two men shook hands, though this time around there was no need to size each other up. They seemed comfortable with each other, and Erin couldn't help but feel a little giddy. Chase only added to her teenage euphoria with his next question, which was aimed at Paul.

"We should grab a game sometime. I have season tickets."

"For the Yankees?"

Chase scowled. He genuinely looked disgusted. "God, no. I won't step foot in that new ballpark. No, I have box seats for the Phillies."

"Even though you live in New York?"

"Yep. My dad grew up in South Philly, only blocks away from the ballpark. He was a huge fan and we would go whenever we could. I renewed the tickets this year, even though he has since passed away."

Paul seemed taken aback by Chase's admission. He resorted to the old standby and said, "I'm sorry to hear about that."

Chase smiled, but Erin saw sadness in his eyes. The look was painfully familiar. "Thank you," he said.

Paul reached out and Chase shook his hand. "I think I'll take you up on your offer sometime. I would love to get away from the office for a night, grab a beer or three, and watch a game."

"Great. Just let me know when and I'll make the arrangements."

Paul smiled at her and though he tried to make it seem lighthearted, Erin knew that he was trying to keep his concern at bay. At least he trusted Chase enough to allow her to go out with him alone.

Chase opened the door for her and was standing at the entranceway. Erin had the overwhelming need to tell her brother that she loved him. She broke away from Chase and walked over to Paul. She gave him a quick kiss on the cheek and whispered so only he could hear, "I love you, you know."

"Yeah, I had a feeling." Paul smiled and then gave her a nudge toward the door, toward the man who had stolen her heart.

Chapter Twenty-Nine

Though she had settled comfortably beside Chase, her head on his shoulder, Erin had been quiet during their ride over to the restaurant. He was struggling with how to confront the situation. Clearly, Erin was hiding something. Chase had seen the look on her face when she received the text message in her kitchen. It was the same fearful look she'd tried to mask when the flowers had arrived at his penthouse. He didn't want to seem like a jealous boyfriend. But Jesus Christ, he'd be damned if he was going to allow her ex to worm his way back into her life!

He helped her out of the car and nodded to his driver. She held on to his arm as he guided her into the restaurant. They were seated immediately, as his reservation was a standing one. He was such a frequent flyer that the owner made certain Chase wouldn't have to wait. Though the atmosphere was comfortable and intimate, the restaurant catered to an upper-end clientele. It took weeks, sometimes months, to land a reservation. The food was incredible and the service nearly perfect.

Chase had gathered from the morning when they had picnicked on his bed that she didn't shy away from rich and fattening foods. She had torn into that burger and those cheese fries without hesitation. He had enjoyed watching her eat. She appeared not to worry about the massive calorie intake. It was a refreshing change from what he was accustomed to. Gabrielle's meals usually consisted of bean sprouts and maybe a carrot or two. Her model body was lean and sculpted in a way that any heterosexual man would crave. She was beauty personified. It was a pity that it was only skin deep.

Chase had dated others since Gabrielle, though they never lasted past a second date. Although each woman had been stunning, not one had had a personality or the ability to engage in a conversation with any degree of substance. He had begun to lose faith that he would ever meet anyone who could challenge him. That was until he saw Erin on the TV monitor.

Chase ordered a bottle of his favorite red wine from their waiter and sat back to enjoy the view. Erin looked incredible in the dress he had selected. His thoughts went to the lingerie beneath and he instantly felt his arousal mount. Later, he reminded himself. Surprisingly, there was something more pressing at the moment.

The waiter returned with the wine and took their dinner order. Chase sipped his wine as he watched the waiter retreat to the kitchen. He had thought about how exactly to ask Erin who this ex-boyfriend was without sounding possessive or demanding. But no approach came off as gracious in his mind.

Maybe it was best that he just come right out and ask. He inhaled and went for it. "The text you received at your apartment earlier this evening…was it from your ex-boyfriend?"

Erin's hand began to tremble, making the wineglass between her fingers wobble. He reached for her glass and set it on the table. She was as pale as the pristine white tablecloth laid out before them. And against the pale backdrop was that look of fear that he truly despised. Chase covered her hand, though it continued to twitch beneath his palm. "Who is he, Erin? I need to know who can make you react like this." The fear in her eyes mingled with another emotion. Pain? Sadness? He couldn't definitely say which, but the thought of Erin being haunted, possibly taunted by an ex, drove him insane.

"He's not worth discussing," she said, never once looking at him.

"Trust me, the last thing I want to do is waste our time talking about someone you used to date. But something is wrong here, I can feel it."

Erin had yet to regain the color in her face. She started to fidget, and just as he was about to demand the bastard's name, Erin stood up and excused herself to the ladies' room. He wanted to physically force her back to the table, but thought that would only escalate an already uncomfortable situation. He watched her disappear into the bathroom and then reached across the table and unsnapped Erin's purse. He slid her cell phone out and quickly reviewed her inbox. It didn't take long. The text she had received at her apartment was the very first one. He thought it was strange that a name wasn't attached to the text, just a phone number. The sight of his own name and the apparent threat infuriated him. How the hell was he going to get through this night without losing it? He wanted to search for more texts, even check her email, but she would be returning at any moment. Chase retrieved his cell phone from his suit-jacket pocket and snapped a picture of the text and phone number. He shoved her cell phone back into her purse. Chase immediately went to his contacts for Sam's number and forwarded the picture of the phone number to Sam, along with a text: *"Mind tracking this number for me?"* He pushed SEND and sat back in his chair.

His timing couldn't have been any better. He looked up to find her exiting the bathroom. Chase stood up and forced a smile. Erin's own smile appeared manufactured, and she took a seat at their table. Chase sat down and though he had a million and one questions to ask her, he simply stated, "I don't want any secrets between us." He pulled her chair next to his, and she took his hand. "I must have you completely," he said, his voice slightly above a whisper. She leaned in, allowing him to take in the floral scent of her hair. He felt his cock grow hard, his desire escalating.

"Chase, dear. I thought that was you."

Chase looked up to see a man and woman eyeing him and Erin.

Holy fuck.

Chase suppressed his shock and irritation and forced what many would probably assume as genuine warmth. He rose from his chair and kissed Victoria Green on the cheek and shook Edward Green's hand firmly. This was not happening.

He had to get through this awkward scene as quickly as possible. Chase decided to do what was expected, and introduced Victoria and Edward to Erin.

"Erin, Edward and Victoria are supporters of the Maya Montclair Foundation," Chase said, looking at Erin.

It occurred to him then that Erin probably had no idea what the Maya Montclair Foundation was. But she surprised him when she stretched out her hand and shook the Greens' hands and said, "I believe with continued support, breast cancer and other cancers will be eradicated in the future."

Intrigued that Erin had done her homework and knew about his foundation, he looked over at her and smiled.

But the Greens weren't smiling. Mrs. Green appeared particularly perturbed, pissed off, in fact. Chase decided to intervene and bring the attention back on him. "So, you will be at the benefit this Friday?"

"Of course. You know we wouldn't miss it," Victoria said. Her lips curled into a wicked little smile, which made Chase uneasy.

"And how about you, dear?" Victoria asked, her gaze fixed on Erin.

Chase didn't want to answer for Erin and assume that she was accompanying him to the event. But before he could concoct a response, Erin answered, "I'm looking forward it." Chase detected an edge to Erin's tone. Maybe she got the hint that the Greens were not her biggest fans.

"Very good. It was nice to meet you, dear," Victoria said with a hint of sarcasm and a dash of what sounded like malicious delight. "Oh, Chase, I'm glad that we ran into you.

Gabrielle is coming home soon and she is looking forward to seeing you."

Chase had had limited interaction with the Greens this past year. And he had taken their absence as acceptance of their daughter's breakup. But it was obvious that they hadn't moved on as they enthusiastically announced Gabrielle's return to New York. It was clear that the Greens assumed that their daughter and her fiancé would continue right from where they had left off.

Chase nodded at the Greens and wished them good night. He watched the couple leave the restaurant. He sat back down and looked over at Erin, who was now staring at him. Chase couldn't be certain what was going through her mind at the moment, but he had a pretty good idea that she was going to ask how he knew Victoria and Edward.

"I don't think they like me very much," Erin said, a smirk forming on her face.

She certainly didn't mince words.

"Unfortunately, I would have to agree with you," Chase said, taking Erin's hand in his.

Erin's eyes narrowed and then, before she could theorize about why the Greens didn't take a shine to her, he said, "Victoria and Edward Green are my ex-fiancée's parents. They obviously carry some resentment that I broke up with their daughter. I'm sorry you were on the receiving end of that."

Chase watched Erin closely. She appeared to be digesting what he had said. Erin took a hearty sip of her wine and placed the glass back on the table. "When was the breakup?" she asked.

"About a year ago."

"Why did you break it off with her?"

Chase took care in formulating a response. He was not ready to divulge the details surrounding his breakup with Gabrielle. But it was possible he never would have to dredge up that disturbing part of his past if he handled things on the front end. At that moment, it became clear what had to be done. A year ago, Gabrielle had given him every reason to question relationships and his trust in women. Now, he couldn't imagine his future without Erin in it. He needed closure to a part of his life that had every capability of tainting that future.

"We wanted different things," Chase said, though the moment he heard himself say the words out loud, he had a feeling she wasn't going to accept such a vague answer.

"Hmm. I see." Erin raised her wineglass to her lips and took a sip. The smile did not reappear. "Looks like I'm not the only one with secrets."

Chapter Thirty

It wasn't the distraction Erin would have chosen, but it seemed to have worked. The run-in with the Greens took the focus off that text message and onto Chase. She should have been relieved, but all Erin could think about was Chase with this other woman. She had never thought of herself as a jealous person, but then again she had never had a boyfriend about whom to experience such an emotion. Erin pictured him using his body to pleasure her, this faceless woman screaming his name as he made her come. The realization that Erin could be so possessive gave her an idea. Perhaps she could use her weakness to her advantage.

"Does it make you jealous that my ex has contacted me?" Erin asked. The waiter had just cleared their dinner plates and was on his way to retrieve two cappuccinos and a tiramisu for them to split.

"That would be an understatement," Chase answered, his expression serious.

"Well, I don't know whether to feel relieved or disturbed to hear that."

He raised his eyebrows and stared at her.

"The thought of you with someone else, with your ex, makes me want to be sick. I'm not used to feeling so…territorial," she said.

His expression darkened and Erin could feel the heat from his gaze. Erin wanted him and from the look on his face, she wondered if they would even make it home. Chase looked away and gestured to their waiter, who was on his way over with two mugs and dessert. Maybe it was a guy thing, or some clairvoyant ability, but the waiter made an abrupt about-face and went back the way he'd come.

Moments later, their waiter walked up to their table with the dessert and drinks in a to-go bag. In the other hand, he held the check. Chase handed the man his credit card and then withdrew his cell phone. He pressed one number and then she heard him tell Marcus to pull the car around.

Erin wasn't the only one who wanted to get home. She needed him inside her, taking her completely, taking everything that she could give. Erin just hoped it was enough.

* * *

She met him with every thrust, every groan. He would pull out of her until only the tip of his cock nestled within, and then he would pound into her, claiming her, taking what was his. Chase lifted her legs over his shoulders and pushed deep inside. Her snug cunt squeezed him like a fist. He wasn't going to last much longer and it bothered him that their intimate connection would be broken.

"Erin, you take it so deep," he moaned.

He felt her tight channel clench down on him and she writhed beneath him, calling to him, to give it to her harder, faster…just more.

"I want all of you," she cried.

"Ahh…Erin…I'm yours…take it all," he groaned. He emptied his seed deep inside her and she sobbed his name as she found her own climax.

He collapsed on top of her, his breathing trying to find a steady rhythm. Fearful that he might be crushing her petite frame, he shifted onto his side and snuggled her close. Even after that incredible orgasm, he could feel his cock twitch against her back as she settled into him. Chase already wanted her again.

She must have felt his cock begin to swell, because she reached behind her and ran her fingers up and down the shaft. His semi-erection instantly turned into a full hard-on as she began to stroke him. "I can't get enough," he said. "It will never be enough."

She turned her head slightly, giving him free rein over her neck. He kissed the heated flesh beneath her ear and then trailed down her neck with gentle nips. Erin squirmed and whimpered, but she never let go of his cock. He could easily come in her hand, but would rather feel her body surround his.

Chase took a nipple in his left hand and stimulated it into a taut point. His right hand navigated first to her hip and then to the neatly trimmed mound between her legs. Her curls were soaked, signaling that she was ready for him once more. Chase slipped one finger in and she gasped. Her heat against his fingers, the warm juices running down his hand and onto the sheets, sent him over the edge and he took her from behind, as she lay on her side. He lifted her leg over his, giving him full access and more depth.

"Too much…too much!" she screamed.

"Am I hurting you, Erin?" he asked, slowing his movements.

"No, don't stop!" she panted.

Chase was overcome with emotion and rammed into her with a sense of urgency and unrelenting desire. He felt his body let go as spurts of semen pumped into her.

Her body shook as she clamped down on his stiff cock. Chase clung to her, soothing her while she trembled with pleasure. They remained in that position, Erin tucked into his arms, for some time. He kissed a wavy golden lock that had strayed from the rest of her gorgeous mane and inhaled her scent.

No. He wasn't going to lose her due to his past. And he certainly wasn't going to give her up or step aside so an ex-boyfriend could reclaim what was now his.

Chapter Thirty-One

Erin hadn't taken a bath since she was nine and pretended she was Ariel from *The Little Mermaid*. But after having Chase for a third time that night in the suds-ridden tub, Erin developed a new appreciation for lavender-infused bubble bath. As she watched the steam rise, she could feel her tension slip away and mingle with the water droplets. The only way he could get her out of the tub as she basked in an orgasm-induced haze was with the lure of tiramisu. She had forgotten that they had brought home the delectable dessert, and Erin suddenly felt somewhat rejuvenated at the thought of it. Chase exited the tub and dried off. She leaned on her elbow with the rest of her body submerged in the water and gazed at his perfect, chiseled body.

"You're staring, Erin," he said, his back to her.

What the hell! Did he have eyes in the back of his head or something?

There was no sense in playing it down. So what if she enjoyed the view? "Would you like me to stop?"

He turned and looked at her. "If I have it my way, you will never look at another man again," he said, his voice steady and so deliciously dark.

Erin swallowed, feeling very vulnerable and what she could only describe as...claimed. And she loved it. Erin felt her face grow hot, and it had nothing to do with the temperature of the bathwater.

"You're blushing," he said as he secured the towel around his waist. He chuckled and then bent down until their eyes were level. For a moment, Erin thought he was going to kiss her. She breathed him in, a mixture of soap and his own heady scent.

His gaze was unwavering, as if he was trying to stare directly into her soul. Erin had to look away. She didn't want him to catch a glimpse of all her ugliness and learn that she carried secrets no one should be expected to deal with. Especially Chase. He could have any woman he wanted. Why would he want someone with so much baggage...one who was so damaged?

Erin needed to play this off. Her emotions were in overdrive. She lifted her chin and, with as much confidence as she could muster, said, "And you're demanding."

He leaned closer, their lips almost touching, and whispered, "You have no idea how demanding I can be." Chase kissed her and she felt it all the way to her core.

Considering her past and the trauma she had experienced, Erin couldn't imagine that it was healthy for her to be involved with someone who had control issues. But there she sat in Chase's tub, her arousal escalating by the second, then shooting off the charts as he alluded to his tendency to be demanding.

What the hell was wrong with her?

He broke away first and said, "You are insatiable, Erin."

"Would you have me any other way?" she teased.

"I plan on having you every way imaginable." He flashed that same smug grin that made her wet and bothered, and walked out of the bathroom. Like an idiot, Erin just sat there. Clearly, he was much better at delivering witty and incredibly sexy comebacks than she was.

* * *

Chase discarded the cappuccinos that had been sitting on the kitchen counter, neglected because they'd had more important things to do, and prepared two mugs of hot chocolate. He set the slice of tiramisu on a plate and retrieved two forks. He heard the tub draining and couldn't help picturing a dripping-wet and very naked Erin rising from the tub.

His cock twitched against his cotton lounge pants. Who the hell was he to call Erin insatiable? He had already had her several times that night, yet he found himself yearning for the next time. He shook his head, trying to gain some sense, some understanding of why he was so addicted to her. No other woman, including Gabrielle, had affected him this way. He shook his head and turned off the kitchen light. He had no intention of visiting the kitchen again that night, or any other room in his penthouse, for that matter. He was more than content to lock himself and Erin in his bedroom for the remainder of the night…for the remainder of their lives.

His timing couldn't have been any better if he'd tried. With two mugs in one hand and the piece of cake in the other, he stood at the doorway to his bedroom, appreciating the view. She was leaning down, her perfect, round ass peeking out the bottom of her white fluffy towel, sifting through his drawers. Erin's hair had been towel dried, though it dripped here and there.

She was sexy as hell.

Erin must have felt his presence and turned abruptly. "Oh God…sorry. I was just looking for something to wear." She seemed embarrassed for some reason and her towel drooped, exposing a two-inch scar just above her hip. He had thought that he had seen and touched every inch of her body by now, but from this angle, the opaque line was clearly visible. She followed his gaze and quickly covered the scar, which by no means marred her beautiful body.

"How did you get that, Erin?" he asked. Although he was curious about how she'd obtained such a wound, he was troubled by how she had rushed to cover her body, as if she was ashamed of it.

She swallowed and then said, "Oh…I got that swimming last year. A seashell got me as I attempted to bodysurf in Ocean City." She secured the towel around her. "Because I had conveniently forgotten that I was no longer ten years old, I earned myself a ride in a lifeguard's Jeep and ten stiches."

Although her story was believable, something nagged at him. Maybe it was the way she could barely look at him or the slight tremble of her fingers that made him want to question the validity of her story. But as much as he wanted to press her, he didn't like making her feel self-conscious or give her the impression that her body repelled him.

He set the drinks and cake on the nightstand. He walked over and stood before her. She looked at him and, before she could say anything, he removed her towel and let it fall to the floor. He dropped to his knees and kissed her scar. "You're beautiful." He felt her quiver beneath his lips. He then left a trail of kisses along her belly to her other hip, where he kissed her gently. Her fingers gripped his hair as he sprinkled her heated flesh with nips and the occasional lick. She whimpered as he reached her breasts, and though he would have loved to have lingered there, sucking her nipples and feeling her quake with each swipe of his tongue, there was something he wanted to show her. He just didn't know how she would react.

He stood and kissed her. She welcomed him as always, and it took him a moment to gather the strength needed to break free of her. He tucked a lock of her hair behind her ear. "As much as I would love you to traipse around my home all day in the nude, I realize that clothes are necessary at times."

Chase walked over to the far side of his bedroom and reached for the closet door. "I got you a few things. I hope you don't mind."

He flipped on the light to the massive walk-in closet and turned toward Erin. She looked at him, though she remained glued to the floor on the other side of the room. It occurred to him that maybe he had made a mistake. Had he assumed too much? He held his breath as she finally walked over to where he stood. She looked past him and peered into the closet.

She didn't say anything, just stared at the closet full of clothes. Dresses, suits, skirts, jeans and t-shirts with the tags still on them took over one half of the closet. His clothes, thanks to his meticulous housekeeper, hung neatly to the right.

"I just want you to feel comfortable when you're here. I don't want you to have to rush home in the morning to get ready for work," he said, trying not to sound like a possessive new boyfriend. Though she remained quiet, he had a feeling she was silently freaking out.

To his surprise, she turned to him, wrapped her arms around his neck and kissed him. Standing on her tiptoes in just a damp towel, she said, "A drawer would have sufficed."

"Too much?" he asked.

"It's always too much," she said. Erin nuzzled into his neck and he shuddered from the warmth of her breath against his cool skin.

But he had the feeling that she wasn't talking about the closet full of clothes anymore. The thought that Erin might also view what was happening between them as "too much" made him entertain the possibility that he was not alone. Perhaps she too realized that they were well past the point of no return.

Chapter Thirty-Two

They polished off the cake and hot chocolates in record time, replenishing the calories they had burned off with all their strenuous activity. Erin was utterly exhausted, and she flopped on Chase's bed after eating the dessert and snuggled into him. Chase held her close as she laid her hand on his chest. His hand came over hers, encasing it right over his heart.

Erin felt his heart beat faster and she looked up at him. "Is something wrong?"

Chase looked down at her, his eyes piercing, determined. "Erin, I need to know who your ex is," he said, his voice steady and very businesslike.

She cringed, not just because of his question, but also his tone. Her tender, mussed, sexy guy had morphed back into the pristine, domineering suit. Erin evaded his gaze and watched her hand on his chest rise and fall with each breath he took. "Why?" she asked.

"Because I saw fear in your eyes when you received that text, not anger, not annoyance."

Erin continued to stare at his chest, buying some time, as her mind entertained possible explanations. She must have been pondering a little too long, because he asked, "Are you in danger, Erin? Has he hurt you?" Chase released her hand and lifted her chin with his fingers. "Is that why your brother escorts you everywhere and why the receptionist in your apartment building has strict orders from Paul when it comes to your safety?"

Shit. Everything was falling apart, crashing down around her. Erin had been deluding herself, living in some fantasyland where she could pick and choose what she wanted to disclose and the other person in the relationship happily accepted the abridged version of Erin Whitley, no questions asked.

Erin looked into his eyes and fought vigorously to hold back the tears. She needed more time...more time before he told her good-bye. She was being selfish, but Erin didn't care. She wasn't ready to let him go.

"What would you do with that information...with his name, I mean?"

Chase's eyes grew dark and ominous. But Erin knew it wasn't directed at her. Still, his gaze was disturbing, and it was then she caught a glimpse of what he might be capable of. "I would use that information to protect you." His voice was eerily calm.

"You are being intentionally vague," she said.

"And you are avoiding my questions," he said, his fingers

gravitating from her chin to the side of her face. He caressed her cheek and she leaned into his hand.

Erin needed to tell him something, just enough to satisfy him for now. "Like your breakup, ours was not mutual. Even after all this time, it appears that he still hasn't accepted it."

"How did he know you were at my penthouse that morning he sent you flowers?"

Erin had no idea what to say. So she just told the truth. "I don't know."

"Why are you afraid of him?" he asked.

Sticking to the truth, even if it was tainted with strategic omissions, seemed to be the safest route to go. At least she wouldn't forget what she had said, and possibly get tripped up in a lie further down the road.

But Erin would need to find the strength to talk about that night, about that bastard, without giving anything away. "He was controlling and…possessive." She felt her throat close up, and Erin knew she wouldn't be able to expand or provide further details.

"I have been told that I can be controlling. And I know that I want to possess all of you," he said.

Erin shook her head, feeling the first tear wind its way down her cheek. She turned away, hoping he hadn't seen that she was falling apart. But she was too late. He sat up, taking her face in both his hands. Chase was nothing like the man who had raped her. And though it was possible that she would regret telling him, he had to know just how different he was from the bastard.

"He never touched me like you do—gentle…respectful."

The scar above her hip ached, though the pain was only in her head. The tears were freely flowing by that point, and she saw his body grow rigid.

"I'll never hurt you, Erin. I think you know that. But it's clear to me, from the look on your face and the tears that I so desperately want to stop, that your ex still possesses the power to inflict pain."

Erin squeezed her eyes shut and for the first time, she wanted to tell him everything, lay out all her secrets. But she couldn't do it. She would lose him. So Erin skirted the truth once again, straddling that ever-fading line. "I don't want you to know who he is," she said.

"Why, Erin?"

"Because I think you'll try to confront him if you know his identity," she said.

"Yes, I would. It's obvious that you're not ready to share that information with me and I would never pressure you to do so. But you leave me with no choice but to arrange for the necessary precautions."

Erin blinked through the tears, wondering what he meant by that. "What are these 'necessary precautions'?"

"You will have a bodyguard with you each and every time you step foot outside your door and mine. No exceptions," he said.

"Don't you think that's a little extreme?"

He raised his eyebrows, and by the stern look on his face, Erin knew she didn't have any right to argue. He was willing to forgo his desire to press her to give up the name of her "ex." She had no other choice but to agree. Erin sighed and then nodded.

"Good. There's no way I would leave town tomorrow morning without knowing you were protected."

"Where are you going?" she asked, trying hard to mask the desperation in her voice. "For how long?"

Chase let go of her face and pulled her closer to him. His fingers caressed the blond waves that had scurried down her back. "I have some business to take care of. But I'll be back for your presentation on Friday."

"Oh," she said. Erin didn't even attempt to hide her disappointment. The thought of not seeing him for a few days, not waking up next to him, made her heart ache.

"And then there is the benefit you agreed to attend with me on Friday night. I know you were put on the spot at the time, but I had every intention of asking you myself if you would like to accompany me."

Erin wasn't by any stretch thrilled about being on the receiving end of the stares and whispered comments that were destined to come the moment she stepped out on the arm of one of the city's most eligible and wealthy bachelors. But he was worth it, and there was no way in hell she was going to let the beautiful women in attendance think he was available. But that wasn't the only reason that Erin was willing to attend.

It had been months since Erin had thought of her work at the hospital. A curious feeling shot through her, and it took a moment to realize where it had come from. It was a jolt of excitement, a glimpse of that fire she had once possessed whenever she pictured herself working as a doctor of medicine, helping those in need.

Was it possible that her dream of being a doctor could be resuscitated?

Tonight wasn't the time to make such an important decision. Though it wouldn't appear to be the case, she had disclosed a lot to Chase over the past few hours. Erin decided it was best to entertain at a later date the idea of returning to the path that she had chosen so many years ago.

"Cancer research is very important to me. I volunteered in the pediatric oncology unit at the Children's Hospital of Philadelphia while attending college. Though it was an emotional roller coaster witnessing children under the unrelenting grasp of cancer, I never forgot the elation I felt when a patient responded to treatment and the doctor was able to tell a very exhausted parent that her child's cancer was now in remission. My mentor was wonderful. He sort of took me under his wing, and it was during that stint I realized what I definitively wanted to do with the rest of my life. I always dreamed of being a doctor, but it was my mentor and the experience I shared with him that made me want to make that dream my reality."

He stared at her, his smile reaching those deep blue eyes of his. Erin felt his fingers continue to circle her back, sending sweet sensations to different parts of her body. "I like to see that."

"See what?" she asked.

"That fire in your eyes. It has snuffed out the shadows that were there just moments ago," he said. "Erin, why did you give it up? This dream that I know you still want? I can see it. I can hear it in your voice."

Her heart started to race. Breathe, Erin.

"I realized after I graduated that I wasn't ready to fully commit to medical school. I needed...time."

Keep breathing. Don't look away. Don't bite that fucking lip!

Chase stared at her. He opened his mouth, as if he was going to say something, and then reconsidered. He leaned in and kissed her. "I'll support you in whatever you do, whatever you choose. I need you to understand that, Erin."

Erin wanted to cry, but she choked back the tears. It meant the world to her that he would support her decision to return to school, but it was his loving tone that did her in. She smiled. But it was time to end the conversation. It had been a risk allowing Chase to see into her past, though it was only a small glimpse. He seemed to sense her desire to shift the conversation in another direction, because he changed the subject and simply asked, "So, you will go to the benefit with me?"

"You do realize that if we attend the benefit together, people, including those at your company, will think we are..." Erin didn't know how to complete her thought.

Luckily, Chase interrupted with, "Together?"

"Um...yeah." It definitely wasn't one of her most sophisticated responses.

"I absolutely hope so. I want everyone to know you belong to me."

Erin melted. He had said those words so easily and with such confidence. She had fallen so fast...so hard.

But reality had a tendency to rear its ugly at the worst possible moment, and she thought it was time she stated the obvious. "But aren't we breaking some workplace rule? Isn't it against company policy for two employees—and in our case, employee and employer—to sleep together?"

"If that is what my company policy dictates, then I will change it to meet my needs. And right now what I need is you." Erin loved the way he looked at her, his eyes dark, those sensual lips only inches from hers. He had the power to ward off nightmarish thoughts and fill her with hope that everything was going to be okay. "And Erin, to set the record straight, we are not just sleeping together."

She loved how honest, how possessive he was with her. But she also took notice that he had refrained from using the L word. It frightened Erin to think of the possibility that his feelings might not mimic her own.

She didn't want to ruin their evening together, especially since she wasn't going to see him for the next few days. So she decided to add levity to their very heavy conversation and said, "So, should I go to the benefit or leave one of the city's most eligible bachelors unescorted and available to countless women?" She knew her attempt to lighten things up had failed when his smile faded. Instead, he looked at her with such a serious expression, she thought he was angry with her.

"There will be no other women for me, Erin."

Erin wanted to believe that. She wanted to believe that he would never hurt her, that her heart was safe in his hands. He must have seen her apprehension, because he rolled her onto her back, his body on top of hers, and said, "I won't hurt you."

Erin's eyes started to well up and she swallowed hard. She put her hands around his neck and drew him close. Though she wasn't ready to tell him exactly how she felt, how far she had fallen for him, Erin could show him. She nodded and said, "I need to feel you inside me."

His mouth came over hers with so much intensity that she felt her entire body react. Chase pulled her boy shorts off in one quick swipe and she moaned with anticipation. Erin watched as he tugged his boxer briefs down, exposing his hard shaft. She licked her lips and, though she would have loved to have sucked him deep, feeling his seed slide down her throat as he came in her mouth, her body craved a more intimate connection.

"Please, Chase…hurry," she begged. He slid into her, her slick channel clenching down on him, now familiar with his massive size. Erin wrapped her legs around him, holding on to him with everything she had.

"Ahh Erin, I'm already so close!" he groaned. His thrusts weren't hurried, but determined, as if he wanted to ensure that every inch of her body had been touched, claimed by his cock. Her orgasm crashed over her, and she screamed for him to come with her.

She felt his body shake as his warmth filled her. She held onto him as the quakes of his climax subsided and then brought his face to her chest. Erin wasn't sure how long they lay like that, with his face nuzzled against her breasts, his one leg entwined in both of hers…and her heart bared to him, completely exposed and wanting to trust.

Chapter Thirty-Three

Chase knew that it would be difficult to leave her that morning, but he was overwhelmed with the feelings that he had experienced after he dropped her off at work. It wasn't fear that seemed to cripple him, but something much deeper, and he wondered how he would go without seeing her, feeling her, for the next forty-eight hours. It was this emotion, which he didn't recognize at first, that convinced him that the plane trip to California was absolutely necessary.

Chase sat back and dialed Andrew Moore, a man who came highly recommended by Sam and with whom Chase would now be speaking frequently. Chase had been completely serious when he told Erin that a bodyguard would be accompanying her from now on. He had expected her to fight him on that, maybe declare that it was absurd and over-the-top. But she conceded, which only made it more apparent that she thought the situation warranted extreme security measures. To add to his worry, Sam had called him earlier and told him that the text in Erin's inbox could not be traced.

Chase looked down at his watch as he waited for Moore to answer. "Marcus, we have a little time before my flight. Turn the car around. There's someone I need to see before I leave."

* * *

"Mr. Whitley, I have a Mr. Chase Montclair here to speak with you."

Paul stared down at the phone as if he didn't recognize the voice coming through the speaker. A few too many seconds must have passed, because his secretary said, "I can tell him to make an appointment if you…"

Paul regained his composure and overcame his initial surprise that Chase Montclair had come to see him. "No, send him in," he said rather curtly. He recognized that his tone probably came off as harsh, and followed it up with, "Thank you, Laura."

It was nine o'clock in the morning on a work day. Why the hell was Chase paying him a visit, and at his office, no less? Clearly, Erin had no idea that Chase was coming to see him. She would have called, texted him, warned him somehow of Chase's intentions. Was it possible that Erin had told Chase about that night, about the rapist?

Paul recalled what Erin had said to him while they had lunch at Monty's. He understood why she didn't want to tell Chase this early on in their relationship that she had been raped. But what he didn't agree with was his sister's decision to withhold the crime from Chase indefinitely. Not that the rape defined who Erin was, but it was a part of her past and, unfortunately, her present. Although she had made significant progress over the course of the year in regards to taking back her life, residual fears obviously remained. The fact that she felt that Chase would view her differently or distastefully if he learned of her secret only confirmed that the battle with her demons still raged on.

Paul was in midthought when Erin's new boyfriend strolled into his office.

Paul stood up and walked around his desk to shake Chase's hand. In the few seconds Paul had to prepare for Chase, he'd decided to appear casual, right where they had left off in Erin's apartment when Chase had offered to take Paul to a Phillies game. But Chase was the one who would set the tone of the conversation as he uttered his first statement. "Erin doesn't know I'm here and I'd prefer it remain that way. But I understand if you must tell her."

Paul thought it was best to just listen. Besides, it was obvious that Chase had his own agenda.

"What's on your mind?" Paul asked.

Chase took a seat and leaned back in his chair, his hands folded. "Erin's ex-boyfriend."

Paul hoped that his lawyer face was secure. Usually, he had no problem remaining calm. Clients could tell him some horrific things, things that would give him nightmares, and he would sit there and listen, unfazed, never rattled. But this was different. His sister was the topic of conversation, and he wondered if his mask would be able to withstand this encounter with Chase.

"What would you like to know?" Paul asked.

"Erin will not tell me who he is. I suspect she's withholding his name from me because she thinks I'll take matters into my own hands...which is absolutely correct. I know that she fears him. So much so that she has allowed me to assign a bodyguard to her."

Paul could feel Chase's eyes boring into his. He suspected that Chase was searching for those nonverbal cues that would indicate Paul was withholding information. But again, Chase surprised him and as he continued, Paul realized that Chase was here, though he was asking a shitload of questions, because he cared for Erin.

"I'm leaving town on business for the next two days. I need to be certain that she is safe." Chase handed Paul a card with the name "Andrew Moore" printed on it and a phone number scribbled beneath. "He is a former secret service agent. His experience in the field is extensive."

Paul took the card and placed it on the desk in front of him. He stared at the card, buying time to gather his thoughts. Chase had come here for some answers, or at least insight into Erin's past relationship. Paul understood why Erin had conjured up this fictitious ex-boyfriend, but she had to have known that a man like Chase wouldn't let go of the fact that a man had sent Erin flowers to *his* penthouse.

Paul decided to stick to the truth as much as he could. "I don't know his name or what he looks like."

"I thought she would have shared that with you. You two

seem very close," Chase said, his voice sounding more curious than disbelieving.

"Erin is my world. We have always been close, even before our parents' accident."

Chase's eyes seemed to soften. "I heard about your mother and father. I'm sorry for your loss."

"Thank you," Paul said, silently taken aback by the genuine concern in Chase's voice. Paul picked up the card Chase had given him and stared at the name, though it was just a stalling tactic. He wanted to give Chase a little more information, just enough so that it appeared he wasn't hiding something.

"I'm her brother, Chase. And that is probably the reason why she didn't tell me that she had a boyfriend who wasn't very kind to her. If I had known, if I had caught wind that she was dating someone who treated her badly, I would have…intervened."

The two men looked at each other, as if they were reading each other's thoughts. From the dark look on Chase's face, Paul gathered that it was possible Chase was wondering just how *badly* this ex-boyfriend had treated Erin. But as quickly as that menacing stare appeared, it evaporated and was replaced by a neutral one.

"Well, I hope you don't mind that Erin is going to have an escort…indefinitely, if need be," Chase said.

Paul smiled and leaned back in his chair. "Mind? Not at all. I just want to know how you got her to agree to have a babysitter. She blasted me when I proposed the idea of a bodyguard after the flower incident."

"Honestly, I have no idea. It's not like she's afraid to give me a piece of her mind."

Paul couldn't help but like Chase. He might be wealthy and a CEO of a major company, but in Paul's presence, in an office Chase had come to this morning before he left for a business trip, he was just a concerned boyfriend who cared for Paul's sister. Paul also gathered that Erin hadn't lost herself, that her stubborn streak and her ability to stand up for what she believed in were both alive and well in her relationship with Chase. But what made Paul even more pleased was that Chase didn't seem to believe that there was any need to snuff out that fire, the passion that always drove her.

Chase stood up from his chair and adjusted his tie. Paul also rose and then shook Chase's hand. "I'll look after her while you're gone," Paul said.

"I was counting on it," Chase said. He smiled and then walked out of Paul's office.

Chapter Thirty-Four

Erin was beyond busy preparing for her presentation on Friday, but she still seemed to find the time to miss Chase...and count the minutes until she was back in his arms.

Pining for a guy was foreign territory for Erin. It wasn't like she was a nun during her college years. Erin appreciated a rock-hard body when she saw one and was thankful for her vivid imagination, quelling lustful thoughts when they overtook her through the release of her own hand. But she didn't expect to feel so empty without Chase, knowing she couldn't take the elevator up to his office and salivate at the sight of him behind that regal-looking desk that Erin loved.

Her cell phone rang and she looked down at the incoming call. Chase seemed to know when she was running on empty. He had called her every few hours since he had left for his trip. It was as if her body refueled every time they spoke on the phone and then started to drain with each passing moment until the next time she heard his voice.

"I miss you," he said.

No hello, just a declaration of how he felt. Erin loved that.

"I prefer that you not go on any more business trips. Can't you hire someone to go in your place next time?"

"Erin," he said, his voice so serious that she knew he'd misunderstood the comment, which was truly meant to be lighthearted and playful.

"I'm sorry, I was just…"

"Don't apologize. I want you to know how difficult it is for me to be away from you and that any future business trips I may need to plan will require your attendance."

Her spirits were somewhat rejuvenated, yet she couldn't determine why his tone seemed so intense. Erin said, "Mr. Montclair, I must admit that your attempt to establish control is a real turn-on."

"My attempt?" he asked. Erin detected a combination of surprise and a touch of humor in his voice, and she knew that he was no longer in that dark place in his head.

Erin sighed and let a small whimper escape by accident as she thought about his lips curving up to form that sly, sexy smile.

"Erin, are you intentionally trying to get me hard?" he asked. That serious tone was back, but now it had a very naughty and delicious edge to it.

The thought of his cock becoming stiff, the head throbbing, made her wet with need. Erin was not as brazen now as she had been a moment ago, and she was thankful that he couldn't witness her face turning multiple shades of pink. "Um…no…I mean, are you?"

She must have sounded like a real idiot, but he had taken her by surprise. Erin thought she heard him groan, as if he was frustrated, and then he said, "I want you to end this call and report to my office. When you are inside, close the door, sit on my leather chair, and then call me back."

Erin waited a moment, unsure if he was really serious.

"Now, Erin," he said, his voice firm.

Yeah, he wasn't kidding.

Erin ended the call and took the elevator up to his office. She had no idea what she was going to say to Lydia. Erin had no reason to be in Chase's office while he was a million miles away. And just as she was about to give some lame excuse for needing to gain access to the CEO's office, Lydia smiled and said, "I just spoke with Mr. Montclair. Take all the time you need, Ms. Whitley. You will not be disturbed."

"Um…thanks." Erin didn't want to imagine what Lydia could be thinking right now. Hell, Erin had no idea what she was doing here!

The office smelled of him, and her heart—and the sensitive flesh between her legs—ached for him. Erin closed the door behind her. She walked around his desk and sat down, feeling cool, comfy leather cradle her bottom. Erin dialed his number and sat back in the seat. "Chase?"

"I'm here, sweetheart."

Erin practically melted, her insides turning to goo at the simple term of endearment.

"Did you follow my instructions, Erin?"

She looked toward the closed door and then said, "Yes."

"Very good. Now, I want you to tell me what went through

that naughty little mind of yours the first time you were in my office."

Holy hell. How in God's name did he know that she had wanted him even then? Just thinking of that night, when she sat across from him, his searing gaze making her want to reach over and tear the clothes off his body and beg him to fuck her on top of his desk, made her folds hot and slick.

"How did you know I…"

"I'll share first," he said, interrupting her. "I watched you enter my office, enjoying the view from my seat."

"Yes, I remember that you didn't stand, or shake my hand," she said, recalling how peculiar that was for a man of business.

"I didn't neglect to stand in your presence. I just couldn't perform such a feat without you knowing how aroused you had made me, how much I wanted to be inside you."

Oh.

Erin was momentarily in a state of shock, her breath leaving her. Erin felt her heartbeat quicken as she digested his words and the erotic tone of his voice. There was nothing she could do to suppress her overwhelming desire to be with him at that moment, to feel his hands caress and claim every inch of her body.

"Why are you so far away?" she asked, barely a whisper.

"I'll be home soon, baby. I plan to make up for lost time, but it seems you may not be able to wait."

Erin swallowed, definitely loud enough for him to hear through the phone, but he didn't mention it. Could he sense just how much she needed him? How responsive her body was just to the sound of his voice?

"Tell me what you were thinking when we first met in my office," he said again.

Erin remembered how he had looked at her from the very chair she was sitting in. She pushed her knees together to quell the relentless throbbing between her legs. "I...I wanted you," she said.

It wasn't that Erin was out of practice when it came to phone sex; she simply had zero experience. Chase, on the other hand, seemed quite comfortable. Erin didn't want to think about how many women had been on the receiving end, listening to him speak so openly and getting heated at just the stroke of his voice. Erin pushed that thought aside, knowing that thinking about Chase with another woman would drive her insane.

"Erin, are you wearing one of those skirts I admire so much?"

"It's a warm day. I thought I'd forgo pants and stockings," she said. Her hand slid to her lap, coming to rest between her thighs. "I'm wearing a black dress...and those black panties that you gave me."

She heard him release a gentle groan. "Take them off, Erin."

Erin didn't hesitate. She reached beneath her dress and pulled off panties that were already soaked through.

"Now, lift your dress up, high enough so that sweet ass of yours is bare against the leather." The sudden chill of cool leather against her heated skin sent shivers through her body. Her sex was now exposed and dripping wet. She needed some relief.

He must have read her mind, though miles away, because

he said, "No touching...not yet." Her hand froze as it hovered over her cleft, needing to put pressure on a clit that was already beyond aroused. "Not until you tell me how you wanted me. What did you want me to do to you?"

Erin could be a patient person when she wanted to be. Right now was not one of those times.

"I wanted...you to take me...from behind," she said, her voice now unsteady.

He didn't say anything. And for a moment, Erin thought they had been disconnected. Suddenly, he said, "Press the button beneath the lip of my desk." There was a sense of urgency in his voice and it made her quiver.

Erin felt for the button with her free hand while she held on to her cell phone for dear life. It only took her a second or two to find and press it. The office was instantly flooded with classical music.

"Put the phone on speaker and set it on the desk."

Erin complied. But with both hands now free, the temptation to touch herself grew exponentially. "Chase, I need to..." she panted.

"I know what you need, baby," he said, his voice confident but soft. "I want you to slip one of those gorgeous fingers between your folds while you imagine that it is my tongue licking and stroking you."

Erin let out a moan and silently thanked Chase for thinking ahead when he'd directed her to turn on the music, drowning out whimpers that would surely turn into screams if she kept going.

"Are you wet, baby?" he asked.

"Yes. Soaked," she whimpered. "Oh God, you feel so good."

"But you want more, don't you?" he said, his voice dark and seductive.

"Ye-yes," she stuttered, as her finger found its rhythm, one that made her back arch.

"Slide your finger in, my love…slowly."

Erin could have come right then when he uttered the words *my love*, but she wanted to extend her pleasure, this sensual experience with Chase. She again moaned, saying his name through rapid breaths.

"Add another finger, sweetheart. I know you need more."

Erin inserted a second finger, stretching her sensitive flesh, picturing his cock thrusting into her tight channel. She was moments from her climax when he instructed her to reach down with her other hand and stroke her clit. Erin found the hard nub and massaged it, moving her fingers in a circular motion. Her orgasm ripped through her, and she cried out.

"That's it, sweetheart, give it to me. I want to hear you," he said.

"Oh, Chase, yes…yes…fuck me, Chase!" she yelled. Erin bucked one last time into her hand and collapsed against the chair.

She was still trying to catch her breath when she heard him say, "Beautiful. You're absolutely beautiful, Erin."

His reverent tone brought tears to her eyes and she was thankful that he couldn't see her. Erin wanted to utter those three little words, words that could change everything, for better or worse. But she couldn't risk scaring him, asking for more than he might be willing to give. Instead, she swapped out the dangerous word for one that was much safer.

"I miss you," she said, before ending the call.

Erin sat in the leather chair for a few minutes, basking in the afterglow. Her mind-blowing orgasm had left her feeling a little loopy and she needed a moment to regroup before returning to the lab. She also needed time for her face to return to its normal color. Even without a mirror, she knew she must look disheveled and flushed.

When she finally caught her breath and was confident that she appeared presentable, she stood up and walked toward the door. Her phone chimed, reminding Erin that she had left it on top of his desk. She hurried over to read the text that had just come through. Maybe Chase was up for another round of phone sex?

But as she stared down at the text and the phone number she did not recognize, that fear, that feeling of sheer helplessness, overtook her: *Do you think Chase will miss you while he's gone? I know I have this past year. I look forward to being inside you again, Angel.*

Every time the bastard reemerged, via flowers, note, or text, it was as if she was violated all over again. He still had control.

Furious, Erin pushed the REPLY arrow, but quickly realized that responding to the sick asshole would only feed his addiction. Erin deleted the draft and left Chase's office in a disgruntled huff. On her way home, she and her new sidekick/bodyguard would be heading to Verizon to change her phone number.

Like she'd told Paul, this monster was a ghost. The police

hadn't been able to come up with even one solitary suspect last year. And last week, when Paul marched her down to the station to report that this freak had come slithering out of his hole, the NYPD had no leads, just like Philadelphia's finest. Although sympathetic, the kind policewoman who had taken on her case had smiled and told her that they would call her if they learned anything, and that she should inform them immediately if the fucker contacted her again. Well, that wasn't going to happen. The police had been unable to help her a year ago. Erin's faith that the men in blue could catch her rapist this time around was, unfortunately, nonexistent.

Chapter Thirty-Five

But doctor, can she mentally handle that information?" Chase asked.

The doctor took off his wire-rimmed glasses and set them on his desk. His fingers formed a steeple as he sat and stared at Chase. The doctor had provided Chase with frequent updates over the past year, as Chase was granted full disclosure to Gabrielle's progress and long-term prognosis. Because Gabrielle was in no shape to make that decision at the time of her admission to the Loyola Ranch, the Greens had given the hospital permission to speak with their daughter's fiancé. Chase knew he should have informed Gabrielle's parents that there was no possible way that he and Gabrielle would ever reconcile. But they had just learned that their daughter had tried to kill herself, and he'd thought that it was best they focus on Gabrielle's recovery rather than the relationship that was beyond repair.

"Gabrielle came to us fragile and frightened. She left as a

strong and confident woman, one who understands the importance and necessity of ongoing therapy. Though she was discharged over three months ago, she continues her weekly therapy sessions here at the Ranch. She has shared with me that she is working again, modeling for some high-end clothing designer, and has even ventured out on a few dates."

Chase processed everything the doctor had said. He had questioned whether he should come. Chase hadn't seen Gabrielle since she was admitted, though he had checked in quite often with her doctors. His inquiries, the need to know that she was going to be okay, were motivated by guilt, not love. The love he thought he'd felt for her evaporated completely the moment he had walked into her apartment that night. He recalled how she looked, straddling some guy he had never seen before and riding him fiercely. Her long, dark hair flowed wildly down her bare back as she arched in pleasure. She had been panting when she screamed her lover's name. Chase had simply looked on, watching his future crumble. And though self-pity could have taken over at that point, and rightfully so, his anger had moved to the forefront.

Thinking about Gabrielle fucking another guy had once made him crazy. He had spent months envisioning her, playing that scene from her bedroom over and over again in his mind. But what really brought him to his knees, what devastated him, was the fact that everything had been a lie: their relationship…even the baby.

Chase shook his head, trying to dispel thoughts of the unborn child, a child that he thought he had helped create. He hadn't come all the way to California, leaving Erin with a bodyguard and her fear, to reopen old wounds. There was a clear purpose to his visit, and the information that the doctor had just given him was the green light he needed to end this once and for all.

"I'm happy to hear that she's doing so well," Chase said, as he stood from his chair. It took him a moment to realize that he truly meant what he had just said. He was happy and relieved that Gabrielle had obviously moved on with her life and had battled back from a very dark place. She may have betrayed him in more ways than anyone could count, but he wasn't an asshole. He wanted to be sure that she was in the right frame of mind, strong enough to hear what he had to say to her.

The doctor rounded the desk and shook Chase's hand. "It was nice to finally speak to you in person. If you have any questions or concerns, please don't hesitate to call me."

"Thank you, doctor. I appreciate everything you have done for Gabrielle." Chase gave him a polite nod and walked out of his office.

* * *

His flight had been delayed due to the weather, but it was still possible to make it in time. Chase didn't want to miss Erin's presentation. Yes, he was interested in her report and in learning about a drug his company might possibly launch. But what he truly wanted to experience, what he had a feeling he would witness, was Erin taking on this project, making it her own. He had seen glimpses of that fire, the confidence that would have served as a solid foundation for a promising career as a doctor. He didn't buy the excuse she had given him while they lay in bed. She had been fully committed to attending medical school, even up until the last night of final exams. And then she'd left Philadelphia and tucked herself away in one of his many research labs for the past few months. All signs pointed to her ex-boyfriend. He couldn't think of anything else that would make her change her mind and choose a career path that didn't appear to suit her.

Chase stared out the window of the airplane and thought about his encounter with Gabrielle. She had said all the right things, even seemed gracious during their visit. But something didn't sit right. And as New York City came into view, he felt the knot in his stomach tighten.

Chapter Thirty-Six

Being a man of means opened many doors, which had allowed Scott Morris to be quite resourceful over the years. And it was time his Angel knew just how resourceful he could be.

He had felt his Angel slipping further away from him. Erin needed to be reined in, reminded of whom she belonged to. And if that meant him contacting a third party to make Erin realize that her new boyfriend wasn't the perfect man she thought he was, so be it. He was more than willing to set aside his desire to go about this all alone and seek assistance from someone who could unravel everything Montclair and Erin thought they had built in such a short time.

Scott looked at his surroundings, appreciating the beautiful potted plants and well-maintained porch. Great care had been given to the flowers that hung from multiple hooks, as they were full and obviously flourishing. He rang the doorbell and waited. A set of footsteps could be heard from the other side of the door. Without a sound, the door opened, revealing a woman who many would describe as breathtaking.

At five foot ten, probably weighing less than one hundred and twenty pounds, and with dark brown hair that flowed uninhibited past smooth shoulders, Gabrielle Green was definitely a vision. And though he could appreciate a good-looking woman when the moment arose, she was flawed. She did not possess that one quality that could send his body into a frenzy. She was not pure. Her body was tainted, thoroughly marked over the years, most likely used by multiple partners.

"Chase is due to arrive in less than an hour. Obviously, I don't want him to walk in on us," Gabrielle said as she opened the door wider. She gestured for him to enter her home.

"But that wouldn't be the first time Chase walked in on a thought-provoking situation." Scott smiled at her, though she returned his gaze with a scowl, making her suddenly look less than gorgeous.

"I told you on the phone that I would hear what you had to say. But I won't tolerate you if you are choosing to be an asshole." She sat down on her loveseat.

Yeah, they were going to get along just fine.

"Gabrielle is such a pretty name," he said, sitting on the sofa across from her.

"Don't bullshit me. Just tell me what I want to know. My mother called me this morning and told me that she saw Chase with a woman named Erin Whitley while she was out to dinner."

He had to quell his anger as his Angel's name passed Gabrielle's full, pouty lips. "Yes, they seem to be a couple."

Her body stiffened and it was clear to Scott that the news that her ex-fiancé had moved on was not sitting well with her. Initially, he had been concerned that too much time had passed, that Gabrielle most likely had gotten over Chase Montclair and was comfortable with the new life she had established on the West Coast. But the jealous look in her eyes suggested she was far from finished with her ex-fiancé.

"I know that there have been others. I'm not naïve enough to think he has abstained this past year. What makes this Erin Whitley any different?" she asked, folding her arms across her chest.

"You'll have to take my word for it," he said, a smile spreading across his face. "Trust me."

"Trust you? I don't know you, and you still haven't proved to me why I should waste another minute on you," she said.

Scott was showing remarkable restraint. It took everything he had not to wrap his fingers around that pretty little neck of hers and squeeze until her smart mouth was silenced for good. Later, he thought. Right now, Gabrielle Green actually served a purpose.

"Let's just say that we could be of great use to each other. Obviously, you still want Chase Montclair. And I have a past with Erin Whitley that I wish to rekindle."

Gabrielle crossed her long, slender legs and sat back in her chair. Her lips curled to form a mischievous smile, signaling that the lightbulb had turned on.

Finally, he had her full attention.

Chapter Thirty-Seven

Erin was already a nervous wreck due to the presentation she was going to give when she realized that she had misplaced the diamond earrings Chase had given her. Erin ripped her bedroom apart looking for them, but she had to face the possibility that she had left them at Chase's penthouse. She looked at her watch and decided that she had time to stop by his place, find the diamond studs, arrive at work, and still iron out the remaining wrinkles pertaining to her presentation. Erin was probably making a mountain out of a molehill, but she didn't want Chase to think that she didn't appreciate his gifts.

Erin stepped out of her apartment only to be greeted by her oversized and very serious babysitter.

"Good morning, Ms. Whitley."

"Hi, Andrew. I need to stop off at Chase's this morning and pick something up."

"Not a problem, Ms. Whitley."

They reached the elevator and he pushed the button to descend. "Please call me Erin," she said, knowing full well the response she would get, being that she had corrected him on the formal use of her name at least a dozen times already.

"I'm sorry that I cannot grant such a request," he said. His voice was stern, but she detected the slightest hint of a smirk.

"Very well," she said. It took Erin a second to realize who she'd just sounded like. She smiled as she remembered Professor Farrell's go-to response for almost any given situation. Guilt and sadness crept in as she recalled her abrupt departure from Philly. She had been so selfish, so anxious to leave her past behind and escape, that she hadn't even given the professor she had grown to love like a father a proper good-bye...and a thank-you. Someday soon she would gather enough courage to pay him the visit he deserved.

They arrived at the penthouse in record time, somehow navigating the typically clogged streets of New York City. As they walked through the lobby of the luxurious apartment building, Erin noticed the clerk at the desk first glance at her bodyguard and then nod. She had planned on begging building management to let her into the penthouse, hoping luck would be on her side since more than a handful of the building's staff had seen her coming or going with Chase over the past couple weeks. But it appeared that luck was not needed, as the two men silently corresponded, and they proceeded to the elevator.

At first Erin had despised the idea of having a bodyguard with her, never having a moment to herself. But she realized she was again being selfish, and if it made Chase...and Paul...happy that she was protected, then it was worth the invasion of her privacy. She also had to admit that the monster coming after her was a living, breathing animal that showed no remorse, a man who had proved that he could get to her again. Paul and Chase were right. A bodyguard was not excessive.

She had to give it to Chase. Andrew had been a good choice. Although he was a bit stiff and reserved, he never pried or even hovered. He knew exactly how and when to keep his distance. It was remarkable how discreet he was; no one, with the exception of Chase and Paul, knew—or at least they didn't let on—that she had a babysitter of the highest caliber.

"I'll just be a second," she said, as the elevator arrived at Chase's floor.

Andrew nodded as they stepped into Chase's foyer. The hollow feeling due to Chase's absence deepened. It had only been two days since she had seen him, but it might as well have been two years. Erin couldn't wait to see him, feel his arms around her as he pulled her close, claiming her as his. She had never imagined herself wanting a man this much. This thought filled her with both excitement and fear. She had fallen so fast...so completely.

Erin headed to Chase's bedroom first, since it was the room they had definitely spent the most time in. She felt her face flush as she recalled their last evening, and morning, together. Staring at his massive king-sized bed now, Erin couldn't help imagining the things he could and hopefully would do with her body that night, after the benefit. Shaking her head in an attempt to refocus, Erin shifted her gaze to the nightstand and then to the bureau. No earrings.

She walked into the master bath and switched on the light.

She spotted their brilliance immediately, the light reflecting off the diamonds enabling her to zero in on their location. Sighing in relief, Erin practically skipped over to the vanity to secure earrings that she vowed she would never take off again. However, in her haste, she dropped one of the earrings to the floor and, as if in slow motion, she watched it roll underneath the door Chase kept locked.

Shit.

Erin bent down on her hands and knees and peeked beneath the door, only to be greeted by complete darkness. She tried to slip her hand through the small crack, but the diamond stud must have grown a set of wheels, because it was definitely beyond her grasp. Panic started to seep in when suddenly it was interrupted by two voices from the direction of Chase's foyer. Erin leapt to her feet, not wanting to be found in her current pose, and headed for Chase's bedroom door. She recognized Andrew's voice immediately but it took a few moments to identify the female he was speaking to. Erin swallowed whatever pride she had left and exited Chase's bedroom.

"Hi, Charlotte."

"Good morning, Ms. Whitley. How are you this morning, dear?" the housekeeper asked, in her typical singsong English accent.

"Well, to be honest, I seemed to have dropped my earring in the bathroom and it rolled underneath the door. I tried to open it, but it was locked."

Charlotte smiled, but it seemed strained this time around. "Not a problem. I'll get it for you."

"I don't want to be a bother," Erin said. "I'll search for the earring if you can unlock the door for me."

"No bother," she said rather quickly, her tone somewhat clipped.

Erin forced a smile on her face and nodded. She looked at Andrew to see if he had witnessed the change in Charlotte's demeanor. But his face remained neutral, as if made of stone. Charlotte excused herself and when she returned, a set of keys dangled from her right hand.

Erin started to follow her down the hall toward Chase's bedroom when Charlotte said, "I'll just be a second."

Erin stopped in her tracks, knowing exactly what she meant to say. Stay here, Ms. Whitley. You are not welcome in that room. The room behind the locked door. What in God's name was behind that door? Erin's brain was entertaining several possibilities when Charlotte returned with her earring in the palm of her hand.

"Here you go, Ms. Whitley," she said, handing Erin the stud. The smile that Erin was accustomed to had returned.

But something lingered behind that smile, leaving Erin with an uneasy feeling in her stomach. She was actually toying with the idea of just coming out and asking Charlotte about that damned door when Erin heard Andrew clear his throat from behind.

Instinctively, Erin looked down at her watch and noticed that she was cutting it close. If she wanted to get to work and have a little time for any last-minute changes to her presentation, she had to leave right now. Maybe it was luck, maybe it was divine intervention, but Erin suddenly felt grateful that she didn't let her curiosity get the best of her and subject Charlotte to her questions about her employer's locked door.

"Oh, thank you, Charlotte. I'm so glad you came when you did. I have to give a presentation this morning and I would have felt naked without these," Erin said, putting the earrings on.

"You are most welcome, Ms. Whitley," she said, her voice filled with that familiar warmth. "And good luck on your presentation. I'm sure you'll do just fine."

"I appreciate that," Erin said, smiling. As Erin walked toward the elevator, she glanced over her shoulder just in time to see Charlotte tucking the ring of keys away in a kitchen drawer.

Chapter Thirty-Eight

Chase had expected her to know how to work the room. But what surprised him was just how comfortable Erin appeared to be presenting in front of the greatest minds in his company. The only time her confidence seemed to wane, though it was for just a moment or two, was when he walked into the boardroom, already ten minutes into the presentation. She had been in midsentence when he entered the room and had stopped abruptly as their eyes met. She didn't smile, but her face turned a beautiful shade of pink, and she continued right where she had left off. He, unfortunately, couldn't suppress his own grin, and he sat down at the head of the long table to enjoy the show...to enjoy Erin.

Board members bombarded her with questions about the drug throughout the presentation. Without hesitation, she answered each and every one of them with a thorough explanation. Even the most skeptical member of the panel seemed to be at a loss for words, as he remained unnaturally quiet at the moment when he would usually infect the lot with doubt and uncertainty about the effectiveness of a new product.

When she concluded her presentation, board members rose to their feet and approached her. Still seated, Chase looked on, watching men and women who usually had no problem ripping apart a proposal that was deemed unworthy, shake her hand and thank her for not wasting their time. She smiled in return. And though she appeared gracious as his pit bulls uttered such kind words, he had a feeling that she had them right where she wanted them. Erin knew when to appear humble and when to tell everyone that she wasn't a woman you could easily break.

And it was at the moment when the last board member had filtered out of the room when she finally looked at him. He had been staring at her for the past hour, not necessarily at her body, though in her pinstripe suit she looked goddamned sexy, but at the way she carried herself. Entranced, he had watched this woman pick apart a tough crowd with unwavering confidence.

A softness blended with that confidence as their eyes met. He had every intention of taking her in his arms and telling her just how much he had missed her. But she beat him to it, as she rounded the table and ran straight into his arms. His mouth came over hers with such force that he thought he may have hurt her. But as he felt her arms encircle his neck and her fingers fist his hair, pulling him dangerously close, Chase knew that she was right there with him.

He wanted to take her right there, lay her out on the table and plunge into her, making her scream his name over and over again. But that would have to wait, at least until after the benefit. Chase wanted Erin to know that there was more to their relationship than just sex. He wanted her to see what he had seen in her today, what she was capable of. With great difficulty, he broke free of her. He did not enjoy the feeling of that abrupt disconnect. Still a bit breathless from their kiss, he tucked a golden lock of hair behind her ear and said, "Your presentation was flawless, Erin."

She smiled, which only increased his need to take her on the boardroom table. "I hope this isn't your typical response to presenters who please you." She bit at his lip, making his erection stiffen even more, though he had no idea how that was possible.

"No one will ever please me like you do. I need you to believe that," he said. He hadn't intended for their conversation to get so intense so quickly, but he wanted her to know just how much he desired her.

She looked up at him, those playful nips to his lip halting in an instant. He watched her swallow and for a second he thought he saw her eyes fill up. Before he could tell for sure, she hugged him, burrowing her head in his neck. And then slightly above a whisper, she said, "I'm yours, Chase. Just don't hurt me, okay?" Chase stood in silence, realizing that she was finally letting him in, allowing him to see more of her in that moment than in the last few weeks combined. "Just…don't break my heart."

Chapter Thirty-Nine

Y ou look absolutely stunning," Chase said, perusing her body with his eyes.

It was just the reaction Erin was hoping for. The disturbing text she had received the day before from her rapist was overshadowed by Chase's presence. Although scary, real and always there, her rapist no longer took center stage in her life. Chase had claimed that role—more specifically, her soul—and she smiled at that realization.

It appeared that her shopping trip had paid off. The deep red, almost burgundy, floor-length dress was definitely a risk. She was way out of her comfort zone with that purchase. Usually, she opted for more reserved attire, the kind that allowed her to blend in with the crowd. But when she'd tried this particular dress on, Erin knew it was the one, even without the saleswoman's coaxing.

"Thank you," she said.

Chase reached over and entwined his fingers with hers. Erin

was about to show him just how much she appreciated his compliment when the limo pulled up in front of the Marx Hotel. "We're here already?" she asked, not even masking her disappointment that she would have to wait even longer to touch him.

He chuckled as he pulled her closer, until she was practically sitting on his lap. "These last two days haven't been pleasant for me either. I can't wait to get you home and show you just how much I missed you." Erin's heart fluttered, not from the heat in his voice, but from the realization that he too might be basing their relationship, or whatever it was, on something much deeper than just sex.

"Me too," she said. Erin wanted him all to herself tonight, a night that had been slated to support a very worthy cause. Erin winced, realizing just how selfish she was being. "I'm sorry. Tonight is extremely important, benefiting cancer research in your mother's name, and all I can think of is how much I want to be beneath you."

He took her face in his hands and she instantly wanted to hide. "Look at me, Erin," he demanded.

Erin stared into beautiful, but very determined, blue eyes. "Don't ever apologize for wanting to be with me." He smiled, as he trailed one finger from her face to the curve of her neck. "It will take everything I have to get through the benefit without touching you."

Chase kissed her softly on the lips and then broke away quickly. For once, Erin was grateful for the separation, as she knew she wouldn't be able to stop the kiss from leading to something much more. They exited the limo and found themselves mobbed by photographers. Chase held on to her hand, pulling her closer with every click and flash of the cameras. Erin didn't know what she'd expected, but it certainly wasn't this. Chase was being treated like a celebrity, and Erin instantly felt uneasy as she realized that she was suddenly in the spotlight. She had flown under the radar for so long that this burst of attention made her anxious.

She needed to relax. Chase, the handsome and extremely wealthy bachelor, was the true object of their attention. She was just arm candy. Chase was gracious, smiling for the cameras and exchanging simple pleasantries. Erin just smiled and said thank you as the paparazzi showered her with compliments on her appearance.

They hustled into the hotel lobby, making a beeline to the elevator. When the doors closed, he turned to her and said, "Sorry about that. I should have prepped you. Don't worry, I'm not in the papers or tabloids too much."

"You don't have to apologize. I was a little surprised, that's all." Erin gave him a quick kiss and then grabbed the lapels of his suit jacket. "I just better not be depicted in tomorrow's news as the flavor of the month, Mr. Montclair," she said, teasingly.

His hands encased hers. "There is no one else I want but you," he said, his voice matching the intensity in his eyes.

The last wall surrounding her fragile heart came tumbling down. And though she wanted to wrap her arms around him and tell him that she had fallen for him, Erin knew that it was neither the time nor the place. She would wait until they were back at his penthouse, while they were making love in his bed, to tell him that she was in love with him.

The ding of the elevator sounded, signaling that her emotions would have to take a backseat for the next few hours. Erin pulled him closer and brushed a kiss over his lush, sexy lips. "I'm happy to hear that." She licked his lower lip, taking in his heady scent and taste. "Because I won't share you…not ever."

* * *

His heart no longer belonged to him. And if he wanted to be truly honest with himself, he had lost it—had given it, rather—to Erin the first time he saw her. He should have been surprised to learn that his damaged heart could find a way to feel again, but as he looked into her eyes, there was not a doubt in his mind. He was in love with this woman.

Chase tucked her arm around his and escorted her out of the elevator. They were immediately greeted by the foundation's chair, whom Chase himself had appointed to take care of the plans surrounding the benefit.

"Good evening, Chase," Steven McConnel said.

"Hello, Steven. Everything in order?" Chase asked, looking around the massive banquet hall. The party seemed to be in full swing as the city's most elite mingled with one another.

"The turnout is even better than last year. Your father would be incredibly pleased."

There was only a handful of people that Chase felt comfortable enough around to discuss his father. Steven was one of them, as he had been a close friend of his father's since Chase was a little boy.

"I'm sure he would be." Chase smiled and then looked over at Erin. "Steven, I would like to introduce you to Erin Whitley."

Steven shook Erin's hand and smiled. "Very pleased to meet you. I hope you will enjoy yourself tonight."

"I plan on doing just that," Erin said, flashing a smile that made Chase's legs want to buckle beneath him.

Grinning, Steven shifted his focus to Chase. "I believe everything has been accounted for, but please let me know if you need anything." Chase nodded, appreciating the man's loyalty and his great attention to detail.

Steven excused himself and left Chase and Erin alone, though their solitude would be short-lived. Chase was expected to meet and greet those in attendance and speak about a cause that was inspired by the other woman in his life. "I want to show you something," he said.

Erin looked positively radiant and when she turned to face him, he swore her eyes sparkled. "What is it?" she asked.

Taking her by the hand, he said, "Come with me."

He led her to an expansive balcony, just off the main hall. A cool breeze whipped through Erin's long blond hair, causing his breath to hitch. She was gorgeous. He squeezed her hand tighter, as if reminding himself and anyone else who looked on that she belonged to him. The weather was absolutely perfect, beckoning the guests to enjoy the outdoors and the breathtaking view of the skyline. Although Chase had lost his mother when he was only five, his father had kept her memory alive by sharing stories about the woman everyone loved, about what made her smile. It was during one of his dad's trips down memory lane when Chase learned of his mother's love of nature, how she appreciated the simplicities in life.

Chase walked her over to a well-lit corner of the balcony that gave the donors a glimpse of the woman behind the Foundation. "She was beautiful, wasn't she?"

Erin looked at the painting of a woman who had died way before her time. "You have her eyes," she whispered. Her hand reached up and touched the face in the painting. Chase was overcome with emotion. He had never missed his mother as much as he did in that moment. He wanted his mother to know the woman who meant everything to him, the woman who he was determined to make his wife.

"I have been told that," he said, struggling to regain his composure. Erin must have heard his voice waver because she turned from the painting and looked him squarely in the eye.

"I think she would be happy to know that you have done much more than just preserve her memory. The research you support will benefit millions, which would make any mother proud."

Chase pulled her to him, caring little that the public display of affection would definitely raise eyebrows. "Do you wish to be a mother someday?" he asked, keeping his voice low.

He had expected her to be taken aback by the very straightforward and untimely question. But she surprised him when she said without hesitation, "I would love a large family, one that keeps me on my toes and makes my head spin, but in a great way." She gave him a quick kiss and as she pulled back, Chase knew he had failed in his attempt to mask the fear that clearly lingered on his face.

Chase knew Erin would be a wonderful mother. She was strong and kind, passionate and incredibly intelligent. She would go to hell and back for her children if that was what was required. But could he say the same about himself?

"Chase, who is your lovely guest this evening?"

Chase was never more grateful to be interrupted in his life. Erin looked at him, clearly confused that her response had invoked such a concerning expression on his face. He forced a smile and looked at his mother's only sister.

"Aunt Melanie, you look wonderful," he said, kissing her on the cheek.

"Oh Chase, you have always been a charmer," she said, blushing.

"Aunt Mel, this is Erin," he said, pulling her to his side. "Erin, this is my mother's sister, Melanie."

Gracious as always, Erin smiled and extended her hand. "It's very nice to meet you. Would it be rude of me to mention that the resemblance between you and Chase's mother is...extraordinary?" she said, looking from Aunt Melanie to the painting.

Aunt Melanie smiled. "You couldn't have paid me a higher compliment, Erin." She looked at Chase. "She was the picture of beauty, inside and out. And she lives on through this young man right here."

Chase blushed, something he rarely did, and thanked his aunt Mel for her nice sentiment.

"Erin, I just love the color of your dress, and the cut is exquisite," Aunt Mel said.

"Thank you, that's kind of you to say," Erin said, smiling.

"Well, I'll let you kids mingle about. I need to get back to John," she said, gesturing to the banquet hall.

"Let me guess. My uncle is scoping out the items marked for the silent auction?" Chase asked.

"Of course. And would we expect anything less?" she asked. Aunt Mel kissed both Chase and Erin on the cheek before she disappeared into the sea of guests in search of her husband.

"I like her. She's very sweet," Erin said. When he didn't answer, she continued, "Is something wrong?"

The realization that he was in love with this woman had hit him like a ton of bricks. And he was willing to risk everything, including his heart, to hear her say those three words to him in return. But what scared him was that he couldn't promise her the future she wanted. A future that consisted of children, his children. It wasn't that he didn't love envisioning Erin growing with his child, he just didn't think he deserved that kind of happiness.

He didn't want to spoil Erin's evening. She looked so content, so carefree that it would be a crying shame to sour her good mood. "I just wish we could sneak away, if only for a moment."

Her eyes softened, the concerned look gone. Chase exhaled.

"A moment wouldn't be nearly enough…for what I would like to do to you," she whispered in his ear.

Chase let out a groan. "Erin, you have a tendency to not play fair." It was difficult to keep his voice steady. "And for that, you need to be punished."

Erin's eyes grew wide as she bit her lower lip. His comment had startled her, but the look she gave him said that she was intrigued, if not turned on. He chuckled. "Come on. We better start socializing before I am physically unable to move without creating a scene." His cock was almost fully erect, and that was before Erin's eyes wandered from his face to the ever-increasing bulge in his pants.

"I promise I'll take care of you before the night is through," she said, her voice husky.

Christ!

"Have I told you that I missed you these last couple days?" he asked.

"Yes. And now you are showing me just how much," she said, her eyes still fixated on his cockstand.

"You need to stop looking at me that way, Erin."

"But why? I quite enjoy drinking you in, even if we are in public."

She was going to be the death of him. He led her into the banquet hall and toward the bar. "You are being a very naughty girl right now," he whispered in her ear.

"I thought that you liked it when I'm naughty?" she asked, her lips pouty and lush.

How the hell could he have gone from sentimental to horny as all hell within seconds? There was only one explanation: Erin.

Chase grabbed her by the hand, bypassing the bar completely and heading straight to the elevator. He pushed the button and watched the elevator doors close in front of him. "Where are we going?" she asked.

"I need to be inside you…if I have any hope of getting through this night."

"Oh," she said.

The doors finally opened at the top floor. "I'm sorry, Erin. But I can't wait." He practically dragged her down the hall. He retrieved the key card to room 519 from his pocket and inserted it into the slot. The door clicked open, and he pulled her into the room and slammed the door shut behind them.

Chase pinned her against the door, mashing his lips against hers. Her mouth opened, allowing his tongue to slide past her teeth. She sucked on his tongue with rhythmic strokes that he felt all the way to his pulsating cock. He tore off his suit jacket and began to unravel his tie. Erin pushed his hands away and completed the task, then went for the buttons on his shirt. Her petite fingers undid every button within seconds. She took a step back and with just the tug of a zipper from some hidden seam, her gown fell and pooled at her feet. Her bra and barely there panties were the exact same shade as her dress, and he swallowed…hard.

"Take them off, before I rip them off your body," he said, his voice filled with desire. It was amazing he didn't come at the sight of her, standing there in her underwear and high heels.

She complied immediately and undressed completely. He unbuckled his pants and kicked them off.

And then she sank to her knees.

"I'm not going to last long if you…"

He gasped as she first licked the tip of the head and then sucked him deep. She moaned as she let him fuck her mouth. He tangled his fingers in her hair, setting an excruciating pace.

"Suck it hard, Erin."

The vibrations from her sweet hums increased the sensation, and he knew if he didn't break free of her, he was going to spill his seed down her throat. It took an act of will to pull away and when he did, he couldn't help but notice that she looked disappointed by the sudden disruption.

He lifted her up and carried her to the bed. "So beautiful," he said, laying her down. She spread her legs and without another word he pushed into her with one powerful thrust.

"Chase!" she screamed, wrapping her legs around him. She grabbed his ass, grinding him into her even further.

"Ahh…Erin!" he moaned.

"Don't…don't ever leave me again," she said, as he slid in and out of her with determined strokes.

"Never…I'll never leave you," he said, his voice breathless, his pants erratic.

He felt a deluge of warmth surround him and her body quaked beneath him. She arched her back as she shouted his name in a state of ecstasy. He erupted inside of her, giving himself to her…completely.

Chapter Forty

I don't think it is at all fair that you look absolutely perfect, with not a hair out of place, and I look as if I have been ravished all night," she said, straightening her dress, trying her hardest to look somewhat presentable after their highly charged encounter in Chase's hotel room.

"You look beautiful. I would be lying to you if I told you that I didn't like how your hair gets tousled and those exquisite lips become slightly swollen as a result of me kissing you deeply," he whispered as they walked hand in hand back to the banquet hall.

Erin was happy that they'd had the opportunity to spend some time together since he arrived back in town, because over the next hour, Chase was consumed by practically everyone in attendance. He shook their hands, thanked them for their contributions and made small talk when necessary. She would have been completely fine with remaining in the shadows, allowing Chase to be the diligent host, but he included her in every introduction and conversation. He also never let go of her. He either held her hand or had his arm wrapped around her waist the entire time. Erin didn't know if he was being affectionate or if he was just being possessive. Surprisingly, Erin couldn't care less which feeling motivated him to want to touch her. The feel of his strong fingers caressing her back or stroking her fingers made her feel cherished…maybe even loved.

"Can I get you a drink?" he asked.

Erin had declined the last time he had asked if she needed a beverage, as she was too nervous at the time to accept. Feeling a little more relaxed, Erin nodded and he whisked her away toward the bar.

"I'm guessing wine?" he asked.

Erin smiled. "I don't think this crowd would appreciate me chugging from a Corona bottle. Do you?"

He kissed her cheek, leaving her skin hot and her heart fluttering. "You can have anything you like. I just recall you enjoying a glass of cold Chardonnay before downing a beer."

Erin loved that he had remembered. Not that he knew the order in which she liked to consume alcoholic drinks, but that he paid attention to the little things, as if they truly mattered to him. "Yes, thank you," she said. And it was during that small window of time, while Chase placed his drink order with the bartender, that Erin turned and found herself face-to-face with Dr. Mitchell Morris.

Not expecting to see her mentor from the Children's Hospital of Philadelphia, Erin forgot how to speak for a moment. Gracious as always, he extended his hand, and when she went to shake it, Dr. Morris gently pulled her to him and gave her a quick peck on the cheek. "Erin, what a wonderful surprise," he said. The warmth of his voice, a quality that she had found endearing during her time as a volunteer, was absent, and when she looked into his eyes, Erin noticed that he appeared to be scanning the crowd.

Erin finally regained the ability to form words and responded, "Thank you. It's great to see you here tonight, though I shouldn't be at all surprised to run into you at a benefit supporting cancer research."

"Yes, it's a small world, especially in medicine." His eyes kept shifting from Erin to the crowd of people. It was so obvious that he was looking for someone that she had to mention it.

"Did you come here with someone, Dr. Morris?" Erin also started scanning the crowd, though she had no idea who she was looking for. "Did you bring your wife tonight?"

His gaze immediately fell on Erin at the mention of his wife. Erin suddenly had the feeling that she had said something terribly wrong.

"She passed away, Erin," he said. His eyes looked tired and grief stricken.

"I'm so sorry. She was a lovely woman, and you spoke of her so often."

"Thank you. That's kind of you to say." He smiled, though it didn't resemble the natural grin that he flashed at his small patients, a grin that Erin knew contributed to one of the best bedside manners she had ever seen. "So, the last time we talked, you were heading to New York for med school."

Erin's hand started to tremble slightly, but before anyone

could take notice, she felt Chase's hand surround hers. The interruption was greatly appreciated, and she embraced the opportunity to introduce Chase to Dr. Morris.

. "I'm happy to finally meet you in person. Your research is remarkable. It continues to provide hope and inspires young doctors to plow forward and beat this devastating disease," Chase said, shaking Dr. Morris's hand.

"You mean young doctors like Ms. Whitley?" he asked, winking at her.

Chase squeezed her hand as if he understood that the conversation had reached a very uncomfortable level. But there was no way to avoid telling Dr. Morris that she had chosen to give up med school for the time being. Erin was just about to inform him of her decision that she had changed careers when he asked, "So, you look like you survived your first year of med school?"

Erin winced internally, knowing that what she was about to say would most likely disappoint him. They had worked closely together, with him taking the time to show her the ropes and teaching a volunteer peon such as herself the intricacies of the profession.

And she had thrown it all away.

Erin had done a successful job convincing herself that she had moved on from her past. But it occurred to her that her position at Montclair Pharmaceuticals, though not menial by any means, was just a way for her to hide from her demons. It was time to reclaim what was rightfully hers.

"I have been working in the research department at Montclair Pharmaceuticals for the past several months,"

Erin said, her voice steady. She looked from Dr. Morris to Chase. "But it's possible that I may have to resign in the very near future."

Chase smiled at her, as if he predicted what she was about to say.

"It seems that med school has come calling once again. And this time, I have every intention of giving it the attention it deserves."

"I can't think of a better reason to accept someone's resignation," Chase said, his radiant smile reaching his blue eyes.

Erin blushed, not knowing exactly what to say. Luckily, Chase chuckled and said, "I would be lying if I said that I wished she would have followed her dream earlier." Chase shifted his focus onto her. "Odds are…we would never have met if that was the case."

She was touched and was apparently staring at Chase like such a lovesick teenager that Erin failed to realize that Dr. Morris had grown white as a sheet. He always had a pale complexion, but at the moment he looked as if he had seen a ghost. "Are you feeling well, Dr. Morris?" she asked.

Dr. Morris pulled a handkerchief from the breast pocket of his suit jacket. He dabbed his forehead with the white cotton cloth. "Oh, just a little warm is all." He returned the hanky to his pocket.

"Are you certain?" Chase asked.

"Mr. Montclair, I've been a doctor longer than Erin has been alive," Dr. Morris said, his tone playful.

Chase smiled, but from the look on his face, Erin got the feeling that he was also concerned about Dr. Morris.

"Yes, sir. Then, please join our table for dinner. It will give you two the opportunity to catch up," Chase said.

"That would be wonderful, but I don't want to intrude. In fact, I believe we have claimed our seats already," Dr. Morris said.

"Oh. Who is accompanying you tonight?" Erin asked, not realizing until after the words escaped her mouth that she had no business asking him about his escort for the evening.

"My son," he said, his voice devoid of emotion.

"Is he following in your footsteps?" Chase asked.

Dr. Morris hesitated and looked around the grand banquet hall. That tired look in the older man's eyes seemed to morph into one that resembled worry. Something was definitely wrong.

"Not exactly," he finally said. Dr. Morris turned, and his eyes seemed to lock on a gentleman who was walking in their direction. "Though he is an oncologist. He left Philadelphia and now practices medicine here in New York."

Erin detected not an ounce of pride in Dr. Morris's voice when he spoke about his son, which she found to be very odd. As the gentleman came closer, it occurred to her that she had met him before. Erin had been volunteering on the oncology floor when Dr. Morris's son had paid his father a visit one morning...

She was discussing a patient with Dr. Morris when Scott Morris strolled into his father's office. Erin remembered how strange it was that Dr. Morris didn't introduce them; rather, he just kept speaking about the eleven-year-old patient down the hall, as if they were the only people in the room.

Finally, Scott Morris walked over to Erin and extended his hand. "You must be Erin Whitley," he said. Erin was taken by surprise, as she had no idea how he knew her name. Erin stood there speechless as he provided her an explanation. "My father speaks about you often. Says we'll be reading about you in medical journals one day." He smiled. "But no pressure."

She appreciated his humor and his attempt to lighten the conversation in a charming sort of way. "Oh, no…no pressure," she said sarcastically. "And you are?"

"His son," he said gesturing to Dr. Morris. "My name is Scott."

A hand wrapped snugly around her waist, thrusting Erin back to the present. She could feel Chase stiffen beside her as he pulled her even closer to him. Erin knew most men could be possessive around other attractive, successful men. It was a territorial thing. But Chase wasn't like most men. And he had no reason to be jealous. She had made it clear to him, over and over again, that she was his.

Erin watched Scott Morris approach. He appeared to glide through the crowd and as he drew closer, she felt her stomach muscles twist in a knot. Yes, he was quite good-looking, maybe even handsome, but her body's response wasn't prompted by his appearance and obvious self-confidence. Something else made her belly do somersaults. She just couldn't put her finger on it or identify the origin of her adverse reaction to Dr. Morris's son, a man whom she had met only once over a year ago.

Erin had no reason, no grounds to justify her uneasy feelings. She leaned into Chase and was relieved to feel his strong arms encircle her…protect her. What was going on with her?

"It's nice to see you again, Erin," Scott said. Erin's stomach turned again as he uttered her name. She forced a smile and reciprocated the expected response.

Chase introduced himself to Scott Morris and shook his hand. The two men seemed to eye each other closely, and again, Erin felt that uneasy feeling in her gut escalate. "Care to join us for dinner?" Chase asked, looking from son to father.

Chase's gaze stayed on Dr. Morris, as did Erin's. Dr. Morris appeared anxious, no longer the calm and collected man who could weather any situation, any medical emergency. He had begun to perspire and again reached for the handkerchief in his breast pocket.

"We would be honored. Thank you," Scott Morris said, forcing Erin to shift her attention from Dr. Morris for a moment. They made their way to their table. Chase was pulling out her seat when he saw Steven walking briskly through the crowd and heading straight toward them. Erin took her seat, positioning herself between Dr. Morris and Chase. Steven came up to their table and excused himself for the intrusion. "May I have a word with you, Chase?"

Chase looked down at her as if he needed her permission. Erin touched his arm and smiled. He bent down and whispered, "I'll be right back."

Erin was relieved to see their table fill up, taking her mind and attention away from the two doctors at her left. She turned to a couple across from her and engaged in small talk, a task she despised, but could successfully fake if deemed necessary.

Erin was doing a good job fielding questions, smiling at people she didn't know and complimenting dresses that she couldn't care less about when she spotted Chase across the hall. He was speaking to Steven, but there was no way Erin could make out what he was saying from that distance, though his facial expression suggested that he was agitated for some reason. Erin watched Chase run his fingers through his hair and then the two men shifted their focus to the banquet hall doors.

It may have been her imagination, but Erin swore that a hush fell over the room. She followed their gaze, though they were not the only men, or women, who were now staring at the beautiful woman who had just arrived...the woman who appeared to have captured the attention of everyone in the room, including Chase.

Chapter Forty-One

As he had done so many times before, Mitchell. Morris stared at his son and wondered where he went wrong as a parent. He and his wife had been married for over forty years, enabling his son to be brought up in a loving and intact family. Mitchell had worked tirelessly to provide for his family, though he had made certain that he was always available both emotionally and physically for his son. He had coached his Little League team, went to the back-to-school nights, and helped him with his homework on the rare occasions that Scott required assistance. Although Scott didn't want for anything, Mitchell always emphasized the importance of discipline and a solid work ethic. But despite Mitchell's best efforts and all those "attaboys" he had uttered, his son had turned into, or maybe he had always been, a monster.

Looking back, Mitchell had always known that his son was just…off. But even with numerous years of medical experience under his belt, Mitchell couldn't explain what was wrong with

Scott. It wasn't like his son had lit the house on fire or mutilated a family pet. He had always come home with near-perfect grades and a discipline report from school to match. He had been a star athlete, earning himself scholarship offers from colleges all over the country. There had never been a solitary incident that would raise suspicion or eyebrows. He had said "please" and "thank you" and kissed his mother goodbye every morning before he left the house for school. From the outside looking in, he had been the ideal son. A son who would make any father proud.

But Mitchell knew better. Even before that horrific night, a night that evoked hellish nightmares and an internal struggle every waking moment of his life, Mitchell knew deep down the vile things his son was capable of. It was just a feeling Mitchell had and kept from his wife. Maybe it was the way Scott had looked at him even from a very early age. There was nothing behind his eyes, no love or genuine respect, only tolerance. It was as if Scott had been buying time all those years, waiting patiently until the day he no longer needed his father financially. And then there was the smug grin Scott would flash every so often, the one that never made it to his soulless eyes, the smile that made Mitchell shudder. As a man with genius intelligence, good looks and no remorse, Scott was the most dangerous person Mitchell had ever known. And the tragedy of it all was that he had looked the other way, hoping and praying that his gut, his usually spot-on intuition, was completely wrong. Mitchell had kept his feelings to himself, never letting on, even to his wife, that the son they had created was derived from nothing less than pure evil.

It would have crushed his sweet wife, and he had decided years before that he would protect her, both mentally and physically, from such a revelation. His wife had been in a fragile state for many years while battling a devastating heart condition. When she took a turn for the worst after a heart transplant, he decided, whether right or wrong, to allow his wife to live out her final days thinking that her lovely boy was the picture of perfection—the picture that many, he feared, saw when they met Scott.

But not Erin. Mitchell had watched closely as Scott shook Erin's hand this evening. He had never seen Erin even slightly rattled. They had worked side by side while tending to patients for over a year. It took a special person to put herself in that position, a position which might require her to tell a helpless mother and father that their child's cancer was too aggressive, that there was nothing anyone could do. But Erin's resolve never wavered in the hospital; at least that was what she portrayed to him. She kept coming back for more, always asking questions, wanting to know everything she could to prepare for a career that was truly meant for her.

But the Erin he had seen tonight was a shadow of the woman she once was. She was still beautiful and charming and clearly smitten with Chase Montclair, but she had changed. That raging fire that he had always seen in her had dimmed. There was something different about her, and it sickened him to know what had derailed the dreams of a woman who now appeared…haunted.

"You're sweating, Dad. Feeling okay?"

Mitchell turned to his son and stared into his cold, lifeless eyes. A malicious smile formed on Scott's face, chilling him to the bone and reminding Mitchell in vivid detail of the night he had found is son lying in a pool of his own blood…

* * *

"Help me."

The garbled plea was barely a whisper, but Mitchell knew instantly that it belonged to his son. Mitchell was leaving the hospital after a long day at work when he received the call. The parking lot was half-full, and as the gruff voice of his son echoed in his head, he picked up the pace and practically sprinted to his car.

"Where are you?" Mitchell asked. He didn't ask his son what was wrong or if he was even hurt, which in hindsight seemed strange.

Mitchell heard his son cough, and in staggered speech he said, "Fourth and Market… in the cemetery."

Mitchell's phone went dead. He tried to call his son back, but it went straight to voice mail. The location his son gave him was only minutes away. He kept his eyes on the road while reaching to the backseat for the medical bag he always kept stowed away for emergencies.

The old, poorly lit cobblestone street was in the old section of Philadelphia. He pulled over haphazardly into a space he was uncertain was even a legal area for him to park in. With medical bag in hand, he entered the cemetery, only to find the most horrific scene he had ever encountered.

Covered in blood, his son was lying on the ground and strug-

gling to breathe, his pants at his ankles. Mitchell ran over to him, and though it was not the time to theorize what had occurred or why his son was bleeding out, he couldn't help himself. It was glaringly obvious and too difficult to disregard the evidence. Mitchell removed the ski mask from his son's face and stuffed it into his coat pocket.

It didn't take a detective to determine that his son was not the victim in this crime. But the inquisition would have to wait, if it was even going to take place. At that moment, Mitchell was unsure if his son was going to survive. He was pale, his pulse and breathing erratic.

"No...no hospital," Scott choked out.

Mitchell knew it was an absolute gamble not to take him to the emergency room, where his son would have complete access to state-of-the-art facilities and care. But, not really knowing why at the time, he complied, gathered his son in his arms and carried him to his car. They drove to his private practice in silence.

Mitchell worked on his son for several hours. Working in the emergency room for a few years, he had seen injuries like this before. Broken ribs, a concussion, multiple abrasions requiring stitches, internal bleeding and punctured lungs were common ailments for a person who had been beaten and left for dead. And Mitchell had no doubt that had been the intention. Scott wasn't supposed to leave that cemetery, at least not breathing. When daylight finally slithered through the blinds of the exam room, his son was sleeping soundly as a result of the heaviest pain meds he had on hand, which weren't that powerful, and exhaustion.

Mitchell sat on the leather chair across from his patient. Scott's vitals were being monitored by various machines, allowing

Mitchell to focus his attention on another matter. He went over to the counter and sifted through his son's belongings in search of his cell phone. The phone was covered in blood, and Mitchell assumed that it had acquired the blood when his son had called him at the hospital. Mitchell clicked into his recent emails and texts but didn't find anything disturbing. He was about to shut the phone down when he noticed the Notes app. He pressed it and found what appeared to be a class schedule. He scrolled farther down and squinted. Detailed daily schedules for an unknown individual had been typed into his phone. Mitchell knew that the schedules didn't belong to his son. Scott had already graduated from college and did not volunteer at the hospital at which Mitchell worked.

Mitchell looked at the unknown person's volunteer schedule in particular. He or she apparently volunteered Mondays, Wednesdays and Fridays from three to five in the evening. Mitchell felt nauseous. He knew someone, someone he had grown fond of over the past year, with that exact schedule. But he didn't want to get ahead of himself. His hospital in particular was a teaching hospital, thus serving as a beacon for aspiring doctors. There were a dozen volunteers within the hospital walls at any given time. He succumbed to false hope that the schedule in his son's phone did not belong to the young lady he had been working with for some time…that was, until he pressed on the camera app. In stunned silence, he leafed through hundreds of photos of Erin Whitley, his talented and most dedicated volunteer…and felt the overwhelming urge to vomit.

But his son's voice stopped him from grabbing the trash can and emptying the contents of his stomach into it. "All these years *of wondering…waiting. Tell me. Are you relieved to know it wasn't your imagination?" Scott asked, his voice husky and somewhat choppy.*

As a father, Mitchell wanted to lie. He wanted to say that it wasn't a relief to learn that his son was a monster, that he hadn't suspected what his only child was all these years. But when he looked into his son's empty eyes, he knew that it served no purpose to negate the truth.

"Where is Erin?" Mitchell asked, his tone laced with disdain.

"At home I suppose." Scott looked at him and smiled.

"You need help, son. I can make sure you get it," Dr. Morris pleaded.

"What kind of help? Rehabilitation? Prison time? What do you have in mind?" Scott asked mockingly.

"Whatever it takes…whatever it takes to help you so you no longer have the need or desire to harm innocent women," Mitchell said.

"It must be exhausting," Scott said. He sighed and slowly shifted his weight while he lay on the exam table. Scott winced, but continued. "To continue to love someone, to put forth so much effort for so long, only to be met with disappointment. Even now, you're trying to help me, your only son."

There was not an ounce of gratitude or appreciation in his child's voice. In fact, it sounded as if Scott was disgusted by him. The last remaining feelings of compassion Mitchell had for his son left him, causing him a pain he didn't know existed.

"Let me be clear. Yes, I saved your life, allowing you to see another day, a decision I most likely will regret. And as long as your mother is still breathing, I will not say a word about what you *are. It would kill her. But make no mistake, Scott. The world will know that you are a rapist and Erin will know who violated her. I will make certain of it."*

Grinning from ear to ear, Scott clapped. "It's a shame that only now, after all these years, do I find you interesting."

* * *

"We need to leave…now," Mitchell whispered. There was no need to keep their voices down. Everyone seemed to be focused on some guests who had just walked through the banquet hall doors. People were whispering and gesturing to their table.

Scott reached for his wrist, preventing him from rising from his seat. "Of course. You don't look well, Dad," Scott said, his voice loud enough to draw Erin's attention away from the woman who had just entered the banquet room.

Erin looked at him. "You do look quite pale," she said, placing the back of her hand on his forehead.

Mitchell took her hand and gave it a pat. "I am a bit tired. I think I'll retire for the night. It was nice seeing you again. Would you mind telling Mr. Montclair the reason behind our early departure?"

"Of course," she smiled. Her eyes looked troubled and he hated himself more with each passing second.

Scott and Mitchell rose to their feet.

"It was nice to see you again, Erin. I would personally thank Mr. Montclair for a wonderful evening, but he seems occupied at the moment," Scott said, gesturing to the brunette at the hall entrance. Scott smiled, and then turned and said, "Ready, Dad?"

Mitchell didn't answer Scott. He watched Erin's face fall as she looked at the woman everyone seemed to be captivated by. It was then that Mitchell knew that Scott was not finished with Erin. She was still the object of his obsession.

Chapter Forty-Two

Scott Morris may have set the stage, but it was up to her to change the tide…a challenge that Gabrielle had been waiting for. She had been patient, waiting for the opportunity to destroy the man she had almost married. And God knows he deserved it. She may have cheated on him, but it was a crime that paled in comparison to what Chase Montclair had done to her. Because of Chase, she would never be able to conceive a child again. She would never know what it felt like to be doted on or fussed over by a man who was bursting with joy because he was going to be a father. Because of Chase, her career had tapered off during her stay in rehab. Because of Chase, she would never desire someone so strongly again. The decision had been made. Chase needed to join her in this living hell he had created.

And from the looks of it, Chase was halfway there already. The scowl he gave her from across the banquet hall spoke volumes. Glorious satisfaction washed over her as she basked in the realization that the first part of her mission had been successful. He appeared not only surprised, but also agitated over her impromptu appearance at his benefit. Gabrielle needed him to feel off balance as opposed to the composed Chase Montclair he usually was—the Chase that was cunning and calculating…her equal.

Gabrielle met his gaze and smiled, an action he did not reciprocate. Instead, he turned and looked over at a round table across the room. It took less than a second to identify Erin Whitley amongst the tabletop of eight. Even without Scott Morris's detailed description of his ex-girlfriend, Gabrielle would have been able to pick her out immediately. She was stunning, a fact that even Gabrielle could admit. But that was not what confirmed her identity. It was the worried look and the daggers the woman was shooting in Gabrielle's direction—daggers that only jealousy evoked—that told her she had laid eyes on Erin Whitley.

"You look exquisite, sweetheart," her mother whispered in her ear as they made their way into the banquet hall.

"Thank you, Mother. I'm so glad I could be here with you and Daddy tonight." Gabrielle gave her mom's arm a gentle squeeze. "You're a survivor. I wouldn't have missed this for anything."

Her mother smiled, but it evaporated quickly when she looked over Gabrielle's shoulder. Gabrielle didn't need to follow her mother's gaze. She knew where it fell. "Don't worry, Mother. Chase visited me in California this week."

"He what?" she asked, her eyes wide as saucers.

"He came to check on me, to make sure I'm doing okay."

"Does this mean you two are getting back together?"

Her mother had always been, and apparently was still, a huge fan of Chase Montclair and his millions. Gabrielle's mother was devastated when her daughter's engagement to one of the world's most sought-after men was called off. Gabrielle never shared with her parents the real reason behind their breakup and what actually prompted her stay at the luxurious Loyola Ranch. Gabrielle had strategically omitted pertinent facts. She never mentioned that the baby she had miscarried didn't belong to Chase. And she never told her mother that she had been caught in the act with her former photographer. Unfortunately, it was impossible to keep her suicide attempt from her parents. She had been foolish to cheat on Chase, a man she knew would leave her if she was caught, a man with the millions she needed to uphold the lifestyle she had always dreamed of. However, it didn't take much to convince her mother that she had made an attempt on her life due to a bout of depression as a result of her breakup with Chase, or that she was now fully recovered…and ready to make Chase experience true loss.

"The conversation we had was long overdue," Gabrielle said, escorting her mother, with her father in tow, to their table.

"But Gabby, I believe Chase is with someone now." Her mother gestured to Erin Whitley's table.

"Yes. She is lovely. Don't you think so, Mother?" Gabrielle locked eyes with the beautiful Ms. Whitley.

"She is just a pretty face. You and Chase have history, a past to build upon." Her mother smiled and then took a sip of champagne, which had been placed in front of her by a very quick and competent waiter.

Gabrielle reached for her own glass of champagne. Clinking her glass with her mother's, she toasted, "May our past only make us stronger."

* * *

"You didn't have any idea that Ms. Green was planning to attend?" Steven McConnel asked.

Frustrated, Chase raked his fingers through his hair as he watched the Greens walk toward their table. "I knew her parents were coming, but Gabrielle is definitely a...surprise," Chase said, keeping his voice low.

"I can ask them to leave, Chase. You know I'll be discreet."

"No. This has to play out...for now."

Steven nodded and moved to the other side of the banquet hall, most likely to be closer to Gabrielle's table. Chase appreciated the fact that his father's longtime friend didn't need a directive. Steven just knew what had to be done and where he was needed the most.

Chase grabbed two glasses of wine from the bar before heading back to his table. He made certain that his eyes didn't drift and accidently fall anywhere near Gabrielle's table. When he reached his table it was clear that some damage control was in order. His sudden appearance seemed to put an end to any conversation that was taking place.

His high-profile relationship and eventual breakup with Gabrielle had captured a lot of media attention. It wouldn't surprise him in the least to learn that many guests were salivating at the opportunity to witness a possible showdown between his ex and the woman he loved. But he didn't care what the people at his table were thinking or hoping to see. The only opinion he cared about belonged to Erin. And from the troubled look in her eyes, he knew that it would take an Oscar-worthy performance to get through the evening as if nothing was wrong. Later, when they were alone and hopefully in each other's arms, he would tell her everything.

Smiling, he set her glass of wine on the table and took his seat. Dinner was already being served, which always seemed to promote mindless but easy conversation at a table. Just as he suspected, the couple to his right commented on how tender their filets were and how the particular vintage they were drinking complimented their meal exactly.

He reached under the table and found Erin's hand in her lap. She tensed when he touched her, a response that was foreign to him. Her body was always so responsive, so willing to reciprocate his touch with either a soft caress or intense passion. But now she seemed to be a million miles away, making Chase question his decision to wait until after the benefit to share his past with her.

"Did you know she was coming?" Erin asked, though her voice was only slightly above a whisper.

There was no reason to be coy. Erin had met the Greens earlier in the week. It wouldn't be difficult to figure out that the woman sitting between Victoria and Edward was their daughter. "No, I had no idea she would show up here."

Erin took a sip of her wine and finally looked over at him. "I'd be lying if I said I didn't feel threatened."

He felt his heart swell as he gazed into her beautiful blue eyes. "I belong to you and you alone."

She blushed. The sudden color to her face was a relief, as it suggested that her distant demeanor may have come to an end. "I must sound like an insecure...jealous..."

"Stop. I can assure you that if the tables were turned, and your ex was the one who walked through those doors, I would need Steven and half the security team to dissuade me, physically most likely, not to approach him and reiterate to him and anyone who would listen that you are mine."

She squeezed his hand from beneath the table. "I'm sorry. I was just so surprised and overwhelmed by my own selfish feelings that I didn't even consider how awkward it must be for you to see her after all this time."

This was the moment of truth, when he should have excused himself and Erin, taken her to the hotel room he had rented for the night, and told her about his relationship with Gabrielle and his trip to California. But for whatever reason, cowardice most likely, he simply smiled and kissed her, never confirming or denying what she had said.

And it was because of that silence, those few sacred seconds, that he would lose her.

Chapter Forty-Three

Gabrielle excused herself from the bland conversation that was taking place between her parents and a couple they had recently vacationed with in Italy, and made her way to the terrace. Chase had just concluded his speech about cancer awareness and the foundation and was finally unattended. Erin Whitley was nowhere in sight.

Gabrielle watched as Chase worked his magic with a group of very wealthy donors, though it was not a difficult feat. He could charm the most hardened of individuals, both men and women, into giving him what he wanted. It was one of his most appealing qualities, and again she wondered what had prompted her to stray when she was with him. Gabrielle quickly pushed that thought aside, as it was both unproductive and painful. Rehashing only opened up old wounds, scars that needed to remain firmly intact.

She waited until he was alone to approach. From behind,

she said, "Your father would be proud of what you accomplished here tonight."

Gabrielle saw his back stiffen as he turned around. "You failed to mention in California that you would be coming here tonight."

His eyes seemed vacant, devoid of the warmth and passion that she had once enjoyed. Gabrielle didn't like the fact that his apparent lack of enthusiasm severely hurt her pride. She needed to refocus and fixate on the one and only reason that brought her here. Chase deserved to suffer, and Gabrielle was confident that she had the power to bring about the right level of pain.

"I only found out this morning that my photo shoot suddenly got moved to next week. I thought it would be nice to surprise my parents and support my mom at the same time." Gabrielle put on her best wounded-bird face. Chase stared at her, as if wondering if she was full of shit. After a few seconds of uncomfortable silence, Gabrielle said, "She is lovely, Chase. Even more beautiful than you described."

Chase glanced around the banquet hall and then moved toward her. "I think it would be best if you two don't cross paths," he said. "Let's give the past the respect it deserves and leave it in the past."

Gabrielle peered over his shoulder and discovered that a very concerned-looking Erin Whitley was approaching. She waited until Erin was in earshot to respond to Chase. Gabrielle batted her eyelashes and feigned innocence. "Chase, I'm not the one who jumped on a plane for California to discuss our past. You might be surprised to see me here tonight. But that doesn't even compare to the shock I felt this week when I opened my front door to see you standing on my porch. You ask me why I have come here to this benefit. That's easy. To support my mother, a breast cancer survivor." Gabrielle tried desperately to withhold the smirk that truly wanted to spread across her face. Erin looked from Gabrielle to Chase, her eyes already filling up.

"You know why I came to you this week. I…"

"But I don't," Erin interrupted.

Gabrielle watched Chase instantly deflate. He closed his eyes as all the color rushed from his face. He turned around to see his girlfriend looking at him, the pain and fear of betrayal clearly evident in those piercing blue eyes of hers. He reached for Erin's hand, but she stepped back, bumping into a waiter carrying a tray of empty champagne flutes. Several glasses fell to the floor and shattered. Clutching her purse, Erin mumbled something to the embarrassed-looking waiter and hurried to the door.

Gabrielle reached for Chase's arm. "Chase, wait. Let me talk to her. I can explain to her why you came to California."

"No, you've done enough." He took her by the arm and pulled her into the hallway, away from prying eyes. Gabrielle was surprised that Chase stayed for a moment and didn't go running after Erin. "You planned this, didn't you? Everything you told me in California—that you were happy that I have found someone—that you were sorry for everything that had happened, was bullshit. Wasn't it?"

There was no need to keep up the charade any longer. The seed of doubt had been planted in Erin's mind. Erin's abrupt departure from the benefit told Gabrielle that its roots had already taken hold and would not be withering away anytime soon, if ever. "You think I could have pulled this off all by myself?" she asked, smiling at confused and what appeared to be desperate eyes.

When he didn't respond, she added, "Seems you have some competition. Erin's ex-boyfriend is quite determined to get her back, says he will do anything to be with her one last time."

Within seconds, he had her backed into a corner, her breath leaving her. "What did you say?"

She knew that she shouldn't be feeling this way, but Gabrielle couldn't dismiss how incredibly sexy he was at that moment, pressed up against her, his voice gruff and demanding.

"Who is he? Is he here?" he asked, his voice sounding panic-stricken.

Gabrielle watched him and wondered why he appeared so rattled. She had expected him to be pissed, crazed with the idea of pummeling someone Erin used to fuck. But it wasn't jealousy that seemed to engulf him, it was fear.

His reaction left Gabrielle temporarily paralyzed. She didn't answer him, even when he grabbed her by both arms and pleaded for her to disclose the name of her accomplice. Chase let go of her and pulled out his cell phone. Seconds later, Gabrielle heard him speaking to a man named Andrew.

"Find her, Andrew...she's everything to me." Chase ended the call and looked at Gabrielle.

Again, she pushed her wounded pride aside and allowed her anger to be front and center. "She's a big girl, Chase," Gabrielle said.

"You have no idea what you've done, do you? Tell me who this ex-boyfriend is."

"Why don't you ask Erin about the company she keeps?" Gabrielle straightened her dress and smiled. It had been rumpled as a result of Chase's inquisition. "Fascinating. She doesn't come across as his type at all."

* * *

Chase had never wanted to inflict pain on a woman before. Even when he'd found Gabrielle fucking another guy in the bed they used to share, Chase didn't have the urge to succumb to such savage thoughts and desires. But this time was different. The woman he was in love with was in danger, and if Gabrielle wasn't going to reveal the ex-boyfriend's name, there was no use wasting another minute in Gabrielle's vile presence.

"I used to spend hours wondering what I did, what I lacked, to make you turn away from me and into the arms of someone else. But the anger that I had has morphed and now it resembles something I can only describe as pity." Chase looked directly at Gabrielle and wondered how he could have ever loved her. Her beauty was only skin deep, whereas Erin's encompassed her entire body and soul.

Chase had turned and began to walk away from her when he heard the words he had always suspected would come. "You're a smart man, Chase. Brilliant, some would say. But you never bothered to do the math, did you?" Through gritted teeth, Gabrielle stood erect and said, "The baby wasn't yours. You were away on one of your business trips when I conceived my child. You were foolish to believe without question that the baby I carried belonged to you."

Chase maintained his distance. And though he felt enraged, a part of him finally found solace. It wasn't like he was happy that she had miscarried a baby. No one, not even Gabrielle, should experience such a loss. Although Gabrielle's affair had made him doubt whether he was the father of her baby, he had never been absolutely certain, and he couldn't help but feel that he may have played a key role in his son or daughter's demise. Until now.

The guilt he had been carrying had made him question whether he could be, or even deserved to be, a father. Now he saw his future. And the only person he wanted to share it with was Erin, the woman who had just left him.

Chase wanted to say something scathing and make Gabrielle wince at the words she deserved to hear. But there was no point, and it occurred to Chase that the heated back-and-forth was probably what she wanted. Instead, Chase smiled and said, "Good-bye, Gabrielle."

Her reaction was priceless, though he wasted no time to savor her stunned silence, let alone the sight of her jaw nearly touching the marble floor. Chase reached for the cell phone that was now buzzing in his pocket, turned away from Gabrielle and walked out of her life once and for all.

Chapter Forty-Four

Mitchell knew why he had kept his son—the child he had created in love with his beautiful but fragile wife—in his life after discovering him lying in a cemetery bleeding and deserving every torturous second. But his reason had since passed. This would be the last night he would see his son. Mitchell would make certain of it. With Scott seated just inches away, the back of the limo suddenly felt like it was closing in on him.

"You don't look well, Dad. Your color has not improved. I think we should go to the hospital for some tests," Scott said, his voice louder than it needed to be.

Mitchell noticed the driver peering into the rearview mirror.

"I'm fine. Just tired," Mitchell said, looking out the side window. It had just started to rain. The sight of the natural occurrence brought him both sadness and fond memories. His wife loved rain and thunderstorms. It was during monsoon-like weather in a tiny, cramped log cabin in the woods that he had proposed and she had said yes without hesitating. They didn't leave that cabin for days. How he missed her smile and infectious laugh.

Mitchell had planned on staying at a hotel tonight. But after what transpired at the benefit, he couldn't get back to the home he had shared with his wife for so many years fast enough. He also needed to get out of New York, far away from his son, far away from Erin Whitley. "Peter, please take me home to Philadelphia. Scott's apartment is just a few blocks from here. We can drop him off on the way."

Peter nodded and turned onto the main road.

"He can be quite stubborn, can't he, Peter?" Scott asked, his tone taking on an annoying playful quality.

Peter didn't answer. It seemed that he too found Scott irritating.

Peter pulled up in front of Scott's apartment. Mitchell knew he shouldn't, but he couldn't seem to help it. Just one last time. He reluctantly looked at his son, and gasped. The features on his son's chiseled face morphed into the soft curves and untainted flesh of a child. His brown hair was trimmed neatly, but appeared somewhat tousled, the way it looked after playing nine innings of baseball with a cap fitting snugly on his head.

But it was an illusion, as it had been even when Scott was that eight-year-old boy. Mitchell felt true despair as he realized that at long last, it was time to let his son go.

"Good-bye, Scott."

Scott stared back at him for a moment, and a smile tugged

at one side of his mouth. Mitchell looked into his son's eyes and shivered.

Peter opened the passenger-side door. Scott stepped out, but not before saying, "I'll check on you later, Dad. You can count on that."

Chapter Forty-Five

M̲s. Whitley, please open up and let me see that you're safe. You know I will not leave unless I'm sure."

Erin pressed her head against the inside of the front door to her apartment. She thought that she would have had a few extra minutes to wrap her head around what she had just learned before Andrew hunted her down. But it wasn't Andrew's fault. He was just following orders. He shouldn't be on the receiving end of her despair and mounting rage.

Erin opened the door to her apartment and invited Andrew inside. He locked the door behind him and proceeded to search each room. When Andrew finally appeared satisfied, he walked over to her. "Mr. Montclair is concerned about your safety."

"Yes, I'm aware. That is why you and I have been hanging out so much lately." Ordinarily, Erin would have smiled, maybe even chuckled, but she was in no mood for light conversation. The pain she had experienced when she learned that Chase had traveled two thousand miles to visit his beautiful ex-girlfriend was overwhelming. It took everything Erin had to leave that banquet hall without causing a horrific scene.

"I must call him, Ms. Whitley. Please understand," Andrew said.

Erin nodded, realizing it was pointless to stop him, if that was even possible.

Andrew withdrew his phone and dialed. Not even a second later, Erin heard Chase's voice, though muddled, on the other line.

"Yes, she's safe. Ms. Whitley is in her apartment."

A few moments passed and then Andrew said, "Of course. I'll stay here until you arrive."

Erin waved her hands frantically as she mouthed, "No. No, Andrew."

"Ms. Whitley wishes to speak with you," Andrew said, holding the phone out to her.

Erin's mouth hung open as she stared at Andrew. She didn't expect her tight-lipped, all-business bodyguard to completely disregard what she obviously wanted. But Erin really couldn't be angry at him. It was unfair to put him in the middle of a lovers' quarrel. Erin felt heat rush to her face, exposing her embarrassment. "I'm sorry, Andrew. I'm not angry with you."

He smiled and placed the phone in her hand. Andrew walked out to the kitchen, far enough away to provide her with a little privacy, but still keeping her in his line of sight.

"I know you're angry with me and you have every right to feel that way. But please let me come over and explain why…"

Those pangs of jealousy and inconsolable pain hit her violently the moment she heard him speak. Furious, Erin cut him off and said, "Explain what? Explain why you flew across the country to pay your ex-fiancée a visit? Explain why you lied to me and told me you were going on a business trip?"

"Erin, please let me come see you."

Suddenly, she heard a knock at the door and then her brother's voice. Now that Erin had a man in her life, they had decided that it was best if they didn't just walk into each other's apartments anymore. No brother wanted to see his sister in a compromising position, and vice versa. They had agreed to give each other a courtesy knock before entering. Erin's attentive bodyguard was already walking toward the door. "Paul is at my door." She sighed. And though it pained her to do so, she said, "I can't do this right now, Chase."

"Please, Erin. You need to understand why I went to California. But more importantly, you are in danger. Gabrielle told me that your ex is determined to get you back, that he will do anything to make you his again." Erin felt her breath leave her and the room began to swirl around. The last thing she saw was the ceiling meeting the floor.

* * *

"Will you always make me worry so?" he asked, his voice full of loving concern.

It took a second for her vision to clear, but Erin would know Paul's protective touch and soothing tone anywhere. Paul was holding her hand as she lay on the couch. "What happened?"

"You fainted." Paul smoothed the hair back from her face, a gesture that her father had used on occasion, especially when he tucked her into bed at night when she was a little girl. "How do you feel?"

More than one word came to mind, but the only thing she could get out was "Foolish."

Erin looked over at Andrew, who seemed to be keeping silent vigil. The expression on his face was one of relief, his stoic composure only wavering slightly. Erin didn't want to put Andrew in an uncomfortable position, but right now it was necessary. "Andrew, I can't speak to Chase right now. Report back that I'm fine, but urge him not to come here."

He nodded, but before excusing himself, he stated, "I will inform him that you're safe and that your brother has arrived. However, I will remain just outside your apartment in the hallway if you require my assistance."

Erin nodded, accepting the frightening truth that constant surveillance was necessary, especially now.

What had happened? Did Chase find out that she had been raped?

Erin simply said thank you and watched her bodyguard leave her apartment. Erin hadn't realized that she had been unconsciously keeping it together until she was finally alone with her brother and her raw emotions. She put her face in her hands, pulled her knees to her chest and wept.

Paul sat down on the couch and took her in his arms. "No secrets, remember. Not between us," he said, his voice steady.

He held her tight as she cried, and when the tears finally started to recede and Erin could again breathe, she told him about Chase's trip to California and the ex-fiancée whom he obviously was still involved with.

Paul refrained for a moment before responding to what she had just said. Erin assumed it was a tactic people learned in lawyer school in order to gather their thoughts before saying something witty or thought provoking. However, the words out of Paul's mouth were simple and straight to the point. "That son-of-a-bitch."

Paul stood up and started for the door. The look of brotherly concern had mutated into something very dark...and very dangerous.

Panic instantly set in. Erin knew what her brother was capable of when he was enraged. She had witnessed it firsthand. And no matter how angry she was at Chase, Erin didn't want him hurt or maimed by her brother.

"Paul, wait. There's something else you should know."

Paul stopped in his tracks and turned around. "Chase doesn't deserve you. And I'll be damned if you think I'll just sit back and let him treat you this way."

"You don't need to defend me. I'll handle it." Erin sat up straight, knowing that what she was about to reveal was even more troublesome. "Before I fainted, Chase called and told me that he was on his way over here to explain why he went to California. But more importantly, he felt the need to say that I was in danger, that my ex wanted me back."

The look in Paul's eyes changed from one of fury to outright dread. "Chase didn't say anything else?"

Erin shook her head. "No, I passed out, most likely from shock, and the next thing I remember was you sitting here on the couch with me." The muscles in her stomach tightened and she said what they both had to be thinking. "Do you think he found out about my rape and the rapist's identity?"

Paul walked back over to her. "Erin, we need to find out what Chase knows or doesn't know," he said, his voice again calm.

"I know. But I can't talk to Chase, at least not right now. I'm so angry, so…"

"Hurt?" Paul interjected.

Erin swallowed, feeling the tears begin to well. "I trusted him, Paul." She inhaled and then said, "I want to be the one to confront him."

"Alright. It will be on your terms, then." Paul leaned down and kissed her on the forehead. He gave her one of his rare smiles and then started for the door.

"Wait, where are you going?" Erin thought that she had made herself clear. She didn't want Paul fighting her battles anymore.

"I'm just going out into the hallway to talk with Andrew. I think until we know anything further, Andrew should stay here around the clock."

"Andrew has a life, Paul. He can't be expected to babysit a grown woman twenty-four seven."

"I'm aware of that. Which is precisely why I was going to ask him how we could maintain coverage, possibly with an additional guard. I'll be right back." He winked at her and left the apartment, closing the door behind him.

Erin had always known that Paul hid behind a mask most of his adult life. He rarely lost his composure, which was surely an asset in his profession. Erin had clung to the belief that Paul would never wear that mask around her. But when he didn't return after several minutes from his conversation with Andrew, Erin came to the disturbing realization that she was not the exception. His mask was securely in place when he left her apartment in search of Chase.

Chapter Forty-Six

With the exception of weekly housekeeping and maintenance checks from Edward Green's hired hands, Gabrielle's lavish apartment had remained untouched for the past year. Gabrielle opened her bedroom closet door and smiled. It was stocked with clothes that she still fit into, a sweet triumph in any model's life. But the momentary feeling of happiness faded as she stared at the king-sized bed, a bed she had shared with Chase…and many others. Gabrielle shook that thought from her mind. She was good at compartmentalizing. She needed to focus on what happened prior to Chase saying that he pitied her, when the legendary Chase Montclair had crumbled before her eyes and experienced true heartache.

A bath. A glass of wine, maybe the entire bottle. That was what she needed and deserved at the moment. Gabrielle retreated to the kitchen, grabbed a glass, a corkscrew and the first bottle she saw on the wine rack, and made her way back to the master bath. She placed her cell phone on the tub's ledge, set it to her favorite Pandora station and turned on the tub's jets. Gabrielle deposited more than enough soap to create a soothing bubble bath. She popped open the bottle of wine and poured herself a heaping glass. She peeled off her gown, a dress that she knew Chase didn't take notice of, and let it and her undergarments fall to the floor.

Gabrielle stepped into the scalding water, though its bite only lured her in further. With wineglass in hand, she sat down and leaned her head against the back of the tub. The jets continued their rhythm, making her more relaxed by the second. The fact that she had downed her first glass and was now working on her second in less than two minutes also contributed nicely to her sedated state of mind. Gabrielle closed her eyes as she savored her victory.

* * *

The sight of Gabrielle, lying naked and wet in a sea of bubbles, did absolutely nothing for him. Scott knew from an early age what turned him on. Purity, innocence…the pristine. Gabrielle didn't possess those qualities. In fact, Scott felt she tainted the world and whomever she came in contact with. Scott stepped further into the bathroom and stared at the woman who lay amongst the suds with her eyes closed. But the only thought that came to mind was that in a few moments there would be one less dirty creature on Earth.

Scott peeled away his disguise, sat on the tub's edge, and removed the cork from the bottle of wine he had brought for such an occasion. The pop of the cork startled the dirty woman, and her eyes shot open. Gabrielle sat up, and though she appeared quite surprised by his impromptu visit, she didn't bother to cover herself. Her perky breasts lay exposed above the waterline as she stared at him with what looked like annoyance. He had hoped she would feel a little embarrassed, possibly even ask for a towel in the presence of a virtual stranger. But she just sat there, looking like the pissed-off dirty whore that she was.

"How did you get in here?" she asked.

She reached for the half-drunk bottle of wine that she had obviously been working on, but Scott intercepted her and poured her a glass from the bottle he had brought.

He ignored her question. "You did very well tonight. And so you deserve vintage of a finer quality," Scott said, pouring Gabrielle a glass of wine rich in color…and side effects.

Gabrielle took the glass and drank heartily. After the prolonged gulp, she licked her wine-infused lips and sighed. "Maybe," she said.

"I don't like this side of you. I was hoping to toast the beautiful and very confident woman I met in California," he said, baiting her.

She straightened and scowled. "I did my part. I put the wedge between the happy couple. Now it's your turn to tear them apart for good."

"Don't worry, sweetheart. That will happen sooner rather than later," he said, pouring Gabrielle another glass of wine.

Gabrielle took a sip and then said, "You don't care to join me, Doctor?" She lifted her wineglass. "Go on, I don't have cooties."

"Of course not. But I have a house call that I must attend to, and I must keep my wits about me." He smiled at her.

Gabrielle took yet another sip. "I'm intrigued, Dr. Morris."

"About what, love?"

"There's no way Chase would have let you sit at the same table as Erin Whitley tonight, let alone breathe the same air as her, if he thought you had been intimate with his girlfriend at some point in time. He's not the sharing type." Her last three words sounded slurred, and he wondered if she had taken notice.

"You do amuse me at times," he said, watching her eyelids begin to grow heavy. She was just becoming interesting. Pity.

She held up her empty glass, motioning for a refill. He complied happily.

"Erin Whitley treated you like a ssstranger, not a lover." Gabrielle smiled, sat back in the tub and gulped her wine.

Scott refrained from commenting on a statement that was meant to sting. He had more important things to do than get into a war of words. He had to know if Gabrielle Green had complied with the terms of their arrangement and from the looks of her, his time was running out quickly.

"Gabby, have you been a good girl? Did you tell anyone about us?" he asked, brushing the hair from her face. Her eyelids were struggling to remain open. The toxin was working beautifully.

She shook her head. "Nnno…and don't call me Gabby," she said, her lips pouty.

"Shh…that's a good girl." He had to keep her talking,

enough to make sure his cover had not been blown. "Does Chase Montclair know about me?"

She shook her head violently. "Only cares about…her."

Scott was almost positive that Gabrielle hadn't disclosed his identity. If she had, Scott was certain that Montclair would have hunted him down by now. Scott took the empty wineglass from her hand and placed it gently on the tub's ledge. He slid her to a sitting position, since she'd started to slump amidst the ever-fading bubbles.

"Open your eyes, sweetheart," he said.

Her eyelashes twitched as she struggled to open them. After several seconds, he stared into glazed-over eyes, once vibrant but blinded to what a woman should hold dear.

"I'm sleepy," she said.

"Yes. But I need you to look at me."

"Hmmph…why?" she asked, barely a whisper.

Scott reached over and smoothed the hair from her face. "Because you need to see what happens to filthy girls."

"But I'm a good girrrl," she said, her voice fading.

"Tonight you were my good, compliant little girl, yes. But one night does not an Angel make." He caressed her cheek and then reached for her shoulder. Her eyes grew wide as he thrust her under the water. She struggled for only a few moments before her body went limp beneath his grasp. Scott was careful not to hold her too tightly. Her death needed to look like a suicide, something she had attempted before, not a homicide. Strange marks on her supple skin would only lead to further investigation.

Scott reached for her cell phone and searched Gabrielle's

contacts. He clicked on Chase's name and began the short and to-the-point text: *"I think I got it right this time. I'm sorry for everything. Good-bye Chase."*

Scott placed the phone on the ledge, but refrained from pushing SEND. He removed a handkerchief from his suit's jacket pocket and proceeded to wipe down everything in the bathroom that he had come in contact with. When he was confident that his presence couldn't be detected, even by the most astute detective, he reached for the phone, pressed the SEND button and wiped it clean. Scott stepped away from the tub and looked at the filthy little girl beneath the suds, the girl that would never be clean, even in death.

Chapter Forty-Seven

W arn him if you must," Paul said as he walked past Andrew. "Just don't leave Erin's side."

Andrew didn't even attempt to stop him. It was as if he expected nothing less from the jilted woman's overprotective brother.

Paul caught the elevator and rode the seven floors down in seething silence. He told himself to calm down, to at least hold off on killing Chase Montclair until he discovered what the piece of shit knew, if anything, about the rape. But the moment he spotted Chase exiting the parked limo across the street from their apartment building, all rational thought went by the wayside.

Paul sprinted across the street, disregarding traffic and any obstacle that would prohibit him from grabbing Chase and pounding his face in, and rounded Chase's vehicle. Paul looked around and noticed that the park adjacent to them would provide the cover he needed to accomplish his two objectives.

Chase slammed the passenger-side door to the limo shut and looked at him. Paul noticed that Chase didn't look the least bit surprised to see him there, fuming and ready to pounce.

"Erin needs to know the truth…and so do you."

Paul couldn't stand to hear his sister's name pour over the bastard's lips. His fist hit Chase's jaw with expert precision, but Chase didn't fall as he expected. Chase shoved him off, but Paul ran for him, backing Chase into the protective shadows of the park, and tackled him.

"You don't deserve her," Paul grunted as he pinned Chase to the ground.

Paul had underestimated Chase's strength, and found himself tossed to the side as Chase maneuvered out of his grasp. Both men sprang to their feet, but it was Chase who seemed to have the upper hand. Chase grabbed Paul and pinned him against an aging oak tree. "You're right. I don't."

"She trusted you," Paul said through clenched teeth. "And she doesn't trust anyone."

Chase's arm was across Paul's throat. "Why is that?" Chase shouted.

Paul and Chase stared at each other for a tense moment. It was as if one was waiting for the other to break. Finally, Chase said, "Why did you tell me that you don't know Erin's ex-boyfriend? It's obvious that you know something. Tell me who he is."

"He can't…and neither can I."

Paul hadn't heard Erin approach. He turned and saw her standing a few feet away with Andrew trailing closely behind.

Chase's arm went limp and he backed away from Paul. Erin stepped closer, positioning herself between the two men.

"The flowers that were delivered to your apartment, the text messages…were not sent by an ex-boyfriend." Erin looked at Paul. He nodded. Her secret was about to be exposed, and if that was what she wanted, he would support her. "They were sent by the man who raped me a year ago while I was walking home from my last final exam."

* * *

Everything made such cruel and sickening sense…almost everything, anyway. Chase didn't know why Erin had kept this unthinkable crime a secret from him. Didn't she know that there was nothing she could tell him that would make him love her any less? All he wanted to do at the moment was take Erin in his arms and protect her.

Chase stepped toward her, but she raised her hand. He froze midstride, and though it pained him to do so, he complied with her command. "Why didn't you tell me?" he asked.

Although tears were already flowing down her face, Erin appeared confident, oddly at peace with her decision to share such a personal event in her life.

Erin walked over to him and touched his face. "This is why," she said. Chase reached for her hand, holding on to the gentle caress for dear life. "I never wanted to see you look at me this way, with such sorrow, with such…pity."

Chase shook his head and just when he was about to tell her how wrong she was, the sound of his cell phone broke the silence. His phone, which lay on the ground at Erin's feet, chimed, signaling that he had received a text. It must have fallen from his pocket during his wrestling match with Paul.

The sudden withdrawal of Erin's hand from his face jolted him, and he felt empty. Erin bent down and picked up his phone. Her face hardened as she looked at the screen.

"It's Gabrielle."

Chase wanted to tell Erin to disregard it, but he needed Erin to trust him. "Read it," he commanded.

Erin looked back at the phone and read the text aloud. "What does she mean when she says, 'I think I got it right this time'?"

Chase looked over at Paul. Although it wasn't possible that Paul could know about Gabrielle's past and her previous suicide attempt, Chase got the sense that Paul knew there was something urgent regarding that message. "Come with me," Chase said, looking at Paul.

Paul nodded, complying with his directive.

Chase turned to Andrew and said, "Take her to my place. Don't let her out of your sight."

"What…what is going on? Paul?" she asked, her beautiful face plagued with hurt and confusion.

"Erin, go with Andrew. We need to check on something," Paul said.

Erin looked as if she had been sucker punched. "A minute ago you two were beating each other's faces in. And now you're best friends?"

"Make no mistake. I'm going with Chase because I believe we may be able to finally find out who the rapist is. I haven't forgotten what Chase has done to you. I can put my emotions aside, the ones that tell me to kill him…for now," Paul said.

Chase walked over to Erin, but the warning in her eyes made him pause. It wasn't the time or place to explain what the cryptic text could possibly mean. She handed him his phone, turned on her heel, and walked in the direction of the street. Although Andrew followed her closely, Chase couldn't help but fear for her safety. If there was any hope of stopping Gabrielle from taking her own life or finding out who she was working with, he had to leave now. It was possible Gabrielle was faking the suicide attempt just to get his attention…but as he hustled toward his vehicle with Paul at his side, Chase got the feeling that she had indeed been successful this time around.

Chase and Paul slipped into the backseat. Withdrawing his phone, Chase shouted Gabrielle's address to his driver and asked him to make haste. Chase then dialed 9-1-1.

"Nine-one-one, what's your emergency?" the operator asked.

"I'm reporting a possible suicide. Gabrielle Green, age twenty-seven, resides at two-twenty-three East Thirty-Second Street. She contacted me approximately five minutes ago via text." Chase reiterated the exact wording of the text to the operator and then added, "She has attempted before, a little over a year ago, with pills and alcohol."

The operator asked him a few more questions that pertained to her previous attempt and then ended the call.

Chase could feel the weight of Paul's gaze. Up until now, Paul had remained silent. But Gabrielle's apartment was several minutes away, giving him more than enough time to provide the brother of the woman he loved with some type of explanation. Lord knew, Paul deserved it.

* * *

"What makes you think Gabrielle knows who raped my sister?" Paul asked, though it gutted him to utter those words.

Chase's face turned a sharp shade of red. Chase closed his eyes and breathed deeply. Finally, he said, "Tonight, at the benefit, she told me that she wasn't working alone."

"What does that mean? What is she trying to accomplish?" Paul asked, his patience growing thin.

Chase ran his hand through his hair. He pressed the button on the intercom and asked his driver for the estimated time of arrival.

"Two minutes sir…lots of traffic tonight."

Chase grunted and then turned to face Paul. "She's trying to destroy me and the woman I love."

Paul had to give the man credit. He had nerves of steel to declare his love without a moment of hesitation. Still, there were too many things left unanswered. Like…why the hell did he go to California to see Gabrielle?

"If you love my sister like you say you do, then why travel to the other side of the country to visit your ex-fiancée?"

"I haven't seen Gabrielle since she left for California, but I stayed in contact with her doctor this past year. He had told me that she was progressing and moving on. But I had to be sure."

"Why? Why not just let her be? If Gabrielle was getting her life back, why would you pop back into it?" Paul asked.

"Erin and I ran into her parents earlier this week while we were out to dinner. They told me that Gabrielle was planning to come home for a visit in the near future and that she was looking forward to seeing me. I was on a plane the very next day and flew to California to tell Gabrielle in person that I have met someone. She needed to know where we stood, that the relationship she and I had shared could not be rekindled."

"Obviously, she didn't take it well." Paul said.

"In hindsight, I should have known something was wrong."

"Why is that?" Paul asked.

"Because she was exceptionally accepting, gracious even, when I told her about Erin." Chase shook his head. "I just didn't know how wrong it was until she mentioned Erin's ex-boyfriend at the benefit tonight."

Paul's eyebrow raised. It was the closest he had gotten to discovering the rapist's identity. "Gabrielle didn't mention a name? What he looked like? Anything?" Paul asked, though he already knew the answer.

"No. Seems like withholding that information was part of her sick game, along with making Erin think that I had been cheating on her." Chase cleared his throat and looked out the window. "I would never hurt her, Paul."

Paul was a born skeptic. He based his beliefs on fact: what you could touch, taste and see. He would often take a gut feeling into consideration when he tried a case, but it never stood alone. He would let the evidence, the cold, hard facts, speak.

So it shocked Paul when he realized that he believed ev-

erything Chase had said…even though the evidence suggested
something else entirely.

The limo pulled right up in front of what Paul assumed was
Gabrielle's high-rise building, though the swirling lights of the
police car and ambulance would have told him that they had
arrived at their destination.

Chapter Forty-Eight

Waiting around was a risk, but Scott didn't care.

He wouldn't be able to be there in person to witness Chase finding Gabrielle's waterlogged body, but being a spectator from afar was the next best thing. Scott retreated to the side alley of the high-end apartment building and waited. The ambulance was the first to arrive on the scene, which wasn't too surprising since there was a hospital practically in walking distance. Chase pulled up in his limo a minute later. Strangely enough, he was not alone. Paul Whitley accompanied him. The dynamic duo sprinted from the vehicle and rushed into the building after the medics. The sight both infuriated and worried him. It was likely that Chase and Erin's relationship was still intact.

Apparently, there was more work to be done. But Scott was not completely discouraged. He would find a way to draw Erin in. He turned and proceeded down the alley toward Manayunk Street. Once there, he could abandon the disguise he had worn to enter Gabrielle's building and blend in with the rest of the New York nightlife. But as always, his head flooded with a multitude of ideas at once. They came as visions, and although many were intriguing, he fixated on one in particular. He smiled.

The grieving process was a wondrous thing, he thought to himself. It had the tendency to bring people together. He pictured his Angel distraught, tucked into his arms as he consoled her. Scott would stroke her back gently until her sobs ceased completely, until they were finished mourning the loss of a dear old man who passed away suddenly.

* * *

Chase heard the familiar tune of Gabrielle's favorite band as he bounded down the hall. Aerosmith's "Dream On" grew louder with each footfall until they reached the bathroom door. He had arrived just in time to see the paramedics pull Gabrielle's submerged body from the tub. They worked on her for over twenty minutes, but to no avail.

Chase and Paul retreated to the bedroom, where a police officer questioned them, wrote some notes and, when he seemed satisfied, dismissed them.

Alone, Chase said to Paul, "I need to make a few phone calls."

Paul looked at him and said, "I'll be in the other room." He started to walk toward the door and stopped. Paul turned around and said, "I'm sorry you found her like that."

Chase nodded, knowing full well that the relationship he

had with Erin's brother was strained to say the least. But still, Paul found it in him to display some compassion.

Chase sat on the bed and stared at his phone. No parent should bury his child. Chase sighed, bypassing the Greens' home number, and searched for Edward Green's personal cell phone number. His thumb hovered above the CALL button for a moment as he prayed for the strength to make it through the impending conversation with Gabrielle's father. Finally, he pressed the button, and as he heard the phone ring, he was instantly transported back in time to when he had made a similar phone call over a year ago. But this time the ending was a bit different. Gabrielle wasn't going to be spending the next year in a luxurious rehab facility in sunny California. This time around, she would be transported to the morgue at Mercy General.

Chapter Forty-Nine

Mitchell sealed the final envelope and tucked the letters into the top drawer of his desk. Running into Erin was the best and worst thing that could have happened that night. Seeing her face and those eyes, which had at one time sparkled with promise, he knew what had to be done. Although he had every intention of turning himself in to the police tomorrow morning, he needed to put his thoughts and a confession down on paper. He also needed to ensure that his son wouldn't get a penny when he left this earth. He would call his attorney first thing tomorrow morning. Tonight, he wanted to sleep in his bed, the bed he shared with his kind and loving wife, one last time.

He turned off the downstairs lights and locked the doors. Although it was almost four o'clock in the morning, Mitchell found it difficult to surrender to sleep. Luckily, the bourbon was starting to take effect. He had hoped that the two-and-a-half-hour drive from New York to Philadelphia would have relaxed him, make him forget about his life, but all it did was give him time with his own horrid thoughts.

Wearily, he ascended the steps. But as he reached the last step from the top, he heard a key turn in the front door's latch. Mitchell closed his eyes and swallowed deeply. He reached for the railing and turned to face his son, the only other person, housekeeper excluded, who had a key to his home.

Scott closed and locked the door behind him. The sight of Scott securing the dead bolt sent a chill down Mitchell's spine. Why was his son here?

"Feeling better, Dad?" Scott asked, moving toward the stairs.

Mitchell eyed him closely. He silently thanked God that his wife wasn't around to witness what her son was, a soulless monster that violated women in the most horrific of ways.

"Tired." From life, from living in denial all these years.

Scott climbed the steps two at a time. In a matter of seconds, Mitchell found himself face-to-face with evil. His hands began to sweat as his grip on the railing tightened.

"You should be lying down," Scott said. Mitchell watched as Scott's gaze drifted to the hand that was firmly holding on to the wooden railing, then to the floor below.

Mitchell turned and climbed the remaining step, but instantly knew it was a mistake. Scott had brushed past him in that moment and spun around. Mitchell felt vulnerable as the flight of steps lay at his back. Scott inched closer and smiled.

It was the smile that gave Scott away. The smile that allowed Mitchell to see why his son had just paid him a house call. Mitchell could scream, even fight it, but in the end, he knew he would lose. He looked his son in the eye and asked, "Where will you go?"

Scott looked at him inquisitively. "What do you mean?" he asked.

"Where will you hide when the world discovers what you have done?" Mitchell matched his son's arrogant smirk.

Scott's smug grin faded. "Your death is intended to serve two purposes. With you six feet under, there will be no need for me to go anywhere."

The temptation to get the last word was strong. Mitchell wanted desperately to tell his son just how foolish he was: Killing him would only bring the truth to light. That thought brought a smile to Mitchell's face. He sighed, knowing that this was how it was supposed to play out. This was his penance.

The last ounce of arrogance drained from Scott's eyes as he grabbed his father by the shoulders. "Give Mom a kiss for me," Scott snarled.

Mitchell lifted his chin, and with a steady voice he said, "I am comforted by the fact that you won't ever get the chance to kiss her yourself."

The last thing Mitchell saw was Scott's face twist in what appeared to be unleashed rage. With his eyes closed, he silently asked for forgiveness.

Chapter Fifty

Erin clenched her eyes shut, though it only sharpened the disturbing vision she had tried to squash. The look on Chase's face when she told him about the rape was exactly what she had expected. He no longer saw her as beautiful, but as a victim who deserved pity, a fragile woman who needed to be handled with kid gloves. Erin wiped her eyes with the back of her hand and cursed at herself.

Erin walked over to the French doors to the balcony and peered at the cars below. From this high up, they looked like slow-moving specs in a vacuum of silence. The central air suddenly kicked on, startling her for a moment. The cool air gushing from the vent above gave her a chill, and it was then she noticed that she was still in her evening gown, a gown that had made her feel wanted. Staring at the deep-red dress, all she felt now was anger. She had been living in a dreamworld, believing that she could keep her past from invading her present and future. She had been a fool.

Shivering, Erin stepped away from the French doors and walked into Chase's bedroom. She went to the closet that Chase had stocked with clothes for her and retrieved a pair of lounge pants, a t-shirt and a fitted hoodie. The last thing she wanted to do was make herself at home in Chase's penthouse, considering what was happening at the moment, but she was not going to be cold and uncomfortable for a minute longer. Erin took the garments to the bathroom and changed. She was zipping up her hoodie when she happened to gaze at the door within the bathroom. Erin knew it would be locked, but she couldn't help herself. She walked over and turned the door-knob. As expected, it didn't budge.

What the hell was on the other side of that door?

Curiosity got the better of her. She went to the kitchen and rummaged through the drawer into which she had seen Chase's housekeeper deposit the key ring. Erin found the keys quickly and returned to the bathroom. With keys in hand, she stared at her reflection in the mirror. Erin experienced a moment of guilt, knowing she was about to invade Chase's privacy, but it dissipated instantly when she thought about the secret he had kept from her. Envisioning Chase and Gabrielle together, Erin jammed the key in and turned the knob.

The bathroom light illuminated the entrance to the room, but the expansive space beyond remained in shadow. She felt for a light switch on the wall, but couldn't find one. Erin crept along the wall until she rammed into what felt like a night-stand. She let out a curse as her stubbed toe throbbed, and she attempted to catch a lamp that was about to fall. Erin rescued the lamp just before it landed on the hardwood floor and returned it to the nightstand. Once it was secured, she flicked it on.

The comforting glow that emanated from the sweet little lamp brought the room to life. And as Erin looked around, a multitude of emotions washed over her. This was no ordinary room, but a fully furnished nursery. She noticed that the room could appeal to either a boy or a girl, as neutral colors were found throughout, warm and inviting like those in Chase's home office. A crib was set up in the corner of the room, with a matching espresso changing table lying adjacent to it. She walked deeper into the room and discovered a beautiful mural depicting the story of Noah's Ark painted on the far wall.

Erin was staring at the animals lined up in twos as they awaited entrance onto the Ark when she realized she was no longer alone in a room that she had no right to be in. But when she turned to face him, Erin noticed that he didn't seem angry, as she thought he would be, but sad. She was just about to apologize for being in what appeared to be a sacred place when he broke the awkward silence.

"I think he…or she…would have liked this room." Chase walked farther into the nursery, looking at his surroundings. He moved toward the gliding chair and picked up a book from an adjoining table. The title was a guide for expectant parents. "According to this book, he or she would have been starting solid foods and learning to sit up by now."

Erin stood there. Speechless. Utterly useless. Numb, she watched him return the book to the table, and then he looked at her. His eyes appeared tired, and as she met his gaze, Erin noticed that they had begun to well. Chase walked over to her and reached for her hand. She had so many questions, so many things swirling in her mind that begged for answers. However, she remained quiet and allowed him to lead her out of the nursery. Erin watched as Chase closed the door, as if attempting to uphold the sanctity of the room on the other side.

Once in Chase's bedroom, Erin regained the ability to speak, though she feared what would actually come out of her mouth. She had not seen this coming, and now she was left unprepared and anxious to say the least. "Chase, why did you keep this a secret?" She sat down on his bed, but he didn't follow her lead. Instead, he paced the room and then made his way to the balcony.

After several seconds of silence, he said, "Gabrielle was almost three months pregnant when I found her in bed with another man."

That explained his unwavering stance that he would never be one to share.

"She didn't look too surprised or even a bit remorseful when I walked in on them. I had no idea how long she had been cheating on me. Worse, it had occurred to me that it was possible that the baby she carried wasn't even mine. That was what devastated me the most." Chase sighed and then walked over to the bed and sat down next to her.

"What happened that night, Chase?"

"I told her good-bye and left her apartment. I went to the elevator, but it was taking too fucking long. I decided to use the stairs, but as I entered the stairwell, I saw Gabrielle running down the hallway and screaming my name. I ignored her and took to the stairs. I was two flights down when I heard a blood-curdling scream echo against the walls. I raced up the steps only to find Gabrielle lying at the foot of the first flight of stairs. I remember how serene she looked. There wasn't a mark on her, at least not on the outside. But within moments, a pool of blood had formed beneath her white nightgown, and I knew that something was terribly wrong. I called nine-one-one and Robert, but it was too late. She had lost the baby. To make matters worse, the surgeon at the hospital botched the D&C procedure, causing irreversible damage."

His head dropped, and Erin could tell he was on the verge of tears. Yet he remained strong and continued to bare his soul. "I visited her in the hospital, but only when I knew she was asleep. I didn't know what to say to her. I felt horrible that she had lost the baby, even if it wasn't mine, and her ability to conceive future children. She was discharged a week later. Gabrielle called and asked me to come over to her apartment. I cut right to the chase and told her that there was no way we were getting back together. I knew the moment I hung up on her that I should have waited. Her loss, her pain was so…raw. I should have given her a little more time to heal before breaking things off with her completely. But I didn't act on my gut. Instead, I sat in my own apartment and threw back a few in an attempt to forget that my pending marriage and child no longer existed. Gabrielle called about an hour later. I barely recognized her voice. She was stuttering and slurring her words to the point that I could hardly understand her. I did recognize a few words, though, such as 'pills' and 'good-

bye.' I called nine-one-one for the second time in eight days.
Luckily, the medics got to her just in time."

Erin stared at him. He was withholding the last chapter
of the story. The text Gabrielle had sent Chase while he was
brawling with Paul in the park came rushing back to her, and
she heard herself ask, "But not this time. They were too late
this time around. Weren't they?"

He nodded. "She was dead before Paul and I arrived."

Erin thought that she would feel a smidge of relief that
Gabrielle was out of the picture, but she didn't. Instead, she
was confused by the feeling of trepidation that suddenly
washed over her. It didn't add up. So much time had passed
since her first suicide attempt. Why now?

"Where was she this past year?" Erin asked.

"Her parents and I sent her to a rehab facility in California,
away from everyone, away from the prying eyes of the media.
We had been successful in keeping our private affairs, including her miscarriage, secret. No one else really knew why
Gabrielle and I broke up or why she decided to move to California.

"But someone else did find out?" she asked. Erin's stomach
began to churn, and she suddenly felt lightheaded.

Chase must have seen that she looked a little uneasy. "Are
you alright?"

Erin nodded and fought through the cloudiness.

Chase looked at her with a disbelieving stare, but ultimately
continued. "After you left the benefit, Gabrielle told me in so
many words that she was conspiring with your rapist."

The churning in her stomach intensified. Erin didn't like

where this was headed. "Conspiring? To achieve what, exactly?"

"To break us apart. I can't think of another reason. Can you?" Chase asked.

Erin's head was spinning. It was all too much. Still, Chase had yet to mention if he knew the identity of Gabrielle's co-conspirator. She had to know. "Did Gabrielle mention who she was working with or provide any clues?"

He shook his head. "No. And I got the feeling that she didn't really know who she was dealing with or what he was capable of."

Chase looked at her with such pity that she wanted to cry. But she pushed it aside for now. Something more pressing had to be addressed. "Gabrielle saw the rapist's face, maybe even knew his name. Are you certain her death was a suicide?"

Chase didn't answer right away. He stood up and walked around the room. Finally, he said, "No, though I believe the police are satisfied in ruling it a suicide based on the text she sent and her previous attempt."

Without warning, he came over to her and dropped to his knees. He took her hands in his. "You haven't asked me why I went to California. Why not?"

"Because it doesn't matter now," she lied. As much as Erin wanted to learn why Chase went to see his ex-fiancée in California, she had reached her breaking point. Erin had to get out of there. She threw his hands aside and stood up. She must have taken him by surprise because he just knelt there, not uttering a word.

He came to, and before she could reach the doorway, Erin

felt him grab her by the wrist and whip her around. "What are you saying, Erin?" he asked, his eyes full of worry.

Erin looked away so he couldn't see the tears forming. There was no way this relationship could move forward, not when it was built upon secrets and lies. She couldn't forget how he'd looked at her in the park, with such pity and sadness. The way he was looking at her now. "I can't do this anymore. I can't pretend that my past doesn't exist. And I refuse to pretend anymore that you could ever love someone so…broken."

The tears flowed as she sobbed into her free hand. Chase drew her hand away from her face and pulled her to him. "You're not broken," he said, his voice laced with anguish.

Erin tore away from him, though it killed her to pry herself from his arms. "No? Then tell me why you're looking at me like that."

"How am I looking at you?"

"I see the pity in your eyes. You feel sorry for me."

He shook his head. "You couldn't be more wrong."

"I don't blame you, Chase. How could I?" Erin stepped farther away from him and yelled for Andrew.

Within seconds, her devoted bodyguard was knocking at the bedroom door.

"Don't leave me, Erin," Chase said.

She wanted to believe that his plea was coming from a place other than pity. But how could it not? In the end, it hadn't mattered how many times Dr. Cahil had told her that the rape wasn't her fault, that she didn't ask for it or provoke it. How many sessions had she spent telling Dr. Cahil how dirty her rapist had made her feel, with the doctor reassuring her that this feeling was normal, that it would fade over time? Too many.

Before all her courage could leave her, she reached behind her and opened the bedroom door. Erin knew that, yet again, she was putting Andrew in an awkward position, but she would have to feel bad about that later. "Being around me is toxic. I have brought nothing but pain...maybe even death into your life, Chase."

He mashed his lips into hers as he slammed her against the bedroom door, shutting it in Andrew's face. His tongue invaded her mouth and she welcomed the assault. But reality slowly crept in, and she begrudgingly broke free of him. "Let me go, Chase. I'm not good for you," she sobbed.

"You're everything to me. You're mine, Erin," he said, his voice raspy and breathless from their kiss.

Erin shook her head, simply because she could no longer form coherent sentences. The pain of losing him was too much. Before he could stop her, Erin reached for the door and ran for the elevator. Andrew hustled behind her. Chase made it just in time to put his hand between the closing doors. The elevator sensors forced the door back open and a moment of awkward silence began. Erin couldn't look at him. His face, a face she loved and couldn't imagine not touching again, would be blurry due to the endless stream of tears falling down her cheeks.

"You belong with me," he said, his voice breaking.

Erin swallowed, and though it would haunt her for many months, possibly years to come, she looked up and stared into his blue eyes. She wanted to melt right there and tell him how much she loved him. But what good would that do? It would only make the situation much worse. Sobbing, Erin shook her head and said, "No. I can't belong to anyone."

Chase's hand fell away, allowing the elevator door to close. Only when the elevator began its descent did it truly hit her that she and Chase were over.

Chapter Fifty-One

Y ou look like crap."

Although Paul's words were spot-on, it didn't mean that Erin wanted to hear them spoken so candidly. "Are you here to add to my misery or be of some use?" she asked.

Paul withdrew a familiar-looking bag from behind him and set it on the coffee table in front of her. Erin wasn't even in the mood for her favorite takeout...or a shower. It had been three days since she had left Chase, and the only time she had moved from the couch was to go to the bathroom. Erin knew from the moment she woke up earlier that morning that work was not an option. She had cried well into the night, leaving dark circles and unattractive bags under her eyes. Tomorrow she would get herself together, just enough to go to work, tie up some loose ends in the office and submit her resignation.

"You know you can stay at my place indefinitely," Paul said.

Erin attempted a smile, but quickly decided it was no use pretending, especially around her brother. He would see right through her anyway. "I'm sorry I came over so late the other night. I just didn't want to be alone...considering."

"This is your place too. Always remember that." Paul pulled out two Styrofoam containers from the paper bag and opened the lids, revealing Chinese food in one and some cheesy pasta goodness in the other. Erin's stomach grumbled, reminding her that she had been depriving it.

"I had a feeling you would be gracing me with your presence. Chase called me after you left his penthouse." Paul scooped a pile of each dish onto a paper plate and handed it to her.

"Did he tell you?" Erin asked, though she knew she was now torturing herself. Erin had no right to ask, but she was a glutton for punishment.

"That you broke up with him? Yes." Paul dumped the last of the Chinese food into the Italian food container and dug in with a plastic fork.

"Did he tell you why?" she asked, her tone laced with frustration. Paul was making her pry the information out of him and it was driving her mad. What the hell?

"Erin, did he tell you why he went to California?"

"No," she said. "And I told him that it wasn't important now."

"So, you didn't even give him a chance to explain?" Paul asked, while shoveling a heaping mound of lo mein into his mouth.

"Oh, like the chance you gave him when you attacked him in the park? You really gave him the benefit of the doubt when you punched him in the face." Erin took a baby bite of lasagna, and though she knew it was delicious, her unsettled stomach was in complete disagreement. She pushed her plate away and sat back on the couch.

"I'm your brother. When it comes to you, I act first and think later. That will never change."

"And now that you have had time to think?" she asked. Erin had a feeling that he knew more about Chase and Gabrielle's past than she did…which couldn't be more irritating.

"I think you need to hear Chase out." Paul smiled, and then continued his gorging.

"Chase told you. Didn't he? He told you why he went to California." Erin couldn't believe Paul was holding out on her.

"He didn't cheat on you, Erin. And that's all I'm going to say on the matter. You will just need to confront him if you want to know more."

Erin wanted to cry happy, pathetic tears. But as much as it was a relief to hear her brother say with such confidence that Chase didn't go to California to sleep with another woman, it didn't change the fact that it was best for everyone if she removed herself from Chase's life, taking her disturbing baggage with her. "I ended things. And that is how it must remain."

"I'll support whatever you decide." Paul finished his plate and tossed it into the empty brown bag. "But that doesn't mean I will refrain from telling you when you look like shit."

Erin threw one of the couch cushions at him, but missed. "I'm going back to work tomorrow. I just needed a day to myself, though the voice mail on my new phone is full with messages from Chase."

"You haven't returned any of his calls or texts?" he asked.

His playful tone had disappeared and was replaced with genuine concern.

"No. I don't know what to say to him."

"But you're going back to work tomorrow...in his building? How do you think that's going to work?"

"It can't. I plan to go in to work, finish up some paperwork and resign," she said.

Paul didn't say anything. He just sat there as if deep in thought. Finally, he said, "You need to stop running, Erin."

"Are you seriously trying to play the role of psychiatrist with me? Because if you are, I find that very funny, and not in a 'ha ha' sort of way." Erin could feel herself getting angry and shamelessly defensive.

"You love him, don't you?" he asked. It was out of character for him to ask such a blunt and painfully personal question. Needless to say, Erin was taken off guard.

"I...I...yes! And that is precisely why I need to walk away from him. You have witnessed what my presence has caused. The psychopath I brought with me from Philly has already infiltrated Chase's life and may have even contributed to Gabrielle's death."

Paul stood up and looked down at her. She felt like a child in that moment. "You're running. And you're not one to give up so easily."

Erin was so fucking mad, but not at Paul. She was pissed off at herself.

"I thought you would understand," she said, feeling that her only ally was changing teams.

Paul sighed and said, "I do understand. If this is what you

want, then I'll support you...and feed you when you appear gaunt."

His comment actually drew a slight smile to her face. Paul smiled in return and headed for the door.

"Where are you going?" she asked.

"To convince Andrew, who, by the way, has been stationed outside this door for God knows how long, to switch employers. I don't think Chase would mind if Andrew was now on my payroll."

Erin hadn't given Andrew a solitary thought all day. How selfish could she be? Very, apparently.

"I guess it's not appropriate that Andrew continue guarding me if Chase and I aren't together." Erin barely choked out the last word. She was happy that she had chosen not to eat her dinner. Because the sudden reminder that she and Chase were over made her stomach roil.

Paul must have sensed her sadness, or at the very least, her discomfort, because he stared at her and said with a touch of sarcasm, "I'll talk to him. I *think* Andrew likes you enough to not want to change assignments."

Erin uttered a rather lame "Thanks" and attempted a smile.

Paul left the apartment, leaving Erin alone with her grief. The empty silence suddenly became her greatest nemesis, as it had the uncanny ability to force her to dwell on her feelings for a man whom she knew she would never get over.

Erin's phone rang from the coffee table. It had been over an hour since Chase had attempted to reach out to her. She thought he had gotten the hint that she wasn't able to speak with him. But she didn't recognize the number that flashed on her screen. Her rapist hadn't contacted her since she had changed phone numbers, but to be on the safe side, she dismissed the call and placed the phone back on the table. Several minutes later, her phone chimed again, but this time indicating that she had received a text. It read: *"No more tears, Angel. I can make you whole again."* How the hell did he learn her new phone number?

Common sense told Erin not to respond, but she had reached her breaking point. She texted the first thing that came to mind: *"Motherfucking coward!"*

Her adrenalin was pumping as she anxiously pushed the SEND button. Erin didn't know what to expect after that. And after a few minutes without a response, she determined that he was not going to indulge her.

Erin got up from the couch and started for the kitchen to fetch a beer from the fridge when she heard her phone chirp. She hurried toward her cell phone and read the incoming text: *"Careful Angel. Only filthy girls, girls like Gabrielle, talk like that."*

Despite Gabrielle's history of suicidal ideations, Erin had her doubts that Gabrielle's death was self-inflicted. And though Erin felt no desire to mourn the woman's passing, she still felt guilty and very much responsible that she had played a role in Gabrielle's demise.

Erin couldn't help but read the text once more. The words served as the perfect reminder, the perfect dose of reality she needed to justify why she had to stay far away from the man she loved.

Chapter Fifty-Two

No good deed goes unpunished. Her mother must have used that saying hundreds of times throughout her life. And now Erin knew exactly what she had meant.

Erin had come to work to clean up her files and finalize any outstanding projects for the person who would be taking over her position. She couldn't imagine just dumping all her work onto someone brand-spanking-new. But within minutes of being in the Montclair Building, Erin knew that coming in to work today was a huge mistake. Everything reminded her of Chase. Knowing that he was only a few flights up produced a level of anxiety that she wasn't prepared for.

Get in and get out.

Her first order of business was the resignation letter. Erin knew that if she completed that task first, she wouldn't change her mind about leaving her job…and Chase. She inserted a flash drive into her desktop, pulled up the document entitled "Resignation" and attached it to an email addressed to Chase's personal secretary. Her finger hovered over the SEND button.

Just do it. Finish this.

She tapped the SEND button and logged out of her email account. It was done.

Erin immediately started on the files and the process of finalizing her reports. If she blocked out all distractions, including the voice screaming in her head, telling her to follow her heart and find Chase, she could be finished and out of the office for good in a little over two hours. She was halfway through one of her lengthier reports when she heard a knock at the cracked door. Erin looked up from the pile on her desk to see Andrew in the doorway.

"Everything alright, Andrew?" Erin looked over his shoulder, but it appeared that he was alone. It was unlike Andrew to disturb her while she worked. He typically remained out of sight, though she always knew that he was near if she needed him.

"Yes, Ms. Whitley. But I have a Dr. Morris to see you. He said it would only take a moment."

"Sure. No problem. Thanks Andrew." Andrew disappeared into the hallway and returned only seconds later with her visitor.

Confused, but pleasantly surprised that Dr. Morris would come pay her a visit, Erin stood to greet her old mentor. But it was the younger Morris who entered her office. All those happy feelings faded at the sight of Scott, though she had no idea why his mere presence made her uneasy. Regardless, Erin forced a smile on her face.

"Scott, this is a surprise." she said, not knowing how to begin a conversation with someone she barely knew. But her fake smile faded quickly as he walked over to her with slumped shoulders and tired eyes. Scott looked exhausted, a far cry from the arrogant and smooth-talking man from the benefit. "Are you okay?" Erin asked.

He ran his fingers through his hair and sighed. "I've been better." He bowed his head. "I would have stopped by to see you yesterday, but I think I was still in shock."

Erin's heart began to race. She had a feeling that she was going to hear something dreadful. Erin's hands began to tremble, her trademark when she was nervous or afraid. This time, both emotions were at play. "Scott, what happened?" She moved toward him, and though that uneasy feeling still lingered, she felt the need to touch his arm.

He rested his hand upon hers. "It's my dad, Erin. He's dead. His housekeeper found him over the weekend…lying at the bottom of the stairs. Police said it appeared that he had fallen and severed his spinal column." Scott looked up at her with tears in his eyes. "I knew he wasn't feeling well at the benefit. I shouldn't have left him."

Erin couldn't believe that the elder Dr. Morris was gone, though she clearly remembered how pale he had looked at the benefit. But there was no way Scott could have predicted this horrific outcome. She felt bad for herself, but it was obvious that the man in front of her was suffering a thousand times more. Erin could definitely relate. The sudden loss of a parent was a traumatic experience, one that she didn't wish on anyone.

"I'm so sorry, Scott," she said, hugging him.

He returned the embrace and after a few moments, he stepped back and wiped his eyes. "I'm sorry. It was selfish of me to come here."

Erin shook her head. "No…I'm glad you came. Your father was always so kind to me."

"I would often hear him bragging about the 'firecracker' he had shadowing him at the hospital. He was so proud of you, Erin." Scott smiled, but his warm words did not comfort her. Instead, he had just confirmed how much of a disappointment she was to those she cared about.

But it was neither the time nor the place to wallow in her sorrows. Scott had already lost his mother this year, and now his father. Both of them…gone. Scott was grieving and she knew exactly how he felt. Erin swallowed back the tears and asked, "Is there anything I can do? Can I help you make the arrangements?" There was a great chance that she was over-stepping her bounds, considering she wasn't family, but she had to offer.

Scott reached up and brushed his hand against her cheek. It was an innocent gesture that was over in two seconds, but that was all it took to make her arms go all goose pimply. "No, but you're sweet to ask. I took care of everything. The service will be this Wednesday at St. Mark's Church."

She dismissed that peculiar feeling and chalked it up to her body's response to hearing that her mentor had died so suddenly. "I would like to come…I mean…if that's okay?" It occurred to Erin that some people reserve such a solemn occasion for family alone. She cringed at her impulsivity.

"The way he spoke of you, people could easily have mistaken you for the daughter he never had." He smiled. "I would like it if you could come, and I think he would have wanted you there as well."

"Then I'll be there," she said. Erin hated funerals, and for good reason, but she had to face that particular demon. Dr. Morris was a gentle soul who had taken her under his wing and shown her what compassion looked like on a daily basis. She had to go to that church and pay her respects.

"Thank you." Smiling, he took her hand, gave it a light squeeze, and walked out of the lab.

Scott Morris might have left, but Erin had the feeling that she wasn't alone. She looked up at the camera for a moment and then walked back to her workstation. This day couldn't get any shittier.

* * *

"He's gone, Mr. Montclair."

"Why the fuck did you let Scott Morris get near her?" Chase growled into the phone.

"I was not aware that he was prohibited from speaking to her, though I was within ten feet of her the entire time." Andrew's voice did not waver.

Chase wasn't pissed at Andrew. He was furious with himself. No man should be talking to Erin, especially a pompous prick like Scott Morris. Chase had no idea why he had formed such a negative opinion of Scott Morris in just one meeting, but he couldn't shake the feeling that something was off about him.

"Just...stay with her, Andrew. Don't leave her alone."

"Yes, sir," Andrew said.

Chase watched Erin on the TV screen. Still unnerved by Erin's recent visitor, Chase buzzed Lydia over the intercom. "Lydia, please get Sam on the phone."

"Of course." Lydia paused and then continued. "Mr. Montclair, I received a resignation letter from Ms. Whitley this morning."

He felt the floor give way beneath him. This was absurd. She wasn't taking his calls or responding to the hundreds of texts he had started to send the second after she had left his apartment three nights ago. Now she was quitting her job! Let her dismiss him when he was standing right in front of her!

"I'll call Sam myself," he grunted.

Chase was relieved to hear Sam pick up on the second ring.

"Sam, I need another background check. His name is Scott Morris, oncologist, here in New York City."

"Hello to you too," Sam said in a sarcastic tone.

Chase didn't have time for pleasantries, even for one of his oldest friends. "I need this as soon as possible."

Sam must have gathered that Chase was in no mood for games. "Does this involve Erin?" he asked, his voice full of concern.

"Everything involves Erin." Chase felt his heart ache as he looked over at the woman on the TV monitor. "Call me as soon as you know something."

Chase hung up the phone and headed for the elevator.

Chapter Fifty-Three

She was kidding herself.

Between her breakup with Chase and Scott's news about his father's sudden death, there was no possible way she was going to be able to concentrate enough to produce a report that was worth submitting. Erin waved the invisible white flag and decided to cut her losses. It was time to leave Montclair Pharmaceuticals and Chase securely behind her. Erin reached for her purse, but the phone within started to vibrate. She withdrew her cell phone and read the text: *"I can forgive you, Angel. Just prove to me that you're not a filthy girl."*

Erin felt her stomach churn. He was threatening her, giving her a crystal-clear picture of what he would do to her if she fell from grace, if she was no longer his Angel. Filthy girls were not worthy, filthy girls died untimely deaths, filthy girls were snuffed out so the world was no longer infected by their existence.

"How?" she typed.

Erin didn't know what possessed her to ask such a loaded

question. But before she could theorize about why she felt the need to converse with him, he responded: *"Say good-bye to Chase Montclair."*

That innate hatred of being told what to do prompted her next text: *"And if I choose to disappoint you?"*

The back and forth with her rapist was beyond surreal. She couldn't wrap her head around the fact that she was having a conversation with the monster.

Her cell phone buzzed: *"Though I have no desire to see you cry or look on as you mourn the loss of Chase Montclair, I will do what is necessary. So, choose wisely, Angel."*

She had been wrong, not about the threat, but whom it was directed to. Erin didn't have any delusions when it came to her rapist's intentions. He had proved that he was more than capable of getting to someone, maybe even making some misguided young lady's death look like a suicide rather than a homicide. Chase was in danger and she couldn't risk his life any longer.

Her eyes gravitated to the mounted camera. She knew Chase was watching, but it didn't occur to her that the voyeur was in the same room as her.

"I didn't betray you, Erin…not with Gabrielle…not with any woman. There will never be anyone else."

Erin squeezed her eyes shut, praying to the powers that be to give her the strength to hold it together just long enough so she could leave without giving anything away. She didn't want Chase to know that she had just made a deal with the devil. Her compliance for Chase's life.

But he still deserved to know that she believed him. She

owed him that much. "I don't know why you went to California, but I believe you. I know you would never hurt me like that," she whispered.

"Then why are you running?" Chase asked.

Erin knew that if she didn't get far away from him in that moment, she would morph back into the sloppy, crying mess who had taken refuge under a blanket on Paul's couch for days on end. "I'm not running. I just can't...I can't be with you."

Chase locked the door behind him and took three steps toward her. Panic set in. She couldn't be left alone with him. Her body ached for his touch, and it was just a matter of time—like a few seconds—until her hormones took over. She needed to get out of the lab, but to do so meant that she would have to walk past him. Erin held her breath so she couldn't take in the scent that was all Chase, and headed toward the door. Her hand was on the doorknob when she heard and felt both his hands slam against the wooden door. Trapped between his arms, his groin against her rear, her resistance was fleeting. His warm, minty breath on the back of her neck was draining the last of her reserves.

"Are you seeing Scott Morris?" he whispered, his lips just millimeters from her heated flesh.

The abrupt change in tone allowed her hormones to fall in line. She had control over them, at least for a moment. The thought crossed her mind to lie. Maybe if Chase believed she was dating someone else, he would leave her be. Erin quickly dismissed it, knowing that Chase would see right through that piss-poor plan.

"No," she said, turning around to face him.

"Then why was he touching you? Why did you hug him?" Chase asked, his voice laced with obvious disdain.

"Dr. Morris, his father, died over the weekend. What you saw on your monitor was me consoling him." Erin couldn't help but sound defensive and more than a little pissed off. If he wasn't spying on her, then he wouldn't have had to theorize about why she was in the arms of another man for maybe a total of two seconds.

Chase's expression changed from one of anger to pure perplexity. "Mitchell Morris is dead?" he asked, backing away from her.

"Yes. Scott said that his father fell down a flight of steps in his home. Dr. Morris didn't look well when we saw him at the benefit. He was pale and appeared nervous for some reason. I can't help but wonder if that had something to do with his fall." She shook her head. "The funeral is Wednesday."

Chase's confused expression mutated back to a look of disgust. "You will not see Scott Morris again," he commanded.

"And you have no right to tell me who I can see." Who the hell did he think he was? "I will talk to whomever I damn well please." Erin stood erect and stared into eyes, consumed with rage.

"I forbid you to see him," he seethed.

"You forbid me? Do you hear yourself?"

Anger was a good thing, as it would make leaving him that much easier. She also thought about the threat to Chase's life, and she found herself uttering words that were meant to hurt him, but instead caused her own already-fragile heart to shatter to pieces.

"We broke up, Chase. I'm not yours...anymore." The last word had barely spilled over her lips when he came rushing toward her. Erin's back flew against the wall as they collided, and his mouth came over hers with grave urgency. Chase kissed her so deeply and with such force that she was already breathless.

"You will always be mine," he said, between labored breaths. "Always." He groaned into her mouth. God, she needed him. God, how she loved him...

That realization gave her the clarity she needed. Shaking her head and crying for what had to be the fiftieth time in three days, Erin tore out of his arms. "You have claimed my soul, and my heart. That will just have to be enough!" she screamed. Erin didn't wait for him to respond and she didn't dare look for a reaction to her raw admission. "Good-bye, Chase."

Erin unlocked the door and hurried down the hallway. Only when she was on the elevator with Andrew standing quietly at her side did Erin realize that Chase had allowed her to leave with not so much as a word of protest.

Chapter Fifty-Four

He should have run after her, but his legs wouldn't budge. They seemed to be in a state of shock, like the rest of his body. Chase had hoped and prayed to all that was holy that Erin had feelings for him that rivaled his own for her. She hadn't told him that she loved him, but it didn't matter. She had given him her heart and soul. But they would never be enough. He had to have all of her.

As much as Chase wanted to relive the moment when Erin had admitted that her heart belonged to him, there were other matters that needed to be addressed. He withdrew his cell phone and called Paul.

"What is the relationship between your sister and Dr. Scott Morris?"

There was a pause and then Paul answered, "Do you mean Dr. Mitchell Morris?"

"No. I'm talking about Scott Morris, Dr. Mitchell Morris's

son. Scott Morris stopped to see Erin at work today and told her that his father had passed away over the weekend."

"Erin has never mentioned a Scott Morris. It was Dr. Mitchell Morris that she used to rave about. She admired and respected him immensely."

Chase couldn't help but feel relieved to know that Scott Morris must not have played an important part in her life. Wouldn't she have mentioned Scott Morris to her brother if he was of some significance?

"I suspect Erin is planning to attend his funeral on Wednesday. I was wondering if…if you would accompany her? I think it would bring her comfort if you were with her."

"She's still not talking to you?" Paul asked, his tone serious and every bit sincere.

"No." Chase walked around the lab she once occupied; her perfume still lingered in the air. "She is determined to believe that we don't belong together."

"She can be so stubborn," Paul said, sighing. "I would talk to her, try to get her to see reason, but it would be useless. Erin will only come around on her own terms, in her own time, never before."

Chase was touched that Paul would consider vouching for him, though he agreed that it wouldn't do any good if Paul pleaded his case to Erin. "I got that very impression just a few moments ago."

"Well, regardless, I wouldn't give up on her," Paul said.

"Not possible." Chase was pleasantly surprised over how easy it was to talk to Paul. It had become less awkward to discuss Erin with her brother. Maybe it was because Chase had laid every card on the table. There were no more secrets.

"Good to hear." Paul hesitated. "Of course I'll take Erin to the funeral. I don't want her going through that alone. She hasn't been to a funeral since our parents died, and I can imagine it will bring up some unpleasant memories."

Chase hadn't thought about that. He had been so preoccupied with Scott Morris that it hadn't occurred to him that Wednesday would be a struggle for her on many levels. "I appreciate you going with her."

"Sure." But just as Chase was about to hang up, he heard Paul ask, "Why did you ask me about Scott Morris?"

Paul didn't miss much. He was in the right line of work.

"For whatever reason, I don't trust him. Don't even bother to ask me why. I couldn't tell you."

"Well, I have a guy who could do a background check on him. It would just take a phone call," Paul said.

"Already working on it. I put in a call to a friend. He'll dig up everything he can on both Scott and Mitchell Morris."

"He is discreet then?" Paul asked. There was a hint of apprehension in his question. Chase couldn't blame him.

"I trust him."

"I can live with that," Paul said.

Chase was pleased that he had earned Paul's trust. But there were still loose ends that needed to be tied, questions that he had wanted to ask before, but which had been put on the back burner due to more pressing matters, like Erin breaking up with him.

"Paul, I can't find any delicate way to ask, but I need to

know what happened the night that...piece of shit...did what he did to Erin. How did he get away with it? How is he still breathing?" Chase knew he was out of line for asking a slew of questions that had to be not just uncomfortable for Paul to answer, but unbearably painful.

It was a good fifteen seconds before Chase heard him sigh. "That conversation needs to take place over a beer. I'll meet you at Nick's. One hour?"

Chase was familiar with the intimate and very secluded tavern on Washington Terrace. "See you then."

It definitely wasn't common practice for Chase to down a beer in the middle of a work day. And he had a feeling that what he was about to hear would require something much stronger than one lonely pint.

* * *

An hour later, in that little bar down the street, Chase sat and listened to Paul describe how he literally took matters into his own hands the night Erin was raped and left a man for dead.

The problem was that the shit didn't die. The rapist was alive and well, here in New York, still breathing, still terrorizing the woman Chase loved, the woman he couldn't live without.

Chapter Fifty-Five

How difficult would it be to just disappear?

The thought had crossed Erin's mind a handful of times over the past few days. But as she sat in St. Mark's Church, the once-passing thought started to morph into a viable option, and Erin felt her attention being divided between the priest and the details surrounding her plan to leave New York City.

"You alright?" Paul whispered.

Erin smiled at her brother. It was thoughtful of him to accompany her to the funeral of her old mentor. She couldn't have imagined attending the service alone. The last time she had been to such a gathering, or even to church in general, was to bury her parents. Their sudden passing was a tragedy that still left Erin more angry than grief-stricken.

Erin reached over and gave Paul's hand a squeeze. He was as stoic as always, his devotion to her unwavering. It was as if Paul's life revolved around two things, work and keeping her safe from any and all threats. He never spoke of his social life or the lack of having one. It wasn't normal for someone to be so consumed. Erin couldn't help but mourn the loss of the man he could have been if it weren't for two gruesome events that he had no control over.

"If I go first, please don't plan on having a viewing or funeral for me." Erin looked around and took in the morbid scene. Hundreds had gathered to pay their respects to a well-loved man, husband, father and doctor. Both men and women were crying into their tissues. "Funerals serve no purpose, except to remind people that, 'Yep, this person is truly dead and never coming back.'"

"We can leave if you like," Paul said.

It had been a while since she had attended mass, but she knew the service was almost over. Shaking her head, she whispered, "No, I can do this." Although Paul nodded, Erin noticed that he had not released her hand.

After the priest's closing remarks, Scott Morris stood and said a few words about his father. They were meant to be kind and heartfelt, but Erin couldn't dismiss the feeling that Scott was going through the motions. Scott's comments seemed almost robotic, devoid of emotion. As he spoke of a man who had never missed one of his Little League games, Erin noticed Scott scanning the congregation. His eyes seemed to lock on hers and she immediately felt uncomfortable. Erin didn't know why Scott made her uneasy. She barely knew him.

Her brief introduction to him over a year ago in his father's office and their coincidental encounter at the benefit, made them nothing more than acquaintances. Yet, Scott had found it necessary to come to Erin's place of employment and inform her that his father had died unexpectedly. She was so surprised by the news that it hadn't dawned on her until now that his personal visit seemed a bit odd. But who was she to judge? Grief can make a person do strange things. It was possible that Scott found solace in the act of telling people personally that his father had passed. Maybe it helped him cope with the loss. Maybe it served as a distraction, preventing him from locking himself in his bedroom for days and cursing at God. She remembered just how dark and unkind those days were after her parents had died, and shuddered.

Erin broke away from Scott's gaze and bowed her head. It would appear she was being reverent, but in reality she needed to shift her focus to anything but what was happening at the current moment. It didn't take long for her to realize what a mistake that was. With her eyes closed and her body still, her mind was bombarded by thoughts of the man she loved, the man she had left...twice.

Erin had replayed the scene in the research lab over and over in her head. There were too many "should have," "would have," "could haves" to count. Maybe she should have told Chase that she loved him. Maybe she should have shown him the text she had received from her rapist, the one she withheld from Paul, the one warning her to leave Chase or something unpleasant was going to happen. But she didn't. And in the end, she was going to prove her brother and Chase right. She was going to run...luring that sick son-of-a-bitch far away from the man she truly didn't deserve.

Chapter Fifty-Six

Scott Morris watched his Angel genuflect and then leave the pew. He had every intention of catching her before she left the church, but she appeared despondent and anxious to make a swift exit. He had planned on thanking her for attending his father's funeral, maybe even working in a consolatory embrace, but her fucking brother hustled her out before he had the chance.

Although it was frustrating having his beautiful Angel so close yet too far to touch, to stroke, Scott was pleased to see that she was following his directive. Chase Montclair did not accompany her, a promising sign that they were no longer seeing each other. Scott had begun to question if Erin was becoming one of those filthy girls he loathed, the kind of girl he at times took it upon himself to silence.

Scott smiled to himself. Erin was still a good girl.

* * *

"How much, Andrew?"

"I can't tell exactly. She asked me to wait for her in the lobby." Andrew paused and then said in a hushed tone, "But without advance notice, I doubt the bank would allow Ms. Whitley to withdraw all her money."

Andrew's words did not bring Chase comfort. Chase stared out the expansive window of his office, and as much as he wanted to believe Erin wasn't capable of running away, leaving the city, leaving him behind, he had to acknowledge that she had the financial means to disappear.

"Andrew, don't let her out of your sight." Chase didn't need to elaborate. Andrew knew where his mind was headed.

"Of course. I'll take her home immediately."

"Where is Paul?" Chase asked, turning toward the speakerphone on his desk.

"He had to go back to the office after the funeral." Before Chase could ask, Andrew said, "I'll stay with her as long as you need."

Chase trusted this man, an act that didn't come easily to him. He knew Andrew would get her home safely. "Thank you."

Andrew ended the call, leaving Chase alone with his thoughts. He turned back around and stared at the setting sun. His feelings of rage melted into sadness and then turned into unmeasured fury once again. He had never felt so empty, as if his soul had been ripped from his body, leaving only a shell of a man behind. Right before Erin had walked out of his life, she had told him that her heart belonged to him. And he had just stood there, speechless. The words were there, bursting to come forth, but Erin had left him in the lab, wondering if he would ever get the chance to tell her how much he loved her.

Chase buzzed his secretary and asked her to report to his office. Lydia arrived within seconds. "Lydia, cancel all my appointments for the next several days. I'm taking some time off."

Lydia raised an eyebrow, appearing perplexed. "Are you ill, sir?"

"I am useless...without her." It was out of character for him to expose his feelings to anyone. But he didn't care. He was tired of hiding.

Chase could hear Lydia drawing near. He bowed his head and then felt her hand on his shoulder. "Love can do that."

Without turning around, he surrounded her hand with his. Her comfort, her simple observation, was exactly what he needed from the demure woman who had always been loyal to him and his company.

"I'll take care of things while you're gone." She gave him a soft squeeze and then walked toward the door. Chase thought she had left his office but was surprised when he heard her say, "Just don't come back here without her. She makes you happy, which makes you so much more pleasant to be around."

Chapter Fifty-Seven

Erin had spent the first couple of months after her rape asking the air, *Why me?* It had taken double the time in therapy for her rage to simmer to a low roar. Only then was she able to let her body refuel with something other than anger and disgust. What she felt was her strength returning.

But once in a while, despite being in therapy, the darkness would creep back in, and she would find herself replaying that night in her head, fixating on what she had lost in the cemetery. Erin could still feel the warm breeze against her face. She could hear the alluring sounds of the city echo in the early summer sky as she crossed the cobblestone street. There had been a sweetness in the air that night, roses maybe; she couldn't be sure of its source. But what she was certain of was the uneasy feeling that had crept up her spine just moments before, leaving every hair on the back of her neck standing on end.

Erin shook her head, praying for the fog to lift, for the visual she tortured herself with from time to time to evaporate with the rest of the steam her scalding shower was emitting. She pinned her hair up in a messy bun and allowed the hot water to caress her tension-filled back. But as always, her mind began to wander and her thoughts were quickly consumed by Chase. Erin knew that the longer she stayed in the shower, naked and accessible, even if it was only to herself, the more she would think of him. And that could not happen.

Although she was uncertain at the moment about how she was going to rid herself of her bodyguard, she was leaving the city tomorrow. The bank promised her that they would have her money ready by ten in the morning. Though they could only allow her to withdrawal twenty-five thousand on such short notice, in addition to the ten thousand earlier today, Erin was hopeful that the meager amount could buy her enough time—and a gun—to accomplish her goal.

Erin sighed and fought back the tears she desperately wanted to shed. She needed to stay strong and not give in to temptation to call Chase one last time, even if it was only to say good-bye. Erin quickly rinsed and turned off the water. She needed a glass of wine, and not one of those wimpy quarter-filled goblets you get at a fancy restaurant.

Erin wrapped herself up in her coveted white fluffy towel and stepped out of her master bath and into the bedroom. And gasped.

He didn't even attempt to pretend that he wasn't snooping through her purse. In fact, Chase had the nerve to count the money right in front of her.

"Where are you going, Erin?" Chase finally looked up at

her. He set her purse on the bureau and started to walk toward her.

Erin wasn't going to ask how he got into her apartment. It made no difference in hell that Andrew was no longer on Chase's payroll. It was blatantly apparent that Andrew still answered to Chase.

"You can't be here. You need to leave…now." It killed Erin to utter those words, but his life was in danger. If her attacker discovered that Chase was still in her life, he would do his best to follow through on his threat.

Chase halted midstride, leaving a few feet between them. Erin secured the towel around her, but it only drew his attention to her breasts. His lips parted as his breathing hitched.

Erin swallowed, and she felt that familiar heat rush through her body. He looked incredible in his dark charcoal suit pants and white oxford shirt. His striped tie was slightly unraveled at the neck and his sleeves were rolled up to his elbows, exposing forearms that didn't need to be flexed to show off how muscular he was. His brown hair looked a bit disheveled, as if he had been raking his hands through those lush locks. Feeling like a complete coward, Erin turned away from him.

"Look at me, Erin," he demanded. He moved quickly, and before she knew what was happening, he grabbed her hand and turned her into him. His beautiful, intoxicating scent filled the air between them, and she knew her defenses had sustained severe damage. Erin could feel his arousal through her cotton towel, and she wanted more than anything to forget, for him to make her forget. But she couldn't afford that luxury. She couldn't be selfish.

And in addition to feeling selfish, Erin felt vulnerable, exposed for the broken woman she was. She had fooled herself this past month into thinking that she could have something that resembled a relationship with someone. But with each passing week, as she and Chase grew closer, her dirty little secret, which always hovered beneath the surface, had become increasingly difficult to keep. Erin felt her breath leave her. He was too close.

Erin wriggled out of his grasp and backed away. "I need to go away for a while," she said, keeping her eyes on the floor.

"Why?" he asked, taking one step forward.

"I…" Erin's towel began to droop. She secured her towel, but it seemed to have a mind of its own and it again started to loosen. "He is *my* problem. Not yours." "He…you mean, the, the…"

"You can't even say it, can you?" Erin interjected. She wasn't trying to be malicious, just realistic. Erin allowed her towel to drop to the floor and she stood before him, her tainted body bared to him. She felt the tears quickly take form as she finally stared into his haunted blue eyes. "My rapist." Erin watched his fists clench and the vein in his neck throb ferociously. His eyes were focused on hers, which only confirmed her fear that he couldn't even look at her used body. "I had never been…I was a virgin before that night. You were the first to touch me, after…"

He took another step forward. "He took you against your will. You didn't give yourself to him. I am your first, and I will be your last, Erin."

Erin shook her head in disbelief. "How can you say that?

How could you ever want…this…after he…" she said, looking down at her naked body.

Chase cut her off and took her in his arms. His mouth sealed over hers and she melted against him. The tears were flowing freely down her cheeks as she kissed him with so much hunger, such determination. He groaned into her mouth and she felt his erection pressing against her stomach. She wanted him to claim her, to mark her as his. She needed it, the feeling of being possessed by someone other than the one who had the capability to haunt her nightmares and taunt her during her waking hours.

"Touch me, Chase. Make me yours," she said.

Chase carried her to the bed. He laid her down gently and then quickly disrobed. Erin licked her lips at the sight of him. She wanted to make him moan and invite him to grab her by the hair as she licked his shaft from root to tip. But before she could satisfy her need to pleasure him, he parted her legs and speared her with his wet, hot tongue. He lapped at her with such vicious precision that Erin felt the first wave of her orgasm mounting. She spread her legs wider, allowing him to take her deep, with no obstructions.

Erin squirmed beneath him. She was so close. But she wanted more. "I…I want to…" She was having difficulty forming words. His tongue, the way his fingers stroked and massaged her clit, was sending her to the edge at record speed.

She was on the verge of orgasm when he stopped and whispered, "Tell me what you want, love. I'll give you anything you need."

As much as she wanted to surrender to him in this delicious

way, she needed something else tonight. "Come with me," she said, breathless.

Chase pressed his lips to her taut and sensitive nub. The gentle kiss on her clit made her shake with pleasure. He climbed up her body, sprinkling soft kisses and nips along her stomach, breasts and neck. She felt his arousal at her entrance, but he seemed to be waiting for something. He was driving her insane.

He hovered over her, his elbows resting on either side of her head. She was panting with uncontrolled desire. Erin wrapped her legs around him, but immediately felt his pelvis retreat, keeping his cock just out of reach. His own breathing, though slightly staggered, was more controlled than hers. "I am your first…and your last, Erin."

She was overwhelmed with emotion.

"Say it, Erin." Erin just stared at him, and though his eyes were filled with warmth, his tone suggested that he was completely serious.

"You are my first…and my last," she said, her voice cracking.

She felt his erection at her entrance once more. "Nothing will make me stop loving you. Nothing. You are mine." He thrust into her with one smooth motion and Erin screamed.

"I must have all of you," he groaned.

"You have it…heart, soul…and my love. I love you, Chase."

His lips covered hers. She sucked at his tongue, mimicking the very motion of their bodies as she welcomed his cock into her blistering heat. Erin heard him moan and she relished the sound.

"Ahh Erin, what you mean to me," he said, sliding in and out of her in an intoxicating rhythm. "What you always seem to do to me."

Erin lifted her hips, meeting his powerful thrusts. "Love me, Chase," she said, breathless and panting with passionate need. She wanted this moment to last, never to let her body and mind be without the feelings only Chase could invoke. But her orgasm was so dangerously close. She needed him with her, especially this time. This time was different.

"I'll always love you, always take care of you," Chase said.

Erin could feel his cock swell and jerk. "I can't hold on any longer," she whimpered.

"Let go, baby," he whispered.

And she did, in so many ways.

With one final thrust he emptied his seed deep within, triggering her own orgasm, one unlike she had ever experienced before. "Oh God…Chase!" She thrashed beneath him, each quake and ripple only maximizing the effects of her climax. "I love you," she said. "Always."

Chapter Fifty-Eight

Scott Morris didn't expect good girls to be perfect. He didn't require his Angels to dress a certain way or have a particular hair color. He could even forgive the occasional expletive slipping from their lips. But what was nonnegotiable, what trumped all else, was that his Angels were innocent. They had to be pure, devoid of the filth that seemed to infest the majority of women today.

Erin had fulfilled that requirement. His mind was suddenly flooded with images of her in the cemetery. She had been so soft under his touch, her body quaking with anticipation. She had never known a man until that night, as her tight cunt confirmed.

He felt his arousal mount.

But as Scott watched Chase Montclair enter Erin's apartment building, his desirous thoughts were taken over by rage and betrayal. His sweet girl wasn't following his directive, despite knowing what would happen if she continued to see the arrogant ass. He had made himself clear. And he had every intention of keeping his promise. Scott sat back in his idling vehicle and punched the steering wheel until his fists were raw. How could she do this to him?

Scott wanted to storm after him and let his threat materialize. This was Chase Montclair's fault. He had corrupted his Angel. But maybe there was still a sliver of hope. Yes, he would give her one last chance. It was possible that she had no idea that Chase Montclair was coming to pay her a visit. If Montclair reemerged swiftly from Erin's apartment, signaling that she had told him to leave, he could forgive her. She would be his good girl, his compliant girl, once more. But as the minutes turned into hours, Scott felt his Angel slipping away from him…toward the dark place where filthy girls reside.

Scott stared at his bloody knuckles. He flexed his fingers and then formed a fist, watching the blood ooze forth from the abrasions Erin had caused. His Angel had fallen from grace, leaving a whore in her stead, one that would surely infect his world if he continued to allow it to breathe his air.

See the next page for a preview of

Cut to the Chase

by Elle Keating

Chase Montclair stared out the window at the world below and prayed that the evil that yearned to infiltrate their lives would just disappear. But it would take more than prayer to lure the sick son-of-a-bitch out of the hole he had successfully hidden in for the past year. Erin and her brother had been on defense too long. It was time they took action and put an end to the madness.

Chase walked over to the bed and looked down at the sleeping woman, the woman he was determined to make his in every sense of the word. He pulled back the covers and slipped in behind her. As if by instinct, she nestled in closer, pulling his arm around her though she was still peacefully asleep. The valiant part of him told him to let her rest. But as he held her naked body close, breathing in the scent of her hair and feeling her soft curves shift beside him, all he could think about was having her all over again.

He rolled her onto her back and gazed at her perfect body

under pure-white sheets. His breathing hitched as he envisioned her in white, walking toward him, smiling only at him and because of him. Soon, he thought. Erin Whitley would be his wife.

Chase pulled back the sheet, exposing breasts that seemed to heed his attention. She began to stir, which was a relief, since his cock throbbed and longed to be deep inside her heat. Not yet. He wanted to hear her. Nothing pleased him more than when she screamed with pleasure. He gently spread her legs and took in the glorious sight. She was beautiful...and wet. Even in her sleep, she was ready for him. He licked his lips and knelt down so his face was only millimeters from her tight, glistening nub. Chase inhaled her scent, which made him mad with desire. He suppressed a groan, as he enjoyed the erotic silence, and licked at her clit. He felt her bottom buck into his hands, and her fingers grabbed his hair in apparent need. With his tongue circling her clit, he looked up and she met his gaze. Though she had been asleep just moments ago, her eyes were crazed and it was clear that she was going to come very soon.

"Oh God!" she whimpered.

He wasn't going to last either. Her cries of ecstasy were enough to make him spill even before he had a chance of getting inside her. Chase lapped at her, tasting her once more before standing up and pulling her to the edge of the bed. He lifted both her legs onto his shoulders and entered her in one determined thrust of his hips. In this position, he was so deep he swore he felt the lip of her womb with the tip of his cock.

"Erin...baby!" He slid in and out of her, which prompted sounds from her that he had heard before, just not as loud or uninhibited. Her body thrashed against his as he pounded into her.

She reached around and cupped his balls as they slammed against her with each forceful stroke. "Never enough, I want it all," she panted.

The combination of her words and the jolting sensations that tingled through his sack from the touch of her hand sent him into a frenzy. He knew exactly how she felt. He could never get close enough, never burrow deep enough. He would never get enough of *her*.

"I love you," he groaned.

He felt her body quake and clench around him as she found her climax. With his name on her lips, he released his seed deep inside her, hoping one day very soon it would take root and grow into something, someone, he would cherish for the rest of his life.

About the Author

Elle Keating was born and raised in South Jersey, where she lives with her husband and three children. It was during her long commute to work, crossing over the Betsy Ross Bridge into Pennsylvania, that her mind drifted. Images of a world with Chase, Erin and their friends came rapidly and sent her writing in order to bring these intense characters to life.

When Elle is not in her favorite coffeehouse, huddled in a corner on an oversized chair and working on the next book in the series, she enjoys being a mom, taking her children from one sport to the next, and challenging herself frequently to be in two places at once.